HARD
TO
BREAK

HARD
TO
BREAK

A MICHAEL GANNON THRILLER

MICHAEL LEDWIDGE

HANOVER
SQUARE
PRESS

**HANOVER
SQUARE
PRESS™**

Recycling programs
for this product may
not exist in your area.

ISBN-13: 978-1-335-44933-7

Hard to Break

Hanover Square Press
22 Adelaide St. West, 41st Floor
Toronto, Ontario M5H 4E3, Canada
HanoverSqPress.com
BookClubbish.com

Printed in U.S.A.

HARD
TO
BREAK

PROLOGUE

WILD BLUE YONDER

1

The Delta flight out of Salt Lake City had a two-hour layover in Seattle so they didn't get up to Juneau until late in the afternoon. Coming into the terminal from the bag retrieval, Gannon saw that it looked a lot like the airports in the lower forty-eight except it wasn't that crowded and the gift shop had a giant stuffed moose in its plate glass window.

When they were halfway down the concourse to the exit, the rumbling luggage cart suddenly got much heavier as Gannon's son, Declan, stopped pushing it. He stood pointing at the green glow of a Starbucks sign.

"What do you think, Dad? Coffee time?" he said.

"Again?" Gannon said skeptically as he slipped out his phone to check the itinerary. "How much coffee can a person possibly drink?"

The super-extra-deluxe spring brown bear Alaskan hunting trip they were about to embark upon had originally been booked for Gannon's friend, John Barber. But when John couldn't go at the last minute, in order to avoid the huge hit on the cancelation fee, Gannon had decided to step in and scoop it up for his son's birthday instead.

Gannon read off the screen. They were to head to a seaport on the other side of Juneau, where a little Piper Cherokee would take them on the final hop to a base camp in the interior of Glacier Bay National Park.

But that was at three, he read. They still had about an hour.

"Yes, okay," Gannon said. "I will allow it. If you hurry. Get me a small one. Black."

"Cookie, too, Daddy? Please?" his six-three, two-hundred-twenty-pound son said, maneuvering around a sandwich board sign that said Alaska: North To The Future.

"Split one?" Gannon said.

"Split one? Come on, Dad. We're headed straight into *Call of the Wild* country. We need to carbo-load."

"Speak for yourself," he called out at his son's wide departing back.

To the left of where Gannon was standing was a huge window, and he squealed the luggage cart over and stood looking out. Beyond the airport tarmac, a bright silver curtain of mist was billowing gently along hills filled with huge pine trees. As he watched, an open airport vehicle went by along the shoulder of the landing strip, its driver wearing a snow hat that said, Yeah, But It's A Dry Cold.

Gannon smiled out at the landscape. Even though he'd been born and raised in New York City, he actually possessed a special affinity for Alaska ever since he was a child. In his fourth-grade class at St. Margaret's, each kid had to do a special project on one of the fifty states and when he reached in and drew out Alaska from the Yankee hat Sister Ann was holding, he had a special feeling about it being *his* state.

Silly as it sounded, throughout the entirety of his life, his sense of fateful connection to its Big Dipper star state flag, (which he had to draw), its state flower, (the forget-me-not), and its main exports, (zinc and oil and fish), had never left him.

"And now I'm finally here," he said out loud to it.

Gannon smiled even wider as the mist parted and a muscular mountain range suddenly became visible in the distance, majestic fissured peaks still thick with snow.

"So far so good," he said as he placed a palm to the cool glass.

The weather was holding up, thirty degrees going up to near forty tomorrow. In the travel guide it said that March was the best time for Alaskan hunting because it was no longer freezing, and it was before what they called breakup when all the snow melted and everything became a muddy mess.

Gannon turned and sat in one of the lounge chairs behind him with his hiking boots up on their bags and hard-pack rifle cases.

"Guess we're about to find out," he whispered excitedly as he scratched at his fledgling beard.

His son had insisted that they both work on their facial hair for the last two weeks. Like pretanning before heading on a beach vacation, he had explained, they should already have a semi-lumberjack-mountain-man look to blend in, to really hit the ground running up here in the wild blue yonder.

Declan was jazzed all right. They'd tagged along on a hunt to Arizona with John Barber for bighorn sheep two months before, and it seemed like he had really caught the bug.

Gannon was more of a fisherman than a hunter by far. But moving forward, maybe hunting would be something he and Declan could share together from time to time.

Especially now that his son was leaving him, Gannon thought with a frown.

2

It was true. Declan was cutting out on him, the bum. He was giving baseball another shot, which meant having to leave Utah.

Gannon was sure going to miss him. Especially after all the time they'd gotten to spend hanging out together at his old war buddy, John Barber's, ranch in Utah.

Though come to think of it, *hiding* out would have been a more accurate term.

Gannon would have liked to have told people that he had taken to the desert-hermit lifestyle for pious religious purposes except it was actually pretty much the opposite. Their sudden need to get off the grid had come about because of a floating suitcase full of money Gannon had come across while out fishing in the Bahamas.

He'd hardly had time to say "finders keepers" and thank his lucky stars before the group of corrupt FBI counterintelligence agents it had belonged to had shown up, trying to kill him.

The problem for them was that Gannon had spent a significant portion of his adult life as a combat-hardened navy SEAL special forces operator. And as he hadn't really felt like being dead just yet, the complications that had ensued from this unfortunate conflict of interests had resulted in the exchange of great amounts of automatic gunfire. Sad as it was to say, more than a few of these up-to-no-good government agents had ended up in the deceased column.

Actually, come to think of it, it really wasn't that sad, was it? Gannon thought.

Since the corrupt-to-the-bone scumbags had thoroughly deserved everything they got.

"And then some," Gannon muttered as he remembered his sweet-natured old pal from the Bahamas, Sergeant Jeremy, whom they had brutally tortured and murdered.

But at least the good news now was that it seemed that at long last all this unexpected and thoroughly unwanted covert combat had come to a close. He had an FBI agent friend of his do a deep dive on the sly to see if there were any cases on him, especially any in the department's top secret counterintelligence division.

The scan miraculously had come back squeaky-clean. Apparently, he was both overt and covert warrant free. It wasn't like he wouldn't still be keeping a sharp eye on their six, but as it seemed the military wing of the corrupt-o-crats wanted to bury the hatchet for now, an ease-up on things seemed appropriate.

Besides, his enemies weren't after Declan, were they? Gannon thought. Hiding his son along with himself had just been a precaution.

And threat or no threat, his son couldn't hide forever. With his birthday in three days, it was time for him to get on with his young life.

Knowing this day was coming, Gannon had worked overtime on his buddy's weekend warrior ranch to get his son to sponge up every SEAL self-defense trick and tactic Gannon could think to teach him. They must have littered over a hundred thousand shell casings on the floor of John Barber's shooting range and shoot house. And for unarmed stuff, he'd spent months teaching him a brutal street fighting version of the martial art Silat, which had been taught to him by one of his old crazy Vietnam vet SEAL mentors.

Packed now with some muscle and tactical technique, Declan was as ready to make his way in the world as he ever would be, Gannon thought. Moving forward, anyone suicidal enough to sneak up on his linebacker-size son to do him a nasty—even a pro—very likely might be in for an unexpected new orifice. And/or a plastic surgeon to reset the broken bones of his face.

Gannon stared out at the striking Alaskan landscape as some large seabird, a crane of some sort, came gliding across the sky.

There you had it, Gannon thought with a sigh as he watched it drift away. There was no more denying it. His little boy was grown now.

One last wistful dream grizzly bear hunting trip, he thought with a grin, and then it would be time to finally cut the Gannon family apron strings with a Rambo knife.

He turned as his son arrived back, balancing two coffees in a holder. He laughed as he spotted the pile of treat bags that were stacked up between the cups. They were almost as high as their luggage cart.

Did this kid ever stop eating?

"A cookie, huh?" Gannon said as his son sat. "Looks like you got us three. *Each.*"

"Very funny, Dad. I got us some breakfast sandwiches as well."

"What? We had lunch in Seattle."

"I know," Declan said, "but cookies are a dessert so I figured, got to have a meal before or, like, it wouldn't be right."

"Enjoy it now, son," Gannon said, finally accepting his coffee as his son tore into the crinkly paper. "But remember, one day—sooner than you think—you, too, will worry about fitting into pants."

3

Bouthier had been busy setting up in the hotel room all morning so when there was some unexpected downtime, he decided to try to squeeze in a quick workout.

The hotel gym was downstairs off the lobby and even before he fully pulled open its glass door, he saw without surprise that it was tiny and complete shit.

The only good thing about it was that its sole occupant, some pudgy thirty-something insurance-salesman-type on the exercise bike, immediately put on the brakes and began gathering up his stuff the split second Bouthier peeled off his shirt.

It wasn't surprising. Six foot and hard bodied with dark pitbull-like eyes, doorway-filling shoulders and a slab of a face that looked like it had been squared into shape with a bricklayer's crack hammer, Bouthier rarely found social distancing to be too much of a problem.

"Before," he said as he tracked the soft bubble butt's hasty exit in the wall mirror.

"After," he said with a gruesome smile as he popped a rock-hard front flex.

He looked around. Without anything real to lift, he decided to do some CrossFit. Burpees, renegade rows, jumping lunges then some dumbbell thrusters with the pathetic 50s.

When the Bluetooth in his ear chirped, he was just done stretching and was bending over about to do his first burpee.

"Heads up. This just in. It is the plane after all," his partner, Llewellyn, said.

"Now you tell me. On my way," Bouthier said with a sigh.

As he came back out into the lobby, the front door of the hotel swung open and in came some grinning Alaskan hillbilly family with a bunch of kids.

There were five kids in all, Bouthier quickly counted. Three girls and two boys, the oldest boy maybe ten. All of them were blond haired and smiling and the dipshit lot of them, even the thirty-something parents, were color coordinated in Walmart blue T-shirts that said Congrats Grammy! on the front of them.

Well, kiss my Alaskan grits, Bouthier thought as he watched the backwoods von Trapps head for the cheap hotel's ballroom. *This is funner than when we done gave that Sarah Palin a ride in the turnip truck. Don't y'all just love going-into-town day?*

As he headed on a collision course with them, Bouthier's dark predator eyes were fastened onto the smallest child lingering at the rear. He was a daydream-eyed, tow-headed boy of perhaps five, the plastic string of a huge shiny Mylar balloon clutched fervently in his pudgy little mitt.

Time for some of his own fun? Bouthier suddenly thought with a raise of an eyebrow.

He quickly glanced over at the check-in desk and saw that the clerk was missing.

Why, yes, he thought, reaching into his back pocket as he picked up his pace. Why, yes, it was.

Arriving in the middle of the lobby at the same time as the cute-as-a-button cluster, Bouthier waited a beat, and just as the five-year-old crossed in front of him, he snicker-snacked open the razor-sharp karambit blade he always carried with a card trick flick.

Bouthier was ten feet past the desk with the blade resheathed when the child began howling.

He glanced back casually over his shoulder.

And had to bite his lip to keep from cracking up.

Because the redneck kid's balloon was missing in action now. Up, up, and away it had gone, hopelessly lost somewhere in the lobby's double-height ceiling.

"Mommy, my balloon! Nooooo! Nooooo!" the inconsolable rug rat wailed to his mother, kneeling now beside him.

"But why did you let it go, Tyler? I told you to hold it tight," she said.

"But it broke! Why did it break?" Tyler bemoaned as he pathetically showed her the now limp short end of the balloon string that Bouthier had just parted as clean as a whistle.

"Because shiny balloons are only for winners, that's why," Bouthier said quietly, unable to stifle the giggles as he finally turned and stepped into the waiting elevator.

"Losers like you, Tyler," Bouthier said as the door closed, "only get the string."

4

The cheap room Bouthier carded into up on three was about as spacious as the bed of a pickup.

But they weren't there on their honeymoon now, were they? Bouthier thought as he kick-slammed the beat-up door behind him.

It actually couldn't have been better because its window provided a clear line of sight to the Juneau arrivals gate.

Llewellyn was bent over the spotting scope by the window, and Bouthier shook his head at his partner's room-filling back. Even taking a knee, his boy Llewellyn was one massive goon.

"Target acquired?" he said.

"Clear as day. He's out on the sidewalk getting a taxi."

"Nevin and Grabowski are on him already?" Bouthier said, referring to their other team members.

"Like maggots on a rotting corpse," Llewellyn said. "They just pulled up at the curb behind his taxi."

"And the target's kid is there, too?"

"The kid, too," Llewellyn said, standing up to his full gargantuan six-foot-six-inch height. "See for yourself."

It was true, Bouthier thought, as he put one of his dark doll's eyes to the scope.

There he was in the flesh, the intrepid Michael Gannon, long-in-the-tooth navy SEAL, and his happy progeny.

Gannon was midsize, maybe five foot ten. Good width in the shoulders. Lean faced. He was fit-looking enough. Not like Bouthier himself, of course. But who was?

Bouthier's eyes narrowed as he thumbed at the zoom.

"Mr. Gannon, you need to lay off the mashed pertaters," he said with a pretty good Irish brogue. "Because faith and begorra that Irish gut of yours is starting to lean a little more toward keg than six-pack, isn't it?"

"Looks like everything's right on schedule after all," Llewellyn said, chuckling behind him.

Bouthier nodded. They already knew all about Gannon's hunting trip itinerary. The printout of it from Control was sitting in a glossy folder on the hotel desk beside him. Along with several marked-off topographical maps of the Glacier Bay territory.

He buttoned the zoom back a smidge as the SEAL's kid handed him one of the rifle cases. Then Bouthier suddenly found himself frowning.

Was all this truly adding up? he wondered. From the startling reports they had gotten, especially the world-class-level confirmed kill count, he was really expecting someone more formidable looking.

The target in his scope certainly didn't give off the demeanor of a killing machine. Fair-haired and bright-eyed with an easy grin, he could have been a youth sports coach, an upbeat daytime game show host, a helpful friendly small-town mailman.

But then again, appearances really didn't always tell the story, did they? Bouthier thought. Take Mike Tyson for instance. He was only five foot ten. Thick and stocky. Built like a gun safe, like he was bolted into the floor. Then one blurring, bobbing-and-weaving second after the bell rang, he was somehow standing in the middle of his much larger opponent's kitchen, ripping down all the cabinets and tearing the door off the fridge.

Or take plastic explosives for another example, Bouthier thought as he watched the stocky SEAL pile the rest of the bags and cases into the taxi's trunk.

One second it was a harmless blob of kindergarten Play-Doh, wasn't it? Then an eyeblink later, they were scraping your sweetbreads off the ceiling with a putty knife.

Nodding at this self-served food for thought, Bouthier was about to turn the camera off when he spotted something and quickly zoomed back in close on Gannon's neck.

"There you go. Now that's more like it," he said with a grin as he scanned the healed-over hickie-like welt just above Gannon's clavicle.

He'd seen such marks before. In his own mirror. It was the burn mark that sometimes got left when the hot tumbling brass shell casings of a rapidly fired automatic weapon got caught in your shirt collar.

Bouthier's stony face creased into a full smile as he watched Gannon settle back into his taxi.

This actually might be fun after all, Bouthier thought as the cab pulled away.

He'd never been on a SEAL hunt before.

5

The bright base camp log cabin was fifty miles deep into the Glacier Bay Wilderness Area and in the crack-of-dawn morning light, it looked like something out of a Boy Scout's dream of heaven.

It had shiny wooden bunks and shiny wooden gear lockers and a massive matte black iron woodstove just off the kitchen that was the size and shape of a small locomotive.

Pausing from stomping snow from their boots on its porch, Gannon looked with his son at the remarkable lake beside the cabin that was somehow the bright blue-green color of a Tiffany jewelry box. Beyond it in the distance, the jagged peaks of the seemingly endless snow-dusted cliffs and mountains they were about to head into looked like something out of Tolkien's Middle Earth.

"This is beyond, Dad. I mean, say huh?" Declan said in quiet awe.

Gannon grinned. In their matching hoodies and watch caps

and insulated hunting coveralls, they couldn't have been more psyched about this hunt if they had tried.

"And just think, the day hasn't yet begun," Gannon said, clapping him on the back as he pulled the door.

"Okay, gentlemen, if you would," their expert bear hunting guide, Chuck Bullard, said, waving them over to the map he had just spread open on the cabin's battered kitchen table.

White bearded, hearty and with a Papa Hemingway thing going on, Chuck Bullard truly looked like an expert bear hunting guide.

Or was Chuck actually Santa Claus? Gannon thought as he and Dec huddled up beside him. Old Santa come south from the North Pole after Christmas to get away from the chirpy elves and unwind by hunting grizzlies.

"Okay, so we're here and we're heading to the base camp that's on the south side of this mountain to the southwest here," Chuck said, tracing a thick finger over the paper.

Gannon nodded, studying the topographical map. They'd just come in from loading up the snowmobiles with all the bags and gear and rifles along with the Marmot tents. The first leg of the hunt was thirty miles in from this base camp, so they'd be sleeping under the stars tonight.

"These lines here," Chuck continued as he tapped the paper, "are old mining roads along the lake. But right here, see, we'll have to cross the frozen part of this river and start heading up and down these ridgelines. Some of the up-and-down runnels are pretty steep, but if you just follow my lead, you'll be fine. You'll probably want to go slow anyway because as the elevation gets higher, the scenery gets quite pretty. A lot of folks say so anyway. Any questions so far?"

"*Gets* pretty?" Gannon said, pouring some more coffee. "You're saying it gets prettier than that lake out there?"

"Don't worry, Mike," Chuck said, raising a snowy white eyebrow at him. "You'll start forgetting about the pretty scenery real fast when we get in close to our base camp and set up the tents and have to start stalking uphill on foot. These brown bears just out of hibernation feed on grass in the upper-level clearings here on the south side of these mountains so it takes a while to hike up there. Now you boys know about bear spray, right?"

"We got some back in Utah before we got on the plane," Gannon said, showing him the key ring canister he'd purchased.

"Yeah, um, that sample size ain't gonna cut it, Mike. Not out here," Chuck said, taking out what looked like a small fire extinguisher of the stuff from a cargo pocket and clunking it atop the map.

"This is more what you're looking for," he said. "It's mace times about a hundred thousand. You get into some trouble, you leave your sidearm where it is and just take this out and pull back the safety cover here and start depressing the trigger. Liberally. A seven-hundred-pound charging, hungry grizzly coming at you at forty miles an hour—even if you hit it between the eyes with that .44 you brought, Mike—will still flatten you like a penny on a railroad track. But if it gets even a whiff of this, it'll immediately put on the brakes and take off."

Gannon smiled as he looked over at his son, who had gone wide-eyed at the words "seven-hundred-pound charging, hungry grizzly."

"North to the future, son," Gannon said, clapping Declan on the back. "North to the future and beyond."

6

A dozen miles into the interior of the bay from the small coastal village, the speeding fishing boat entered the narrow mouth of an inlet.

Bouthier, no fan of things nautical, was glad for the Dramamine he'd taken as they rocked around a jut of pale ice-coated rocky shore.

The stony coast they zipped past was feldspar mostly with bits of quartz in it. Bouthier could tell by the hard gray fragments of it, the angular grain. Though he appeared to be a meathead, Bouthier knew a few things. He had actually planned to be a petroleum engineer like his daddy before he had gone into the service.

He turned his attention to the boat. It wasn't a trawler, but it wasn't exactly a rowboat either. There was enough room to lash the two snowmobiles to the gunwale, and the wheelhouse on it was able to fit the four of them along with all their gear and the two-man boat crew.

Bouthier blew into his hands and rubbed them as he watched Captain Pete trim the throttle. He, like his son, Young Joe, standing beside him at the wheel, wore his long dark hair in braids. They were genuine Alaskan native Tlingit Indians.

Of course, they were, Bouthier thought as the vessel carved them a dogleg right back to the south through the inlet toward the grizzly hunting area.

You had to have Indian scouts if you wanted to head 'em off at the pass.

Bouthier checked his watch.

"Hey, Joe. What's the name of the bay again?" he called over.

"Disenchantment," Young Joe said, turning.

Bouthier smiled.

"Perfect," he said, winking at Llewellyn beside him. "Word of the day."

Young Joe turned and came over to them with a map.

"We'll arrive in about twenty minutes right here to put you in," he said, pointing.

"How will we get the snowmobiles off? There's a dock?" Bouthier said.

"Yes. Then see here, you just head in due north five miles and right here in off this trail is where you can set up your ambush. Right here where the trail's tight."

"They'll be coming that way? You're certain?" Llewellyn said.

The Indian nodded somberly.

"They have to," he said. "The mining road is the only way in from their base camp. And around the end of it here is where the guides always set up a minicamp to stalk."

"That's a pretty confident plan, Joe. You know about ambushes, do you?" Llewellyn said, winking at his buddies.

"A bit," the boyish-looking black-haired Indian said, calmly blinking at him. "I walked point in the mountain division in Afghanistan. Plus, I've hunted this area since I could crawl."

"What you hunt?" Grabowski said from the other bench.

"Moose mostly," the Indian said.

"Moose. Oh, I love me some moose. You cook it?" Nevin said.

"Hey, moron, can it, would you?" Bouthier said as Young Joe left to stand back next to his father.

Llewellyn leaned over.

"Been meaning to ask you, bro. Why are we here on this assignment?" he said.

Bouthier looked at his tall homely partner, at the comically high reach of his knees as he sat. Bouthier, who didn't like anyone, sort of liked Llewellyn. The Detroit native was quick on the uptake and quite good in a tight spot. He especially liked the fact that for all the man's size he was very quiet when he needed to be.

What was crazy was he wasn't even military. He was former Company, an analyst of all things. Rumor was, before that he'd been a shoe-in for valedictorian at West Point but got kicked out for trying to slit a roommate's throat during an argument. Bouthier wholeheartedly believed this story.

"You didn't read the report?" Bouthier said.

"Of course, I did. But I mean, why us specifically? Us four. We're all usually team leaders. We never work together. Plus, we were all taken off other jobs. I've never been taken off another job before. You?"

"No."

"We're also all getting double bonuses for this one. You ever get a double before?"

"No," Bouthier said again.

"Exactly. And we're probably the best operators in the firm."

"Not probably the best," Bouthier agreed. "We are the best."

"They need a dream team for one guy and his kid?" Llewellyn said. "Who the hell is this guy?"

"I don't know, but I hear he likes to play pretty rough."

Llewellyn looked around at the four of them, the armory piled at their feet.

"No one's this rough," he said.

Bouthier calmly looked out at the desolate vista as they entered a narrow channel. On both sides was nothing but more rock. Bouthier examined it. There was more limestone here, argillite. All of it was sparse and windswept. It was like boating through a cave tunnel with the roof ripped off.

"That's pretty much what I said when they told me about the job," Bouthier finally said. "You know what they told me?"

"What's that?" Llewellyn said.

Bouthier slipped out his karambit and slowly shaved at the edge of his thumbnail with its razored sickle. He did this nervous habit quite often, and the nail bed there was red and raw and calloused with scar tissue.

"You better watch your ass with this guy," he said, licking at his thumb.

7

"You've got to be kidding me," Gannon said as they came level atop the next ridgeline.

Under the crystal-clear spring light yet another line of blazing white peaks rimmed the horizon, the dark hollows between them blue as inkwells. At who knew how many miles beyond them to the right, a towering blue-hued glacier, the first one Gannon had ever laid eyes on in his life, sparkled in the distance like a gemstone.

Then he heard his son howl happily as he zipped past, and he quickly twisted back on his own snowmobile's throttle, his stomach dropping as he tilted off the brink into the next roller coaster downslope.

At first in the deep loose snow, it felt like he was in free fall, like he was riding a bicycle down the greased side of a tilted skyscraper. Then the skis caught traction, and Gannon smiled at the wind in his face, the snow flying. He couldn't remember the last time he'd had this much fun.

They'd bottomed out way down at the end of the ski-slope-like hill and were a quarter way up the next one when Declan suddenly slowed and stopped. As Gannon throttled alongside him, Chuck, in the lead, spun around and came back.

"What's up?" Chuck said.

"I don't know," Declan said. "The engine sounds funny all of a sudden, and it feels like I'm getting less power."

Chuck hopped off his Artic Cat and peered down at Declan's dash display and tapped it. Then he tapped it again.

"Shit," he said, keying it off. He bit off his gloves and tipped back the snowmobile's front hood.

"The engine gauge is pinned past the redline," he said as he tinkered with something. "Dammit. Knew it. The crankcase is filled with oil. Could be a crack in the pump or maybe the O-ring split. That's probably it. They go sometimes. Just one of those things."

"Fixable?" Gannon said.

"Not out here," Chuck said, standing and looking back up the steep slope they had just come down.

"Can we double up?" Gannon said.

"No," Chuck said. "All the gear wouldn't fit."

"This sucks. I'm sorry," Declan said.

"Not at all," Chuck said, patting him on the back. "Not your fault. It's not even a problem since we haven't gotten too far yet. How about this? We'll leave this one here, and Declan, if you ride back with me to camp, we'll get you the other snowmobile from the shed. If it's okay with you, Mike, might be better if you hang by yourself here with all the gear. I'm actually a bit low in the gasoline department."

"No problem, Chuck. That's fine," Gannon said, turning and going into the packs for the coffee thermos.

"Appreciate it, Mike," he said. "It shouldn't take us too long. Maybe an hour and a half."

"Any Yukon Cornelius tips for me while I'm waiting?" Gannon said as he found the thermos. "Any grizzly around here, you think?"

Chuck gave him a pensive look as he pulled his gloves back on.

"Grizzly? No. Shouldn't be. You should be good to go. Actually, there is one...but no...no... Don't worry about it. You're good. You'll be fine."

"Whoa, wait a second," Gannon said as he watched their guide un-bungee some gear to make room for Declan. "There is one what? Don't worry about what?"

"This is sort of the hunting area for a roaming wolf pack," he said. "But not really. Honestly, we're talking its farthest outskirts."

"Oh," Gannon said, his turn to be wide-eyed. "A roaming wolf pack. Is that all?"

"You know it, brother. All part of the package," Chuck said, winking as he gave him a fist bump. "And if you see some, have at them. Here at Bullard Hunting Incorporated, we always toss in wolf stuffing free of charge."

8

Gannon exchanged a wave with Declan as Chuck deftly spun their snowmobile around. He watched them roar back up the long ridge they'd just come down. When they finally went out of sight at the top, the chainsaw sound of their engine immediately ceased as if someone had hit a mute button.

It was the amount of space, Gannon thought as he took in the vast bowl-like valley he was parked upon. Alaskan dimensions were on a different level. The Glacier Bay Park itself, just this park they were in, was over five thousand square miles, which made it two times larger than the state of Delaware.

He found the thermos and some chocolate-covered pretzels and leaned way back onto the snowmobile's packs, snacking as he scanned the surrounding ridgelines. But there was nothing. No movement, no wolves, no deer. Not even birds. All around in every direction, there was just random clusters of pine trees and some gray rock outcroppings that stood out here and there like constellations in a white universe of snow.

There were no grizzly around, that was for sure, he thought, peering into a sparse tree line below him at a diagonal to his left. Because you'd notice them. From space, he thought as he tossed a pretzel up and into his waiting open mouth. On Chuck's website, some of the brown monsters he'd helped to bag looked like they were about the size of a small school bus.

A sudden rush of cold wind coming down the ridge sent his next tossed chocolaty pretzel flying. The gust roared in his ears and almost ripped his coverall hoodie off his head before he could get a hand on the string.

People wanted to gush about forest bathing, Gannon thought, closing his eyes.

How about glacier bathing? he thought, turning his smiling face into the polar vortex. That'll put a little hair on the chest.

As Gannon leaned even farther back into the gear bags behind him, he began to wonder how the hunt would eventually go down. He really wanted Declan to take the shot if at all possible.

One of the wisest observations he had ever made in the theater of combat was that the best men in every unit he was ever in, the ones you made sure to get right beside when the shit started going down, were all hunters. To a man, they were all southerners and westerners who by puberty had been taught by their daddies how to go out into the woods with a rifle and come back with enough meat to get their family through winter.

That was the real reason why they had come up here. Call him crazy, not being able to know what the future had in store for his son as he went out into the world by himself, he wanted Declan to know how to survive. Hell, that's why Gannon had really scooped up the trip. He wanted to put a cherry on top of all the training they'd done, to give his son a glimpse of what he was capable of if, God forbid, he ever found himself in a tight spot.

That's why after the kill, to hopefully hammer this rite of passage home, he was going to present his son with the other gift he had brought for him.

Gannon took it out of his inside coverall pocket. It was a stainless-steel Rolex Submariner watch that had been a gift to Gannon and to everyone in their SEAL unit from a rich army general after a top secret mission they had successfully completed.

The watch originally had an ace of spades carved into it with the name of their unit, but for his son, Gannon had the case back replaced. Now inscribed upon it was a quote by the ancient Greek general, Thucydides.

He is best who is trained in the severest school.

Gannon passed his thumb over the engraving. He wasn't exactly a scholar of Greek generals or anything, but it was just that it was one of the truest things he had ever come across in his life.

Gannon had the watch repocketed when he thought he heard the drone of a motor.

He lifted the coffee tumbler from out between his legs as he sat up and looked back over at the ridgeline where Dec and Chuck had left. He was thinking he would see them coming back. But even after a minute, no one showed.

Was it a plane? he thought, squinting up into the sky.

Another ten seconds passed before he realized he was looking in the wrong direction.

He'd just turned up the steep slope in the direction they'd been heading when he saw the two dark snowmobiles top its crest.

He immediately sat all the way up.

There were two men on each of them.

He tracked them as they descended. Like him they were wearing winter hunting coveralls and they had rifles strapped to their backs.

They were coming from *out* of the wilderness? Gannon thought, puzzled. Another hunting party?

He watched them rip down the steep white contour of the

hill, getting closer. They were going fast. Then they seemed to slow and bunch together, talking to each other. Then they came faster again straight at him.

There was something weird about it, Gannon thought. Off-putting. Chuck was one crackerjack guide. He would have mentioned another party out here in the bush. *Right?*

Without knowing why, Gannon suddenly didn't trust it.

He stood up off the snowmobile fully, a tightness coming into in his chest.

Roaming wolves came from somewhere in his mind.

No, he thought as he watched the four men close in on him down the cold white hill.

He didn't trust this at all.

9

By the time they arrived, Gannon, who had been straddling his snowmobile, was sitting off on one side of it.

Sitting *casually*, Bouthier noted as he laid off the throttle. Their target was leaning back with his legs straight, his ankles crossed, his boot heels in the snow.

Not a care in all the world, Bouthier thought as he squeezed the snowmobile's brake.

After his skid became a full stop, Bouthier turned off his snowmobile then looked up the way they had come. It had been bright at the top of the slope, but it was shadowed down here. He looked to the left and right. The hills around. No sign of the guide or the son. No one in the pine trees. He stifled a smile as he listened to the silence. They must have gone back for something.

Bouthier looked over at Gannon, his lean, lined unsuspicious face, his fair beard, his blue eyes looking calmly but alertly into his own.

Sometimes it happened this way, Bouthier thought. Like catching three cherries on a slot machine. Or a hundred-dollar bill blowing up the middle of a Vegas sidewalk. Absolute zero resistance. Easy as falling off a log.

"Morning," Bouthier said.

"Afternoon, you mean," Gannon said, smiling and lifting the coffee canister at them in greeting.

"It's still morning, isn't it? Only just eleven," Bouthier said without checking his watch.

"Is that right? Thanks for the update," Gannon said, his eyes still calm and alert above his grin.

Bouthier smiled himself as he scanned around the massive natural amphitheater some more. Getting a feel for the terrain, letting his adrenaline tamp down a bit. Taking his time with it. There was no need to rush.

He didn't know if it was the lack of pollution or what have you, but the vividness of Alaska was just incredible, he thought with a sigh. Good bombing weather.

"So, how's it going?" Bouthier finally said after a yawn.

"Mighty fine," Gannon said nodding. "Out hunting, are we?"

"Yep. Going for bear this morning," Bouthier said. "You, too?"

Gannon took a sip of the coffee.

"Yeah, I'm loaded for bear," he said, lowering the thermos. "How'd you know?"

"I'm good at guessing," Bouthier said, pointing at the rifle case at the back of Gannon's snowmobile.

His unwisely unopened rifle case, Bouthier thought, glancing at the tightened-down clasps.

"Out here by yourself?" Bouthier said.

"Oh, yeah," Gannon lied casually. "Just me."

Bouthier cocked his head at the second snowmobile with the hood up, the gear beside it, and the heavy tracks in the snow leading back down the trail.

"With two snowmobiles?" he said.

"Oh, yeah," Gannon repeated with a nod. "I always bring two in case one conks out on me. Good thing, too, as it turned out. Unlike you guys. You like doubling up, huh? Must be hard to figure out who gets to ride bitch."

They all stared at him. In the silence, you could hear the whip of the wind. Up the slope, it carved a corkscrewing skein of snow into the blue-tinged air.

"Come on, fellas. That was actually kind of funny," Gannon said, sitting up. "Not even a smile?"

"You're a real wise guy huh, Mike?" Bouthier said. "That's your name, right? Mike. Mike Gannon?"

"You really are a good guesser," Gannon said, lifting the coffee to take another sip.

Then he let thermos drop and emptied the small canister of key ring bear spray he'd been palming behind it straight into Bouthier's eyes.

10

Chuck Bullard hadn't been playing about the bear spray.

All four of them—plus even Gannon himself—in a split second of him setting the spray off were moaning and tearing up as they tried to cough and spit away the burning, horrible reeking, skanky mist.

Lurching to his right through this agony, Gannon fell more than climbed aboard his snowmobile.

Then he yanked back the pull cord and found the throttle and went tearing off down the hill.

He'd already thought a little bit ahead so instead of straight down, he went in a diagonal toward the nearest left-hand tree line. He needed to get himself some cover or at least a little time. A half a minute or so would do it, he thought. Just time enough to unpack his loaded .44 Magnum and see what in the world was up.

He was leaning forward and down, half hanging off the far

side of the Arctic Cat so as not to get shot when he felt the thing begin to skid on him. Because of the weird angle and the steepness, he saw that the front right ski was starting to lose its grip and was carving sideways into the snow.

"Shit, shit, shit," Gannon said as he felt the back end begin to swing.

Counter-steering, he'd just gotten straightened out when he heard the first shot. Not hearing the telltale click of a round coming past him, he ignored it. Probably a warning shot up in the air to get him to stop running.

Yeah, right. Warn this, Gannon thought, leaning down even lower with his head just above the handlebars, his heart hammering.

He was spinning back the throttle as far as it would go when it happened a split second later.

What he hit under the snow, Gannon never found out. A tree trunk or maybe a large rock in a buried-over creek.

Whatever it was, it caught both front skis of the racing snowmobile stiff, and the back end lifted up underneath him like a tripped catapult.

There was an almost pleasant carnival-ride-like feeling as Gannon was immediately shot over the handlebars and sent rocketing airborne off the slope. He had just enough wherewithal to tuck his chin down as he entered the midlevel boughs of the first pines in the tree line. He was still doing about thirty miles an hour when this happened, and there was the loud crack of a branch, followed almost immediately by the crunching sound of his cheap helmet as it made impact with a tree's thick trunk, and he was free-falling backward.

Some moments later as the blackout of shock subsided slightly, he found himself facedown, trying to get up from the snow. But he was having trouble. His arms were weak and he couldn't feel his legs or think clearly. He was also having trouble breathing. He had hardly gotten up on all fours, gasping from the wind knocked out of him, before he collapsed again.

Oh, he was screwed up, he thought, lying there facedown in the cold snow. He knew he was. Concussion for sure. Maybe worse than that. He'd been in major accidents before.

Everything was slow motion now. Everything detached and graying in and out.

This wasn't a rub-it-off moment, was it? he thought, pawing at the snow as he tried to raise himself again and failed.

11

He must have passed out because the next thing he knew, he was turned around on his back, staring up at pine tree branches.

"Well, well. He lives after all," Bouthier said from where he knelt beside him. "At least your breathing is sounding better. Talk to me, bud."

Gannon said nothing. He tried to breathe. It was difficult, like breathing through a bar straw. There was also a sharp pain along the right side of his chest. He wondered if he had cracked a rib.

"That was a bad move, Mike," Bouthier continued. "Real bad. Haven't you ever heard the expression, you can run, but you can't hide?"

"Especially with the way he drives," Llewellyn said.

"My partner's right, friend," Bouthier said. "I mean, I've heard of great escape attempts before, but your strategy of plowing straight into a tree face-first is a new one."

Gannon tried to squirm away as a hand explored his pockets. But it was useless. He was too weak. He closed his eyes.

"Come on, talk to me," Bouthier said.

"Who?" Gannon finally gasped.

"Who what?" Bouthier said, smiling. "Who am I? You want an introduction?"

"Who's your next of kin?" Gannon gasped out.

"What?" Bouthier said.

"The people who have to bury you," Gannon gasped painfully. "What are their names? They'll need to be informed."

"You're going to kill *me*?" Bouthier said with genuine amusement.

Gannon suddenly opened his eyes then and stared at Bouthier, hovering above him. Examined his face, his features. Objectively. Like Bouthier was a still life that Gannon was intent on painting.

Then Gannon passed out again.

"Is he dead?" Llewellyn said with concern.

"No," Bouthier said from where he knelt, listening at his chest. "His heart's still beating."

"I don't know, dude. Look at the helmet. He really ate that tree. You think he'll make it?"

"Yeah, I do. Might have a hairline crack in that thick skull of his, but this dude looks pretty old-school tough."

Bouthier turned as Grabowski and Nevin arrived on the other snowmobile back from their recon. He put a hard stiff arm to Grabowski's thick chest as the idiot leaped off the snowmobile and reared back to give Gannon a kick in his nuts.

"What are you doing?" Bouthier said.

"What does it look like I'm doing?" Grabowski said, unsuccessfully trying to throw off Bouthier. "Giving this funny bastard some payback. I'll show him who gets to ride bitch."

"Not so fast," Bouthier said, easily tripping Grabowski backward into the snow before waving a finger at him. "Step off and go punch a tree or something, would you?"

Bouthier knelt again, checking Gannon's pulse at the neck. "The contract is only half if he's delivered dead, dimwit," he said. "No messing with my valuable merchandise."

PART ONE

DARKEST BEFORE DAWN

12

John Barber arrived at the airport in Juneau on a Delta flight twenty hours almost to the minute after Mike's son, Declan, gave him the frantic call. What he had heard had flat out stunned him. The whole way up, he was hoping he'd land to find it was all just a big mistake.

But there was no mistake, he saw immediately in Declan's devastated face as he pulled open the airport hotel door.

"John, they took him," Declan said frantically as Barber came in. "Somebody took Dad!"

"Slow down, son," Barber said, patting the kid on his back. "We'll find him. That's why I'm here. Come on. Sit down. It's going to be fine."

Barber turned to the burly white-bearded man who stood from where he was sitting by the desk.

"Chuck Bullard," the rattled-looking hunting guide said as he offered his hand.

"John Barber," Barber said, shaking back.

Barber took the fifth of Jack Daniel's he had brought with him out of his bag and cracked the seal.

"Thanks for waiting with the boy," Barber said after he poured three healthy drinks into some plastic water cups he found on the desk.

"For waiting? Are you kidding? I feel completely responsible for this," Bullard said, staring at his drink before he downed it in one shot.

"Join the club," Barber said as he sipped at his own drink, "since I was originally the one who booked the trip. But we need to scratch all that. Just tell me what happened."

Bullard did. It took him three minutes to lay out how Declan's snowmobile had died. How they had gone back to find Gannon's snowmobile smashed up beside a tree. How they followed the tracks of two other snowmobiles to an abandoned logging dock on Disenchantment Bay.

"You said on the phone that the troopers were called?"

Bullard nodded.

"They put up a helicopter to search. Said a bear could have grabbed him, the idiots. I told him he's been kidnapped. Showed them the tracks. Damn meatheads just stared at me like I was speaking Chinese. I still can't believe this. We never had a client who got as much as a scratch. Who the hell would kidnap a hunter?"

Barber and Declan exchanged a look. They both knew who. But as Barber had advised Declan on the phone, Chuck Bullard or the state troopers or anybody else didn't need to know about all that. At least not yet.

"Can I talk to you in the hall for a sec, Chuck?"

"What's up, John?" he said when they were outside in the empty corridor.

"Mike and Declan were brought in to the base camp by plane, right?"

"That's right."

"You hear any other plane traffic that morning?"

"No, I didn't."

"Okay. Let me throw you a hypothetical. Might sound a tad nuts."

"Shoot. Anything," Bullard said.

"If men who weren't from around here came to grab my friend, Mike, by boat, who would they most likely hire to bring them in and out?"

13

There was only one bar in the tiny Tlingit fishing village of Awdiggan on Disenchantment Bay, and it was coming on 11:00 p.m. when John Barber walked through its front door with a .44 held openly in his hand.

Chuck Bullard had brought him to town and had wanted to join him to watch his back. But Barber had told him to stay at the dock and to keep the engine of the rental boat running.

"Be back in a minute," he had said.

About half of the two dozen or so Tlingit Indians who were in the double-wide trailer swiveled all but in unison as John Barber stepped from the door to directly behind the bar. When he ripped free the plug for the music and the TV, he had everyone's complete attention.

"Hey, folks!" Barber yelled in the stock-still silence.

The only light in the place left after he had shut the TV came from a Molson beer neon sign beside it. Barber smiled coldly in its green glow. Then he placed down the Smith & Wesson 329PD on the bartop before him. With its black scandium alloy frame and titanium cylinder, it was a formidable-looking revolver. He placed his hands down atop the bar on either side of it like a preacher at a podium.

"My name's John Barber," he said. "And I'm looking for my friend, Mike Gannon. He was taken out of the bear hunting area two days ago. It was by one of you slime bag pieces of shit because there was no air traffic in the area, and it's the only other damn way in or out.

"Now," he said as he held the .44 up for all to see. "Me and my other friend here have decided that no one is leaving until I get told what the hell happened. You get me? No one. Now you can go ahead and try to sneak out a pistol of your own. Have at it. Or sneak a call to the cops if you want on your cell phones or whatever. Bring in the Alaskan state troopers. The SWAT. But first you take a good long look in my crazy blue eyes here to check to see like I give a shit.

"Because they may get me in the end," he said, "but let me assure you, if I know one thing, it's this. Every last damn one of you is going to be well on your way to the happy hunting grounds by the time they breach that cheap-ass trailer door. We understand each other?

"You sick of living? You feel like today's a good day to die? 'Cause I do. In fact, I'm looking forward to it now that my best friend in this world is gone. Now you tell me what the hell happened to him and you tell me now!"

There was a heated murmur in the back of the crowd by a pool table. Then there was a scuffle that was followed quickly by the meaty sound of a fist loudly smacking a face.

An old man stepped forward a moment later. He was wearing a Seattle Seahawks baseball cap along with a very faded and worn looking Carhartt coat that seemed too big for him.

"Yes, old man? You have news to report?" Barber said.

"Are you police?" he said.

"No, I'm just a crazy man out looking for his long-lost buddy," Barber said.

"I will tell you about your friend on one condition."

"Which is?"

"You leave here after you are told without harming anyone or having anyone here who was involved arrested."

John Barber glared at him.

"That's a pretty tall order, old man, since I don't know what the hell happened yet."

"Then start killing us," the old Indian said, "because it's the only offer you will get."

John Barber took a deep breath.

"Fine. What happened?"

"You are right. Your friend was taken out of the hunting area."

"Alive?"

He nodded.

"Who took him out?"

"Four men."

"Americans?" Barber said.

He nodded again.

"Men like me? Hard men? Soldiers?"

"Yes, they were soldiers. Very heavily armed," he said. "They paid in cash for a rented boat and guides. Then they left with your friend in the boat. They didn't tell us their names. We have no idea who they were. Like you, they came through that door unannounced. That's all we know."

"But my friend was alive? You're certain?" Barber said as he holstered the .44.

"Yes," the old man said, nodding. "He was injured, but he was breathing. He was still alive."

14

Three thousand miles to the east, in the soft gold light of daybreak, a vintage vehicle appeared at some speed over a rise on a back country lane in Nokesville, Virginia.

It was a 1961 Porsche 356 cabriolet colored in pearlescent green tea and behind its wheel, Adrian Bright's lips pinched together a little tighter as he drew the car in close along the low hedge that bordered his remote rural vacation property.

At the last possible second, he suddenly spun the wheel hard right as he kicked the clutch, sending the car into a perfect drift. Bright actually laughed and a small and rare genuine smile crossed his face as the fishtailing rear end just cleared the mailbox as it sailed gravel among the wildflowers.

He bumpily zipped the car down his drive. It was lined with a half dozen apple and pear trees and at the end of it was Bright's stone farmhouse. More gravel crackled merrily under the Porsche's expensive Italian Pirelli racing tires as Bright swung it around the circular drive and just under the lip of his rising garage door.

He let the garage door close behind him before he cut the purring engine and then he turned to his left. Bright was a car enthusiast among other things, and in the immaculate bay beside him was nothing short of a work of art, a '73 Jaguar E-type that he'd been restoring for the past three years.

It needed a new transmission and a bunch of other things and would take maybe another year to truly finish it especially with his crazy schedule. But that was okay, he thought, smiling at it.

Adrian Bright, if anything, was a very patient man.

He got out and keyed in the security code above the meat freezer before he climbed the garage steps. There was a mirror just inside the mudroom door, and he stopped and smiled at himself in it, checking his teeth. He looked at the middle-aged balding blond man in a smart casual jacket staring back at him. His face was as bland and puffy as vanilla pudding now that fifty had come and gone, wasn't it? But the blazer brought out the blue in his still sharp eyes.

He smiled again as he remembered the perfect drift past the mailbox.

"I still got it," he said with a wink.

He frowned as he stepped farther into the cold empty house. Usually upon arriving home after work during the week in Georgetown, Juanita would have the thermostat set the way he liked it and CNBC on in his study with his Pellegrino chilled and waiting. But staying alone in their country house while his wife, Claudette, visited her mother in Florida, they'd given Juanita the week off.

The things I do for love, Bright thought with a sigh as he kicked off his loafers.

He was outside wearing his jogging stuff three minutes later. One of the neighbor's cows gave out a hearty bellow as he walked through the garden past the pool. Adrian bellowed back even louder and laughed.

Why his wife always claimed to hate their country place so much, he'd never know. He absolutely couldn't get enough of it.

"What isn't there to like?" he said to himself happily as he passed under the tangle of their climbing rosebush.

Past the lap pool, house and garden, the sound of excited yelping was already ringing out as he crunched up the kennel's gravel front path. There was full-on baying by the time the chain-link fence jingled. He glanced at the clipboard hanging off the fence where Thomas, his caretaker and dogwalker, noted things. But there was nothing.

"There you are. You miss me?" Adrian said with a laugh as he quickly unlocked all the gates and dropped to the Astroturf as Stanley came running.

A fairly hard drinker in his time, Bright used to have a stiffener or three after work. But, wow, was this better, he thought as he lay flat on his back, scruffing at his buddy. Like being reborn.

After he and Stanley were friends again, he got him going first with a game of tennis ball fetch before he unlocked the front gate and took him out for their jog. As usual, the cows on the other side of the stone wall along the back meadow took off like a shot as they approached.

"They fear you, Stanley," he said to his dog. "See that they always fear you."

15

When they were done with this fun, back at the kennel his smooth little fox terrier stayed right at his heel as they went through another gate to the agility course.

Bright smiled as Stanley headed straight as an arrow for the jump bars without prompting. What a dog, Bright thought, as he watched him slalom through the weave poles and bolt over the teeter-totter for the tunnel. Pure white except for his half golden brown face, Stanley was handsome and active, smart and playful, curious and quite nimble and acute.

He wasn't just the best fox terrier Bright had ever had, he thought watching him. He was the best fox terrier Bright had ever laid eyes on. His compact body was just compact enough, his long face just so.

Which was why he was really thinking of actually going for it and placing him at Westminster.

But should he really? Bright thought for the umpteenth time.

Was it really time to try for the bigs? True, he had helped a friend's Burmese mountain dog to score best in breed in Eukanuba last December. But Eukanuba was not Westminster, was it? Not by a long shot.

It was his wife's family that had gotten him into dogs. The Everetts—descended from the famed Richard Everett, who founded Springfield, Massachusetts, in the early 1600s—had been dog people from the *Mayflower* times. His wife's father, Edward, had actually won at Westminster with Coco, their pug, in the early eighties. Claudette was nine at the time, and she told him she never forgot that moment of pure elation. It was the jewel in the crown of the Everett family pride.

He watched Stanley give off a high-pitched bark as he shot into the tunnel like a rocket.

Then he closed his eyes, visualizing it. He and Stanley parading with the silver cup under the hot Madison Square Garden lights as her elderly father (whom he didn't get along with and who had actually tried to drive Claudette away from him) ate crow.

Claudette, his tall thirty-nine-year-old still-smoking-hot swan of a wife, would simply swoon.

Why not? he thought to himself as Stanley barked again as he emerged from the tunnel's other side.

"Why not dream the impossible dream?" Bright said.

After another half an hour, Bright put Stanley up and went in and took a shower. Ten minutes after that, he was in his robe rummaging around in the fridge. He tentatively sniffed at a catering tray of veal piccata from a twenty-first birthday party they had thrown for Claudette's cousin, Georgina, the week before. Good thing too, it turned out, as deciding to stay in the country until his wife's return he'd been basically living off it for the past three days. It was pretty slim pickings without Juanita around.

A tad sketchy, he thought as he clattered the tray onto the glowing white marble countertop.

"But beggars can't be choosers," he said with a sigh.

He'd just peeled back the cold foil when he got the call on his work phone.

"And we have liftoff," said Bouthier.

"Is that right?"

"Well, just about. Gannon is on the plane. It's about to take off."

"Collateral?" Bright said.

"No collateral," Bouthier said. "We lucked out. The kid and guide weren't there. No witnesses. He was alone. He might have suffered a slight skull fracture and there's some bruised ribs in the takedown. But all other vitals are fine."

Bright nodded. He'd had problems with contractors in the past, but Bouthier apparently was as skilled a professional as advertised.

"Excellent work. Pass on my thanks to all involved."

Bright hung up and plated some veal. The microwave hummed.

The Gannon file was quite the little hot potato. After the issue at the Chilean embassy in London, some said action should have been called for, but it had been nixed by someone for some reason. But then Gannon's name came up again mixed in with the San Francisco airport abortion where a Pentagon artificial intelligence asset as well as a Senior Executive Service member had lost their lives.

This had set off even more alarm bells. An SES member's death was the biggest of all no-no's, completely unacceptable. Bright himself was SES. Which was why eventually he'd come up with a plan to deal with the troublesome former navy SEAL.

Bright smiled as he thought about what was now in store for the SEAL. It was going to be a surprise all right. One the troublesome impudent upstart wasn't going to forget.

Oh, yes, Bright thought as the microwave started to beep. Things were working out swimmingly.

Several birds with one stone was what Mr. Bright was all about.

16

Cold on a cold floor, Gannon woke up on his side.

The vibration against his numb face and a raw metallic whir in the air told him immediately he was in an aircraft aloft. When he opened his eyes, he realized there was some kind of hood over his face, and when he tried to move, the cold steel of the handcuffs he was wearing behind his back bit into his wrists.

He lay motionless, evaluating. He was still wearing his hunting coveralls but they'd taken off his boots and socks to put another set of cuffs on his ankles.

There was also a bandage on his head, and he could feel that his ribs were taped up. When he took a breath, he felt a stitch on his right side.

Slowly and carefully, he began to piece together what had happened. The four men on the snowmobiles. The hard-faced leader of them. He winced at the terrible memory of being thrown over the handlebars.

After that there was nothing, a full blank.

He thought about Declan then. Would they have harmed or captured him as well?

No, he decided with a breath of relief. At least he didn't think so. He'd been alone, thank God. The only use of his son would be to get to him. And they had him now.

The cuffs clicked at his back when he tried to move his arms. *Boy, did they have him.*

It was pitch-black under the hood. He listened to the drone of the aircraft. The cold floor rumbled slightly beneath him as they hit a little turbulence.

He wondered what time it was. It felt like night.

Yeah, he thought. But which night?

Assuming he was now in the hands of the corrupt intelligence scum he'd been banging heads with, he realized they were most likely renditioning him somewhere outside of the US.

His head dropped to his chest.

You have to be kidding me, he thought. He knew what was coming. He'd be brought to some foreign hellhole where they'd drug him and interrogate him with torture. They'd want to find out who and what he knew about them, where the money and diamonds were that he had found in the Bahamas, the people he'd been talking to, all the people who knew.

Then what?

Then they'd kill him was what. Dump his bloody and burned broken body in an unmarked hole or dissolve it in muriatic acid.

Then after they erased his body, they'd erase his memory. If his name ever found the light of day again, they'd probably lie about it. Say he was a PTSD-crazed veteran domestic terrorist they'd stopped in the nick of time from blowing up a federal building or a preschool. Use the lie to polish up the alphabet agencies' dwindling respect with the public and get their anti-terror budgets up higher.

You had to give these blackhearted devils their due, he thought. They were clever. Everything they did was a double blind.

Gannon closed his eyes.

As an eight-tour veteran of the so-called War on Terror with the SEALs, he had worked with spooks. Several times. And to be honest, he hadn't found even one that he had liked all that much.

Because with few exceptions, as a group, they were all basically very arrogant, nasty, bratty, childish, rich Ivy League snobs. They truly seemed to think that because they had money and their daddy got them into Yale that they weren't just smarter than you, they were truly better than you, as in inherently more important and of superior worth.

That the United States of America had actually been formed through a bloody war with the British Crown to do away with all that terrible and animalistic blue-blood birthright royal bullshit didn't really seem to occur to them all that much.

Because of this, they often treated blue-collar tactical people not so much like co-workers or brothers in arms, but like brainless footmen who weren't fetching their bags fast enough.

Added to this incredibly unpleasant demeanor was the fact that they all seemed kind of nuts, deeply depressed, outright sociopathic, passive aggressive. After watching that movie *American Psycho*, Gannon had thought, there you go. Polished Park Avenue killers with confident good looks, impeccable preppy clothes, and funny sick little smiles.

He wasn't the only SEAL who had observed their uniquely unpleasant peccadilloes either.

And now his screw-loose managers had him, didn't they? They had to be pleased. He was like a butler who had run off with the silver. Can't have that. Not fitting.

That's why he needed to be punished now. Slowly and pain-fully and very firmly brought back to heel.

Maybe you should have stayed off the grid a little longer, huh, dumbass? Gannon thought, opening his eyes.

17

Screw the pity party! Gannon yelled at himself in his head. *Do something!*

He wriggled himself up into a seated position, waiting for someone to yell at him or maybe strike him with a rifle butt.

When it didn't happen, he wondered if they were watching him with a camera. He sat there, expecting to hear a door open. But that didn't happen either.

Which meant what? He was alone, he decided. At least for the moment.

Under his palms was some stiff carpet. As every military plane he'd ever been on had been floored with rubber and steel, that meant he was on a commercial jet.

Probably one of the CIA's little corporate ones.

Just like the crashed one in the Bahamas that had gotten him wrapped up in this mess, he thought.

"Golly gee, Mike," he whispered to himself. "How ironic."

When he reached his bound hands out to his right, he felt some kind of canvas cargo netting straps. As his hands probed around at them, he thought about those choose-your-own-adventure books from when he was a kid.

You have just woken up handcuffed in the luggage hold of a corporate CIA jet. What do you do?

As he thought on this, he remembered playing the Oregon Trail computer game with Declan when his son was in grade school. The best parts were when the nonplayer characters would offer you hilariously stilted and ridiculous propositions about what to do next.

"You have now been bitten by a rattlesnake. Is it a deal?" they would joke.

"Yeah," he whispered under the stifling black hood. "Tee-frickin-hee."

He began to wriggle backward and after a second, he heard a click down by his ankles.

"Shit!" he said.

They weren't taking any chances, were they? They had his ankle cuffs chained to something else to immobilize him.

When he reached back as far as his aching hands would allow, his fingers could just reach the cold curved wall of the aircraft's fuselage.

He played them over the metal wall, searching. For what, he wasn't sure. A loaded Glock would be nice. Maybe a nifty pair of bolt cutters. And then a parachute and the handle to the exit door.

But after a minute or two, the only things he found were some open steel ribbing and some screw heads. Even after straining for five minutes until he thought his back would snap, he didn't get anything for his trouble except a scratch on his thumb as it caught a sharp burr or something sticking up on one of the screws.

He lay back down on his side and let out a breath as his lower back throbbed. He was rubbing at his sticky slightly bleeding thumb when a thought slowly began to occur to him.

He sat back up and wiggled back over to the plane wall again. Pushing back with his hands, he felt at the screw head where he'd encountered the burr. After a moment of probing, he found the burr was actually the sharp end of a thin wire coming off the screw. Tracing the wire, he realized it led to another screw head along the curved ribbing.

Maybe the constant vibrations of the aircraft over time loosened the screws so they used a little piece of thin steel wire to keep them battened down tight? That sounded right. They did the same thing with speedboats.

He strained back, pushing with his thumb painfully, until he was able to just get his fingernail in under the sharp edge of the tight twist of wire. He gritted his teeth as his thumb slipped and the sharp tip of the wire end went painfully in under his thumbnail.

Instead of pulling it back out, Gannon gritted his teeth even more as he pushed even harder with his thumb, digging the metal tip even deeper in under his nail. Then he bit at his lip as he pushed with his thumb at the wire, trying to move it.

Sweat was dripping down his face two full minutes later when he stopped. As he unstuck himself, he didn't think he had moved the wire at all. But when he checked it again with his forefinger, he realized it was sticking up a little tiny bit more than before.

Gannon closed his eyes under the hot and sweaty smelly black hood as he painfully jabbed the end of the wire in under his thumbnail again and began to push at it with all his might.

18

Nine hundred nautical miles south of the nose of the jet where Gannon lay abducted, at an outdoor veranda behind a hotel in the small beach town of La Crucecita, Mexico, the Jennifer Lopez 2011 dance hit "On the Floor" suddenly began to play.

Directly beneath one of the speakers at the table closest to the sand sat two men and a woman. The shorter of the two men, a rough-looking portly little man with a mustache who needed a shave, suddenly smiled as he pointed up at it.

"Hey, Lou. Check it out. They're playing your song," he said.

The woman giggled at this.

"Go ahead and join in when your part comes up," he continued. "We won't laugh. We promise."

The taller man, whose name was Louis Salazar, loudly clacked down the Stoli and soda he was drinking onto the glass tabletop as he shook his bald head.

Because whenever anyone said that he had a kind of a Pitbull the Rapper thing going on with his look, Lou went bananas.

It wasn't like that at all. There were *major* differences. First off, Lou was much taller at six-one while Pitbull was only five-nine. Plus, he had brown eyes while Pitbull's were blue. Lou was also a Dominican from New York while Pitbull was some little Cuban cat from Miami.

Besides, Lou had been rolling like this since the tenth grade up in Washington Heights, shaved head and always crisply dressed. If anything, he told people, Pitbull was copying him!

"How many times I have to tell you?" Lou said.

"But come on, man, you even have that little soul patch thing he's got," said Lou's buddy, Manuel Herrera, pointing his own after-dinner nightcap at Lou's chin. "You could be his professional impersonator."

"Mine was there first, Manny," Lou replied, as he shook his head some more. "He must have seen me somewhere at a club or something. I'm telling you, I hate the little Cuban shrimp son of a bitch. I should sue him for ripping me off."

"He's such a liar," Herrera said to Alessandra Cota, the table's third occupant sitting across from them. "You ever been to a nightclub with him? After a few more drinks, he starts sounding like him. He probably sings like him in front of the mirror when no one's looking."

Lou smiled over at Alessandra as she laughed. She had hardly touched her Cuervo. Of course, she hadn't. The lady had manners to burn. Attractive and regal and cultured, the high-class South American even laughed demurely.

"Yeah, okay, ha ha. Whatever," Lou said coldly to Manny. "Don't believe me. Have it your own ignorant way then. You're the one who brought it up."

Then after a beat, Lou, looking out at the darkened beach, growled in a perfect imitation of Pitbull's low whiskey voice.

"Brazil, Morocco, London to Ibiza."

And that actually got the both of them going.

Oh, yeah, Lou thought, laughing himself as he stirred some ice cubes.

Fun was being had by all this Friday night in ol' Mexico, he thought. Party time was in the house.

As they cracked up, Lou did a quick and methodical scan of the other tables and the rear lobby of their playful white stucco hotel with its thatched roof. Despite the beachy setting and all the laughs, they weren't here on spring break. Quite the contrary.

They had business to conduct, a serious-as-cancer business meeting that would take place tomorrow afternoon up in the Sierra Sur mountains high above the town.

They were heading to this thing that was called the Concurso. The Contest. Some mysterious happening all the major cartel bigwigs put on once a year.

It was like some kind of convention, a rare truce and meetup between all the top Mexican players, a gesture of industry solidarity.

And at the heart of it was some sort of mysterious event.

Was the Concurso a sporting event? Lou wondered for the hundredth time. A horse race? An orgy? A satanic initiation? All four?

No one knew. Because attendees couldn't talk about it and actually didn't. Which for Mexico, where gossip was all but officially the national pastime, that was truly saying something.

The important thing for them was that their invite to it through Alessandra meant they were being given a job interview at the tippity-top of the drug smuggling food chain.

Which was exactly what their up-and-coming yet still floundering little operation needed quite badly, Lou thought.

They had a nice little network going on, the three of them, a one-stop discreet ground-and-air service for getting lucrative contraband from the Amazon jungle to Brownsville, Texas.

Pudgy, fun-loving Manny was responsible for the Mexican ground part. Head lieutenant of the Tamaulipas federal highway department's night shift, he was in charge of arranging which cars would be studiously ignored along the last stretch of the smuggling routes into the US. And even more importantly, which ones would be protected with Mexican police caravan escorts to ensure deliveries didn't get stolen by rival cartels.

Lou himself was the in-between air freight part of it. The proud owner of three Cessna 414s hangared at an off-the-beaten-path airfield in Honduras. It was he and his pilots who did the careful and stealthy leapfrog stuff from the South American jungles to Manny in Mexico.

But Alessandra was the straw that stirred the drink. Widow of a Colombian who had been a high-up in the Cali cartel, Alessandra Cota, the chestnut-haired former runner-up for Miss Venezuela, was their lovely and essential South American liaison.

With her elegant manners and serene courtly demeanor, the attractive thirty-something was the most unlikely of crooks possible. Lou often felt he and Manny were more like her pilot and chauffer rather than her drug smuggling partners.

What a nice girl like her was doing in a jungle like this, Lou didn't know. What he did know was that she was definitely the final piece to the puzzle for the whole operation.

Because getting into the lucrative South American cocaine fields was about as easy as a new broker getting into Manhattan real estate. With so much money involved and so little trust, it was all about nepotism. Who you knew rather than what you knew.

Even with Manny, they'd been getting nowhere. They were working with some real low-level Panamanian flakes he knew before Alessandra herself had approached them through another of Manny's corrupt cop friends.

She had heard Lou and Manny were up-and-comers with some planes and a solid pipeline across the US border. It was she who had suggested they take her on as a full partner to be their sole South American broker.

No problem there, Lou thought, watching her stand across the candlelit table.

"Well, gentlemen, we have a long day tomorrow, if you will excuse me," she said, pulling on her wrap.

"I'm telling you," Manny said as they watched the back of their partner's toned fitness-model body cross the sand. "This Concurso will blow your mind, Lou. Up into that mountain jungle tomorrow, it's gonna just kaboom that shit bye-bye."

"Yeah, I'm more interested in the mind-blowing amount of cash we're going to be seeing once we finally make this connection," Lou said.

They both thought about that as they listened to the roar of the Pacific waves.

"But wait, how do you know, man?" Lou finally said.

"Know what?"

"About the Concurso. You've never been there before."

"This is true," Manny said, winking. "But I've been told by those who have. They say once witnessed, you leave a changed man."

"Changed, huh?" Lou said, yawning as he stood himself. "That might work out for you then, huh, Manny. Who knows? Maybe after it's said and done, you'll be taller and better looking."

"Screw you, Pitbull," Manny said, laughing good-naturedly as Lou left. "Go trim your soul patch, would you? And don't forget to say hi to J-Lo for me tonight in your dreams."

19

Up in his third-floor suite, Lou neatly hung up his suit and put on the hotel's fluffy bathrobe from the closet.

There were some Stoli minis in the fridge, and he poured himself another drink and took it with him to the window. He smiled as he saw Manny still down at the beach bar, hitting on one of the waitresses. The little Mexican meatball just didn't quit, did he?

Manny, he thought, smiling. He actually liked the guy. At least a little.

Or did he really? Lou wondered. Wasn't it just because Manny was easy to manage because he wasn't that bright?

That was it, Lou thought as he yawned and turned and walked over and sat back on the bed. Bingo. Manny was easy to snow, to get over on.

That's what it was all about, wasn't it? he thought. The secret of his success. To be good with people, good at making friends, especially with other men. Camaraderie was his specialty. That was the key to it really.

He sipped his Stoli and sighed with a smile, allowing himself a rare pat on the back.

He really did have actual charisma, didn't he? He was calm, funny, a good listener, patient. People liked him. And he liked them back. Or at least liked playing with them. Staying one step ahead. It was like a game.

That was the way to do it. Be a man's man. Be suave. Set it up so that the others were too busy—wanting to be friends with him, to play golf with him, or to watch him expertly hit on women—to ever get in his way.

That's exactly how he had roped in Manny at a club in Cancun the year before.

It had ended up working like a charm. He knew how much Manny liked to party, what a horndog he was. Some sloppy drunk divorcee from Belize had been hitting on Lou at the bar and when Manny came by, Lou drunkenly bumped into him and asked him to do him a favor by pretending to be his friend so he could blow her off.

He just introduced her to Manny and left. That's all it took. Two nights later, when he had "accidentally" bumped into Manny again at another tourist dive, Manny had high-fived him.

He couldn't stop thanking Lou for his lucky night with Ms. Belize. He had to buy him a drink, had to. It was like they were long-lost friends.

That was all she wrote. A month later, they were thick as thieves in business.

It had been serendipity. And Lou's silver tongue. And his balls, of course.

That was his best quality, wasn't it? he thought with a smile as his eyelids began to flutter. His incredible amount of balls.

20

His eyes shot bolt open a second later when he heard his phone chirp. It was his real phone. His personal phone.

"Shit," he said as he knocked the drink to the floor as he searched for it on the bedside table. It wasn't there. He looked around and leaped up when he spotted it on the desk.

As he crossed to get it, he wondered if his wife, Marcia, had texted him.

But no. That was impossible, he thought. He'd told her he was working. She knew not to contact him when he was at work.

He lifted the phone. It was a text from the phone company telling him his data was seventy percent used.

He tossed the phone back down and clutched his head in his hands.

It wasn't just his data that was running out on him here, was it? he thought.

"What the hell are you doing here, Lou?" he whispered to himself as he slowly sat down on the edge of the bed.

That was a good question.

Because he was in an in-between sort of place, wasn't he?

Just go back and tell her, he thought to himself for the five-hundredth time. Stop this crazy bullshit and get on a plane, go back home and lay it all out to Marcia, Mr. Balls.

But how? he thought, massaging his temples. *How?*

He really could have kicked the ever-living shit out of himself. Everything had been going so well until he got the call two months before. It was from a girlfriend from high school of all places.

Well, not just from high school. He had bumped into her at a club in Manhattan a few years after he had gotten married. She looked really great and gave him her number. She kept calling him and then he slipped and he slept with her.

He thought, that's it. Never again. It was just the one time. He broke it off. Clean, he thought. It ended up being the only time he had ever cheated. The only fricking time! And there had been opportunities. Oh, how there had been opportunities!

Then two months ago, fourteen fricking years after this one indiscretion, he gets the call from her. She spills the beans. How he had knocked her up that night. How she'd kept the kid, a daughter named Amy, who was now a teenager and wanted to talk to her father.

In complete freak-out mode, he was going to fight it until he saw Amy's picture. He knew there was no mistaking it. It was like looking into a mirror. Then the hard sell started coming soon after. Could he send her some money to help with the kid? They had hit some hard times.

His old girlfriend was living in Vegas now. She was still looking okay, but she seemed like a drug addict by the sound of it.

Hate to bring your wife into it, she said. We really don't have to. Just need some money. A hundred grand would do it. Or maybe two. Didn't want to be a pest.

Which was why he was here in Mexico, acting like a damn maniac.

To get that money.

It wasn't even the threat of being exposed, he thought. It was the girl, Amy. His *daughter* Amy, he corrected himself. She was so sad and a little overweight but pretty. She reminded him of pictures of his mother, young. And what the hell kind of life did she have with this nut of a blackmailing drug addict mother in Vegas?

He was really doing it for Amy, to support her.

Yeah, right, Mr. Clean, Lou thought, rolling his eyes. Who the hell are you kidding?

He needed the money so his wife didn't find out. He loved Marcia so much and this would destroy their marriage. Destroy it. Right when they were going to go off into the sunset together.

Because he was about to retire from this insane life. They were in the process of selling the apartment in Brooklyn. They were going off to live in the low country. A brand-new house where Marcia had picked out everything. The cabinets, the counter-tops. She was from upstate New York and had never really liked living in the city. She was so happy she was about to head home to a new uncrazy, calm country life. It was like her reward for putting up with Lou and his completely crazy life.

They were going to do all the things they couldn't because of the kids. Make up for all the lost time. Take it easy. They loved playing golf together, and Marcia was going to have a real garden. He owed her that. Owed her so much. Everything in fact.

And this revelation of his stupid idiot weak moment would destroy her. Just wreck her. Another kid? Are you kidding? She might even leave him.

He thought about that.

Then he stopped thinking about it.

Because that wasn't going to happen.

He was going to walk that tightrope one last time, he thought, nodding. He was going to go up against the killers with a smile and a freaking shoeshine one last time and come out of it flush.

He was going to get the money. Set up one or at most two massive coke runs. Play both sides against each other. Get his cut finally. His out. His cover.

Didn't he damn well deserve it for all he had put in? he thought, lying back.

One more time. Just for himself. And then the rest of his life would start the way they had been planning.

He poured and lay the cool of his drink to his forehead as if to soothe his worries.

One more time, Lou thought as his eyes finally shut. And he would be home free.

21

Gannon snapped awake like a hit switch.

Dammit, he thought as he realized the vibration and sense of movement was gone.

The last thing he remembered was shivering as he fell asleep on the cold moving plane.

Now he was stopped dead and it was very hot, and he was sweating like it was going out of style.

He was still in the hunting coveralls, still cuffed behind his back and at his feet, and still wearing the hood over his head. But he wasn't on the plane anymore.

He tried to remember leaving the plane. But he couldn't. Not even the slightest trace of a memory. The bastards must have injected him with something in his sleep.

He thought about that. How sick that was. To creep over and inject something into someone while they were sleeping. What the hell even was it? Ketamine? Quaaludes? Snake piss? It could have been anything. It made his skin crawl, made him want to throw up.

I'm going to kill somebody, Gannon thought.

Stow that for later, he thought. *Liquid nitrogen that shit. Analyze.*

He was on his back on something hard, a prison cot maybe or a concrete floor.

That it was so hot seemed to reinforce his first depressing theory about being renditioned to another country.

Or maybe not. Maybe it was Florida, he thought.

Like I said, he thought after another beat. *Another country.*

He could tell it was daytime by the faint light through the smelly hood. As he listened intently, he began to hear the weird echoes of people talking coming from somewhere. He tried to make out if they were speaking English, but they were too far away.

Good golly, did this suck, he thought as he lay there, filthy and sweating.

He knew the point of handling him this way, keeping a hood over his head, making him hungry and thirsty and dirty and itchy. The constant stream of stress and dread and physical irritation was to weaken his spirit, soften him up, infect him with despair to erase any potential defiance.

Good luck with that, he thought as he probed his tongue down to the floor of his mouth and felt the piece of steel wire he'd managed to loosen from the bolt heads on the plane.

Astringently metal-ish with notes of dirty carpet and the faintest creamy wisp of aircraft engine oil, Gannon thought crazily as he licked at the smooth piece of thin metal.

We here at *Wire Enthusiast Magazine* can confidently give it a 91-rating going away.

Not exactly an ace up his sleeve, he thought, licking at his skinny little metal secret.

But at this point he'd take anything at all.

22

The Escalade the cartel sent to the beach hotel was a slick pearl gray beast with black tinted windows. Twenty minutes up above La Crucecita, a flock of pigeons scattered before it as it swung off the curving asphalt onto a dirt road.

Lou looked out its back windshield to see if the Ford F150 escort vehicle with them would follow. It did, the two young *sicarios* strapping AR-15s in the bed of it, laughing at each other as they ducked down their black bush hat covered heads to avoid the jungle underbrush's low-hanging fronds.

"Are we having fun yet or what?" said Manny beside him, thumbing back his black cowboy hat to show off his swag Rick Ross—style sunglasses.

Dressed to the nines and seemingly coked to the gills, Manny seemed even more amped-up than usual. As if in direct contrast, Alessandra, beside the driver, was placid, unruffled.

He watched as Alessandra said something to the driver to make him laugh then touched up her lips with some gloss.

In her pale flowered silk dress and nude heels with her hair done, she could have been a bored aristocrat on the way to a charity event.

Yeah, Lou thought. Alessandra was the shit all right. Smart, quiet, played her good looks like a virtuoso. She fluttered among all these psycho killers like a butterfly, didn't she? he thought. One with ice in its veins.

Lou brushed a finger nervously over his soul patch as he looked at the back of her done-up hair.

He had good reason to be nervous. Now he was entering the sanctum sanctorum.

Alessandra had used her connections to get in with someone she said was a real player, a group that was referred to as El Aleman.

El Aleman, Spanish for "the German," was actually a name Lou had heard before. Some people that he knew in the drug trade talked about El Aleman Group with a kind of fearful reverence.

If Alessandra's connection came through, they'd be made. Made in the shade drinking lemonade in fact. They'd be doing a hundred kilos a week or even more. After one run, they could practically get another plane. After two or more, you were looking at exponential growth, corporation level money. The potential money that would roll in would be mind-boggling.

Lou only needed a fraction of it off the top for his own personal marital issues, of course.

And then he'd retire.

Sure you will, said a little voice in Lou's guilt-ridden mind. *Sure you will.*

23

"Wheee!" Manny called out like an idiot as the Escalade bucked in and out of a trail hole.

As they straightened out, Lou's eyes suddenly fell upon the vehicle's fifth occupant he hadn't noticed before, a small statue of Our Lady of Guadalupe glued to the dashboard.

Oh good, that's just what I need, he thought, staring at it. More guilt.

Lou knew all about Our Lady of Guadalupe from his grandmother. Every time he would visit her on University Avenue in the Bronx, before he could get his cookie, she would give him a plastic saint card that he would have to read over and over until he could recite back the pertinent stats from memory.

Our Lady of Guadalupe, he remembered, was the venerated version of the Virgin Mary who had appeared before Saint Juan Diego near Mexico City in the 1500s. He knew all about Juan Diego's famous tilma cloak that had miraculously been embossed with Her image from a bouquet of roses Our Lady had given him and how this image was the only one in Christendom that showed the Blessed Mother pregnant with Jesus.

Since he was in the middle of the commission of a litany of sins, as Lou looked at the little statue, he wondered if praying for help was even appropriate.

He decided to say a Hail Mary anyway. Then an Our Father as well for good measure. How could it hurt?

When he was finished, they were slowing. They were coming on a switchback turn on the jungle hill and through a gap in the foliage in the distance was the green splattering stream of a lovely waterfall.

Lou tracked the line of falling water as it wound down the jungle slope and then he stopped as his eyes almost bugged out of his head.

Because peeking out from the triple canopy below to his right was the top of a pyramid.

It was made of stone and was the size of a small office building. It had crumbling gray stone steps at its center with terrifying primitive carvings along its sides like you'd see on a totem pole.

Lou instantly remembered what Manny had said about *Ancient Aliens*. It could have been a still from the show, a pale Stone Age archeological site just sticking up out of the palm trees there in the middle of Mexican nowhere.

"Man, you gotta be joking," Lou said, feeling the hairs rise on the back of his neck. "Do you see what I see? They got all that old Aztec stuff around here?"

"No, man. It's not the Aztecs," Manny said, popping the gum he was chewing. "It's even freakier, bro. This is the area that belonged to the Mayans who were like before the Aztecs. The ancient, ancient ones."

"This whole mountain is a Mayan burial ground, right?" Alessandra asked the driver.

The cartel driver turned. His ageless stony face might have

been the model for some of the pyramid carvings below. He nodded cryptically.

"See? How many times I gotta tell you?" Manny said, clapping Lou on the back painfully. "We're about to come into contact with some interplanetary multidimensional shit on steroids, Lou. Nazca Lines, star gates, Puma Punku, here we come!"

Lou unbuttoned another button on his silk shirt as the pyramid slid away out of sight to his right. When he looked up, his eyes locked on Our Lady again. He tried to read if Her young serene face was sad or angry at him. Both, it seemed.

He didn't blame Her.

He looked away as they flowed deeper into the jungle.

He felt pretty much the same way about himself.

24

It was coming on three itchy, stifling hours of hot and dull agony later when Gannon reared back at the sudden loud scuff of a boot by his face.

Then the hood was suddenly pulled.

Gannon winced and pinched his eyes shut tight at the scorch of the sudden bright light. It was a full minute later when he could hold them open long enough to take a look around.

And immediately felt like closing them again.

He was on a kind of plywood cot with no mattress in a small room with cracked plaster walls. A prison cell, he thought at first until he realized that bright daylight was flooding in through a window above him. Prison cells rarely had windows and this was a normal-looking one without any bars on it.

Not a prison then?

He turned the other way. Whoever had pulled his hood was gone, and there was an open door to his left that led out into a scoured stucco corridor. Ten feet into this narrow hallway along the wall was a cheap-looking industrial gray metal tray on wheels.

It was a hospital, he realized, staring at the cart's rusty wheels. Some kind of rundown hellhole country hospital.

"Shit, shit, shit," he said.

As he attempted to sit up fully on the cot, there was a loud metal clicking and clacking by his feet, and he looked down to where his ankle cuffs had been passed through a thick reddish iron chain.

A pulse of terror passed through him as he stared at the rusty links. They looked about a million years old, like slave block chains or something. Like something you'd see in a ye-olden-times Middle Ages dungeon.

He looked up as there were what sounded like car horn honks from outside the window. Then he turned at another scuff of a boot.

The figure who stepped in through the open doorway was about six feet tall and bodybuilder-jacked and was wearing camo military fatigues. Even with a black ski mask on, Gannon immediately recognized it was the muscled-up jackass who had taken him out of Alaska.

Gannon looked at the camo. It had little square digital dots in it, splotches of black and orange against light green. Not US military, Gannon thought. But he'd seen it before. Did the British SAS use it? No, it was some other NATO country. What was it called? Flecktarn, he remembered.

He definitely recognized the weapon in the guy's thigh holster. It was a Colt M1911 .45 in a blackened finish. It was the government model. Big five-inch barrel. Eight in the magazine plus one in the pipe.

Gannon stared at the gun for another second then finally looked up at the guy staring back at him.

Like the .45, the guy's eyes seemed to have a blackened finish to them as well. Like a doll's. Button eyes, they called them when he was a kid.

NATO fatigues? Gannon thought again, trying to figure things out. Was he in Turkey?

As Gannon tried to rack his memory, he noticed how slow going it was. His mental acuity seemed blurry, wooden. It was the blow to the head he'd taken, he realized. Still some cobwebs. Concussions took a few days or sometimes even weeks to clear. Or was it the mystery injections?

"Hey, nice fatigues. Belgian?" was the first thing that Gannon could think to say after another few seconds.

Button Eyes wouldn't say. He kept staring.

"French?" Gannon tried.

"A medic is on his way up here," Button Eyes said in perfect unaccented American English as he bent and undid the handcuffs. "He'll clean you up and get you dressed. You give him some trouble, you're going to be carrying around your teeth in your pocket."

"Got it," Gannon said. "Could I just get a drink, man? I need some water. I'm dying of thirst."

But Button Eyes had already turned, and the door of the closet-size room slammed shut hard enough to raise the dust.

25

The incline the Escalade was climbing suddenly leveled. There was a pause and then a sudden rumbling shot through the car as the dirt path under the tires became cobblestones.

Coming out from under the jungle trees into a sunny clearing, they began to bump alongside a wall. Lou looked up at it. It was comprised of yellowish stone blocks and had to be about three stories tall. Running along the top of it were whitewashed parapets and just underneath them were architectural moldings, elaborate cornices, entablatures.

As they came in closer, Lou began to spot people walking along the parapets. Even from some distance, he could tell how attractive the women were. They were wearing white, showing a lot of skin. Everyone was wearing sunglasses.

Lou had gone to the famous horse race at Saratoga Springs in New York and that was the vibe he immediately got. Upscale rich people in festive summer mode, partying.

"What is this? A castle?" Lou said up to the driver.

"It's been many things," Alessandra said. "It was a presidio originally. One of Cortez's. Then they tried to build a cathedral. But that was abandoned and then they finally turned it into a prison in 1920 when the communists came to power. But even that fell through. It's been abandoned and closed for years, since the 1970s."

"How do you know all this, Alessandra?" Manny said. "You've been here before?"

"No, but my husband was," she said, turning. "When the Concurso began, my husband was invited to the first one with his business partner, Alberto, who we are going to meet today."

"You tell us all this now?" Manny said, wide-eyed. "I thought we were partners."

"A lady likes to retain an air of mystery, Manuel," Lou said. "Am I right?"

Alessandra, turning, smiled as she slipped on a pair of sunglasses.

Lou slipped on his own as they slowed behind some other SUVs already parked before the old prison's wide-open iron gates. Slick-looking security people in suits were wanding people and taking cell phones. Having thought about that already, Lou had left his back at the hotel.

Both of his phones, he thought with a swallow.

As the doors finally popped, he looked forward at Our Lady one last time, resisting the urge to cross himself.

The svelte, handsome security guard who greeted them outside wore his dark hair slicked back into a ponytail.

"Ladies and gentlemen, welcome to the Concurso," he said with a flourish of his metal detecting wand. "Please present any and all cell phones or weapons, and if you could please raise your arms out straight up beside you. Yes, that's it, senorita. What excellent form you have. Might I say, you look very beautiful today.

Thank you. And you two as well. What a handsome group. Yes, that's it. Arms up. Just like that, senor. Perfect."

A footpath of cobblestone led them in beneath an arch. At the other side of it, the compound's interior was even larger than it looked from the outside. To the left and right, the walls ran what had to be two football fields long or more, and at the corners stood what looked like four-story-high parapeted guard towers.

Centered between this rectangle of stone walls was the huge prison itself, a massive three-story slab of brick and concrete. Lou looked up at its tall high windows. They were glassless now and the iron bars and casings within them had gone dark with rust.

Taking in the hot desolate prison yard, Lou was wondering why the hell anyone would want to meet up here when there was the high whine of a speaker being turned on. The strains of a Spanish guitar started up and a moment later, it was accompanied by a loud and catchy salsa beat.

When a crooning voice suddenly started rapping along to it, Lou smiled, looking around to see where it was coming from.

"You've gotta be shitting me," he said, as he backpedaled and turned and spotted the stage set up atop the guard tower in the corner to their right.

As he stepped back some more, he saw they had the whole nine up there. Scruffy pretty-boy guys with guitars, bleached blonde female backup singers.

Lou was still smiling and shaking his head at this when a waiter with a tray appeared from somewhere behind them. The flute of pink champagne Lou accepted with a thanks was pleasantly cold under his fingertips.

Lou laughed as Manny raised his own glass and started bopping along to the salsa. Then he laughed some more as Alessandra, rolling her eyes, let the short, goofy pudgeball turn her in a spin.

"Very funny, you two. Enough. These people don't work with fools," she said, as the waiter gestured them on for the guard tower to the left.

26

Salsa pop wasn't exactly at the tippity-top of Gannon's playlist, but when he heard some start up from somewhere through the doorway, a not so small beat of relief pulsed through him.

Not exactly "Born in the USA," but it sure as hell beats the Muslim call to prayer, he thought.

So he was where? Mexico? Gannon thought brightly. Mexico didn't seem so bad. He'd take Brazil at this point. Hell, Argentina. Because once he got out of this, he could walk home if he had to. Just head north, right?

Yeah, he thought. For several thousand miles.

Whatever, he thought, listening to the guy singing his lively Spanish-language pop song. He'd catch a bus. Or ride the rails. Hire a coyote. He'd take any damn positive at all at this point.

Sitting there in the heat as the happy horns blatted on, a funny memory from his teenage years in the boogie-down Bronx suddenly came to him.

In the summer in the nineties when Sammy Sosa and Mark McGwire were battling to break the MLB home run record, he remembered how the Dominicans in the adjacent neighborhoods would drive around blasting salsa music with Sosa's climbing home run count scrawled proudly on their rear windshields in soap.

Not to be outdone in this highly competitive cultural home run contest automotive parade, he remembered how his crazy friend, Joe, began to soap in McGwire's bombs across the rear windshield of his own beater along with a huge shamrock as he drove around blasting U2 and "Danny Boy."

The door opened a few minutes later and Gannon sat up straight as a short clean-shaven Hispanic guy of about seventy came in pushing a rolling tray. He was wearing gray business slacks and a white dress shirt with his silver hair cut short and neat.

Was he an actual doctor? Gannon thought.

Then he frowned as he noticed the tattoo. The guy's shirt was rolled up neatly to midforearms, and Gannon could see someone had written something in Spanish up the back of his left arm in cheap blackish green prison ink. Someone with terrible handwriting.

The first thing the illustrated old man did after he undid Gannon's handcuffs was to offer him a chicken-and-rice plate he'd brought along. Gannon, not having eaten in who knew how long, didn't bother to ask for utensils. Scooping at the food with his dirty hands, he devoured the greasy, tasteless meal to stripped bones and licked-clean foil plate in about two minutes.

He washed down this incredibly welcome repast with the four plastic bottles of lukewarm water he was handed one by one. After the old guy neatly retrieved the tin and the empty bottles into a little plastic bag, he removed a plastic bucket of water rimmed with white dishrags from the cart and gestured for Gannon to take off his clothes.

Gannon stripped off the rancid coveralls. After his plaid flannel shirt and T-shirt and jeans and underwear followed, he stood in the center of the room naked, shamelessly scrubbing at himself with the warm-water-soaked rags. After another minute of extremely satisfying scrubbing up of every conceivable nook and cranny, he dropped the rags—not so white now—with a loud splat to the stone floor.

Finally fed, watered, and cleaned, Gannon rolled his neck and took a deep breath and then looked down at the neat old guy again as he bent down and removed a stethoscope from his cart.

He didn't know what the prison tat was about, but the guy really did seem like a doctor, Gannon thought as he checked his heart with the stethoscope. After the guy took his blood pressure, he gestured for Gannon to sit back on the bed. Gently and expertly, he changed his rib tape and then began to take off his head dressing.

As he took his pulse a second time, Gannon tried to read his arm. Like most born-and-bred New Yorkers, Gannon's Spanish pretty much began and ended with the *No se Apoye Contra La Puerta* sign from the NYC subway. Not surprisingly, the tattoo said something else. Was it the Hippocratic oath?

When El Doc was done with all that, he said something in Spanish and Gannon, still sitting in his birthday suit, stared at him, puzzled. How do you say, "Turn your head to the wall and cough" in Spanish? he thought as the guy went back into his bag.

"How am I looking?" Gannon said.

The old dude nodded that he was good as he brought out a change of clothes from a duffel bag that was atop the cart.

When Gannon finally saw what was in the bag, the chains on his still-cuffed legs rattled as he leaped to his bare feet. A sudden almost irresistible urge shot through him to smash a hard straight right into the nice neat little genteel old guy's temple.

"What the hell is that? What kind of crazy bullshit is this?" Gannon said angrily.

As he said these words, Gannon realized something very important. Clean and fed and out of the cuffs and his heavy hot stinking clothes, he was feeling somewhat normal again. Not a hundred percent back in the pink yet, but getting closer. Quickly.

He stared at the spot on the old man's jaw below his ear where he could easily break it. He needed the anger, he realized. Anger was adrenaline, energy, life force, forward motion. That's what he needed now. All the anger he could muster up.

"Hey, you tatted-up dirty old scumbag," he said. "Are you deaf, you old coot? I said, what the hell is this shit?"

The old doctor wouldn't say as he handed him the folded white underwear and white shorts and a white numbered shirt. A pair of white cleats came out of the bag next, and he placed them down on the floor next to Gannon's feet, sizing them. Satisfied, the old man handed him something else. It was a pair of white socks. They were athletic knee socks.

"What the hell is this? Halloween?" Gannon said, working himself up. "I'm talking to you, dipshit. You think I'm going to wear this, think again. Get me some real clothes now, comprende? What kind of nonsense is this?"

There was a sound and Gannon turned as Button Eyes appeared in the open door.

He was chewing something. He had a dried sausage or something in one hand and as Gannon watched, he peeled another slice of it off with a curve-bladed knife.

Gannon's eyes went to the knife. By its silver color and dark splotches, Gannon knew it was vintage carbon steel. There was something dirty about it, he thought. Backwoods homemade dirty. It looked like something Uncle Cletus used to cut linoleum with before Aunt Petunia plumb went missing.

"We having a problem?" Button Eyes said, chewing, letting him get another good look at his trailer park sling blade as he carved off another slice.

Staring at the knife and then staring at its owner's black canine eyes, Gannon almost went for it then.

He'd definitely get sliced, but once he throat-punched this buffed-up fool and got a good grip on that M1911, it would be a whole new ball of wax now, wouldn't it?

Besides, who knew when he'd get another chance. Or what kind of shape he'd be in when that happened.

Gannon squinted as the dice rolled in his head.

Then he remembered the leg chain. He wasn't sure if he had enough slack.

Shit, he thought as he let the moment pass.

For now, he thought.

"Sorry," Gannon finally said, suddenly smiling from ear to ear. "I was being rude, wasn't I, senor? Where are my manners? It must be this dreadful heat."

He bent and accepted his new tighty-whitey underwear El Doc was holding out to him.

"I'm actually more of a boxers man," he said. "But this is fine. Just fine."

27

What I'm going to do next, I'm not sure, Gannon decided after he reluctantly dressed in the rest of white soccer player outfit and let himself be re-cuffed at the back.

But taking too much more of this bullshit, he thought as his cleats clacked loudly off the stone as he was led out of the room and down the dusty paint-cracked corridor, wasn't going to be it.

The next time he turned, there was another flecktarn-clad soldier walking along with Button Eyes and El Doc. He was a tall, thin jackass. Had to be six-six. This one had opted for a nifty balaclava instead of a ski mask.

When Gannon glanced at him a second time, he noticed his camo uniform seemed small for him. The cuffs of his fatigue pants hardly cleared the top of his combat boots.

"How's it going, sucker?" Private Too Tall said.

Gannon stayed silent, kept walking.

"How's that dent in that head of yours feeling?" the tall guy said merrily. "You really like hugging those trees, huh? Environmentalist?"

Gannon smiled as he suddenly recalled a gem from his Bronx childhood.

"'The flood is over, the land is dry,'" he said.

Gannon turned, grinning.

"'So why do you wear your pants so high?'"

"Look at Mr. Navy SEAL ice-for-blood. Sometimes the bear gets you, huh? How you liking your south-of-the-border vacation so far, commando shit for brains? Better than spring break, you think?" the guy said.

"Oh, you know it, brother," Gannon said, turning back with another easy grin as he clacked along. "I haven't had this much fun since your mother gave me around the world for a handful of Newport loosies. Or was it your sister who went first? It was hard to see through all the crack smoke."

Gannon laughed at the blistering slap that was delivered to the back of his head a split second later. It was followed by the loud scuffle of Button Eyes holding the tall guy back.

Pay dirt, he thought, chuckling. You'd think stupid mother jokes wouldn't work past the schoolyard to trigger the dumb. But you'd be wrong.

"You really are a funny guy, huh, Mike?" Button Eyes said a second later as he pushed him forward down the hall again.

He really was feeling better after a meal and a scrub, wasn't he? Sharper. This was almost fun.

"Oh, yeah. I got a million of 'em," Gannon said as they hit a set of stairs and he was shoved to go up.

The stairs spiraled upward. They were made of stone blocks. Like the chains in his room, it all looked like something out of a castle.

But it wasn't a castle, Gannon realized as they passed an arrow slit-like window and saw the side of what looked like a prison building across a yard.

At the top landing was a thick steel door. From under it came the salsa music, louder now. Gannon suddenly noticed the smell of cooking.

It was the scent of fried dough, he thought. It smelled like carnival French fries.

What in holy hell was this? Gannon thought.

"Let me ask you a question," Button Eyes said as the Latin dance music suddenly stopped.

"Oh, sure, anything," Gannon said, not looking at him. "We being such great pals and all, fire away."

"You wouldn't happen to have any soccer playing in your background, would you?"

Gannon almost jumped as a loud rat-a-tat-tatting hum of something, some sort of heavy equipment by the sound of it, suddenly started up outside the door. Following it came a kind of collective cheer.

"I said, have you ever played any soccer?"

"You need glasses?" Gannon said, still just barely able to hold it together at what in the name of Sam Hill could be making that awful sound.

"Come again?"

"You already know I'm American, right? And now that we're locker room buddies, you know I'm confirmed biologically male," he said.

"So, no soccer," Button Eyes said.

"Nope," Gannon said. "Never played soccer. Or Barbies."

"Shame," Button Eyes said, making a tsking sound.

Behind the thick door, the terrifying humming got louder.

"That's just too bad," he said.

28

Button Eyes pulled the door open and Gannon was pushed out onto what appeared to be the top of a castle watchtower. Off its sundrenched parapet beside him there were tall palm trees, hazy green hills. When he craned around, farther to his left he saw an ocean sparkling in the lower distance.

Elevated terrain, he thought, scanning the vista. A mix of jungle and desert. He looked up at the sun almost directly above.

It was Mexico, he thought as Button Eyes shoved him forward to the right across the watchtower's stone landing. Southern Mexico. That was the Pacific, right? Had to be.

Then he looked over the tower's low inside wall and he immediately forgot about all of that.

"Holy shit," he said.

"Oh, yeah," the tall guard said in his ear again. "Let's hear a one-liner now. What's wrong? Cat got your tongue?"

Almost directly across from where Gannon stood was a soccer field on the roof of the three-story cell block jail building.

A new green Astroturf one edged with bright white lines and bookended at either end with netted goals.

Under the harsh sharp light of Mexican noon what he couldn't help but notice immediately was that along the sides of this professional-looking field, there was no railing. The neat white boundary lines of the field went directly around to the edges of the building's roof itself, and instead of a barrier or guardrail there was nothing but four stories of air.

And that wasn't the only attention-getter.

Completely surrounding this oddly repurposed old prison was a thick parapeted wall and other watchtowers, and walking along the top of the wall were crowds of people.

Gannon stood gaping at the white canvas tents, the waiters bearing trays, the bandstand, the parade review seating. There were maybe a couple of hundred people or more.

"Why, lookee here. Here comes your ride now," Too Tall said as the rolling scissor lift that was making all the industrial noise loudly came around the far wall of the prison. It belched out some more black diesel smoke as it headed right toward them.

Gannon, still in shock, started laughing half hysterically as he looked at it and then back at the field and then back out at the festive crowd atop the walls.

The Hispanic men who stared back at him were hard-looking ones wearing expensive sunglasses and gold wristwatches with their summer suits. The women with them were long legged and busty arm-candy types with tousled hair. Their summer dresses were barely battening down the cleavage as the bright sun glittered off the shiny clasps on their designer bags.

"This the big reveal?" he said, smiling back at his captors. "My big a-ha moment? I'm the attraction at some south-of-the-border carnival? The circus comes to town even in shitholes, huh? Learn something new every day."

"I knew you'd like it," Button Eyes said.

"Like it? Why, it looks like a Miami rap video shoot or something, doesn't it? I've never seen something classier. Please tell me there will be twerking."

Private Too Tall smiled under his balaclava.

"Look at him. Still trying with the macho man act," he said.

"So, let me guess. I'm supposed to play a soccer death match or something," Gannon said, ignoring him. "On top of a building with no guardrail on the sides for super-sloppy extra-double-dare style and drama, huh? That's real creative. What will the degraded scum of the earth think of next?"

"Oh, keep it up," Too Tall cooed. "We're about to see *exactly* how macho you really are."

"For real, who are these pieces of shit?" Gannon said to Button Eyes. "These are cartel scumbags, right? That's the big master plan? Bring him down to Mexico. Feed him to the cartels. That's it? That's all you got?"

The thunderous hum of the lift got louder as it got closer.

"Don't tell me your intel bosses have some kind of working relationship with the drug cartels," Gannon said. "Egads! So, you're saying CIA really does stand for the Cocaine Importing Agency? Imagine the shock! Next, you'll tell me the war on drugs is a scam, too. Is nothing sacred?"

The lift arrived. Button Eyes made a higher gesture with his hand at the operator below. As its platform zipped up a little, he hopped up on the parapet and undid its gate with a loud clank and an iron groan.

"Get up here and into the lift so I can uncuff you," Button Eyes said.

"And if I don't?"

Gannon's teeth clicked together instantly as Too Tall suddenly jabbed him in the back of his neck with a clacking electric stun gun. The sudden shock was like a sucker punch, like something exploding straight up through the top of his head.

It felt like every muscle in his body spasmed at once as he collapsed to his knees.

Even after the cattle prod was removed, his head was ringing and aching like he'd just been slapped over the skull with a baseball bat. He was still half grayed out as they heaved him up. Then he was sitting on the hot metal of the lift as his hands were freed.

The gate groaned as Button Eyes slammed it shut. The lift hummed and belched again as it began pulling him away.

"What am I supposed to do now?" Gannon yelled back as he got to his knees.

Button Eyes shrugged from the parapet.

"Sounds like a personal problem," he said.

Gannon got to his uncertain feet as the lift swayed and bumped him across the prison yard.

"And, oh, I forgot to thank you," Button Eyes called.

"Thank me?"

Button Eyes lifted his camo sleeve back to show the Rolex Submariner Gannon was going to give to his son for his birthday.

"Buh-bye now, bitch," Too Tall said, buzzing the clacking stun gun on and off as he waved with it. "Don't forget to write!"

29

Piedmont Heights was a fly speck in the central northern part of Maryland near the border of Pennsylvania.

It was a sleepy little town but coming on eleven in the morning that Saturday, it was a bit more awake than usual as three dozen people and counting gathered outside its town hall where a truck towing a flatbed was pulling in.

The flatbed looked like a parade float with a podium and flags and red, white, and blue bunting. Adrian Bright, standing with the videographer on the sidewalk, gestured the driver forward a smidge to make sure they were getting the Americana of the town's eighteenth- and nineteenth-century brick buildings as well as the foothills of the Blue Ridge Mountains in the northern distance in the shot.

Bright had started his new political consulting side gig almost as a lark a few years before and had really taken to it. Transitioning out of the government in the next year or two, he knew he had his choice of corporate landing spots, but he wasn't done with the DC game just yet.

"Perfecto," Bright called up, as two young campaign staffers unfurled the red-and-white Ginny For Senate banner from the second-story balcony of the bed and breakfast beside the town hall.

It really was, Bright thought, folding his arms as he looked around. He had been worried about the weather, but it had turned out just perfect. It was cool but nice and bright with just enough wind to keep the Old Glories billowing beside the podium.

The larger than expected crowd was a bonus. But not completely necessary. This was politics after all and what was necessary were the optics.

"How's this? Are we getting all of it?" said the video guy.

Bright squatted down and looked at the monitor again.

Oh yeah, they were getting all of it. Even the helpful small-town police officer who was now directing traffic beside the bunting to complete the God Bless America, Fourth of July parade atmosphere they were looking for.

"Roll 'em," Bright said as he gave the tech a thumbs-up.

Bright was still smiling to himself when he looked up and saw a white-haired hearty man in a blue suit and bright red Scottish plaid bow tie wave at him through the crowd. It was Ginny's dad, *Admiral* Paul Mickelson, and he was smiling as broadly and proudly as the father of the bride, wasn't he? Bright thought as he took the happy man's powerful hand into his own.

He was just getting started.

"Adrian," the admiral said. "At first when you said to come all the way up here so far from the Beltway, I really thought you were crazy. But wow, I'm stunned. The rumors are true. You really are a genius."

"Guilty as charged, Paul," Bright said taking a little bow.

And why not? It was Bright himself who had insisted on the

location for Ginny's announcement that she was running. He and Claudette had found the hokey gem years ago as they passed through to go skiing and he had tucked it away.

A moment later, the two men turned at the applause as the small-town mayor, a clean-shaven roly-poly sixty-something wearing a VFW cap and a rumpled suit, exited the town hall and mounted the flatbed.

The gifts just keep on coming, Bright thought, drinking in the Norman Rockwell painting on the video monitor. No one was actually playing a banjo as of yet, but who knew? The day was young.

He stood back up as Ginny came out of the Ford Expedition beside the platform smiling and waving.

An athletic blue-eyed brunette in her late thirties who was quite easy to look at, candidate Ginny Mickelson made quite the entrance. Like the father, there was a healthy energetic American sheen to her. She looked like a model for a Coca-Cola ad from the fifties. Or maybe from one of the raunchier pulp fiction covers of the same era, Bright thought, as she had quite the tight little figure.

The mayor introduced her and helped her up onto the platform.

Then Bright's heart warmed as she hit everyone with her smile.

It was her room-lightening smile that did it, made him agree to sign on. There was something genuine in it.

Because that was really the part that separated the wheat from the chaff. Appearing to be genuine.

Bright knew that firsthand.

He watched as Ginny took a deep breath then a nervous look around.

She even did nervous kind of sexy, didn't she? Bright thought. My, my, my was Fox News going to be selling a lot of Viagra this election year.

"Hello, everybody. My name is Ginny Mickelson," she said.

"You may not think you know me but you actually do. Because I'm just like you. I love Maryland. I love our incredibly beautiful state not just the part of it down south linked to all the special interests. No, I love all of Maryland. Most especially places here like Piedmont Heights. Places where the Little League baseball fields are going to be full in the next few weeks and the church pews come tomorrow morning."

Bright smiled at the actual cheers he heard around him.

He had helped on the speech, but she had improved it, he saw. Owned it. She was really getting this.

She was a star. You could feel it right here and now in her big stage debut. He felt a flutter in his stomach. It was like opening your portfolio to see a stock had jumped fifty percent.

Bright received the phone call from Bouthier as she was wrapping things up.

He thought that the riveted hicks wouldn't even notice if he whipped out his sat phone right there in the open. But he ducked into the alley beside the town hall anyway just in case.

"What's the story? It's over? Mission accomplished?" he said hopefully after he picked up.

"Almost. Gannon's on his way in," Bouthier said. "You told me to record it, but I wasn't sure if you wanted it on the live satellite feed so you could watch."

Bright almost laughed.

What a funny joke. As if Gannon meant something to him. Gannon was work. A data point. One about to be deleted from Bright's spreadsheet. He was a piece of paper about to be cleared out of Bright's in-box.

Watch? he thought. Watch what? It would be like watching the erasing of a number from a ledger.

"Can't now," Bright said. "I'm right in the middle of something. Save it and I'll get it later from you when I'm in the office."

"Will do," Bouthier said.

30

In the corner watchtower of the prison opposite the elevated bandstand, Lou stood with Alessandra and Manny.

On the exterior of the tower, there was bleacher seating, but here on the inside, where they stood, it looked very much like a modern stadium's VIP skybox. There was carpet and nice wood paneling, portable air conditioners every five feet blowing cool air. By an elaborate buffet table at its center and at a long bar at the crowded room's opposite end, good-looking people in stylish clothing were mingling.

Lou was in the center of the room by its sole window, holding his second ice-cold bottle of Corona Light. Actually, technically he was white-knuckle clutching at it like a falling man gripping the edge of a cliff.

Because as usual, he was trying to act laid-back and suave and casual.

But he was having some incredible difficulty at the moment.

"Are you kidding me?" Manny said beside him, looking out the window to where some white dude in a white soccer uniform was being scissor-lifted over to the prison roof soccer field.

"I mean, are you seeing this?" Manny continued. "Did I tell you? No damn walls on the sides and four stories straight down. Look at that gringo! My boy must be shitting cinder blocks. So, this is what the Concurso is! I knew it, bro. That's why it's a secret, man. We're about to see some ancient gladiator fight-to-the-death-style shit going down!"

"Uh-huh," Lou said mechanically as he lifted the bottle and lowered it without drinking.

"Still nothing," Alessandra said in an annoyed voice from Lou's other side.

Lou looked at her. If the current insanity had raised her blood pressure one iota, she was remarkably skilled at concealing it. Constantly working her phone, Alessandra had explained that their contact was with the host of the festivities. But apparently, the heavy hitters were still busy at the moment. They just needed to cool their heels until their host was free to say hello.

"Do you believe this?" Manny said again.

"I guess," Lou said, really not believing it as he lifted the bottle again, managing to drink a little this time.

"Okay. Our contact just texted. We're ready now," Alessandra said, suddenly looking up. "Look lively, gentlemen. It's time to say hello to our new business partners."

Snapping out of his shock, Lou placed down his bottle on the buffet table and slipped in beside Alessandra as they walked.

"This guy is El Aleman, right?" he said. "That's our new partner? The El Aleman Group, right?"

Alessandra stared at him for a beat.

"Yes, you're right. It is," she said quickly as they pushed outside. "At least maybe if you don't screw this up."

They came out into the heat and blatting sound of the scissor lift and stepped under a white tent. In the shade of it, a small outdoor seating stand was set up and Alessandra led them around to the front of it where half a dozen men in pastel summer attire were seated, sipping cordials. As at Saratoga Springs, Lou saw that some of the pretty women sitting in the row behind had binoculars.

"Alberto!" Alessandra said happily as one of the seated men, a professorial-looking Hispanic wearing eyeglasses, stood and gave her an air kiss.

He was a lawyer or something. Had to be, Lou thought, looking the man over. In his new designer jeans and crisp new dress shirt, he looked awkward, like a politician out among the unwashed trying to get the blue-collar vote.

"Alberto, these are my friends I was telling you about. Louis and Manuel."

"A pleasure," Alberto said, nodding at them. "And if you would let me introduce the three of you to our host and my boss, James."

They all watched as the guy sitting next to Alberto stood.

James was a blunt-faced white guy in his early forties with hay-colored hair shorn tight. When he smiled broadly, his slightly gapped front teeth were very white against the deep tan of his rugged face.

Not very handsome and not that tall, yet there was something about him, Lou saw immediately. Something in his gray-green eyes and the constant half smile on his face and the way he held himself easily like an athlete. There was an arrogance, a cocky secret knowledge, that seemed to make all the difference.

James inspected each of them back. Lou wasn't exactly a slouch in the ding-ding measuring contests that were part and parcel of the cutthroat drug business. But as James looked baldly into his own eyes, it was not easy to hold the icy intensity of the man's gaze.

Yeah, he was a smooth operator all right, Lou thought. In the tailored single-breasted navy dinner jacket and white linen pants, he looked like David Beckham at Wimbledon.

"Everyone, a pleasure to meet you," he said in perfect Spanish. "I'm hearing very good reports about all of you."

"Thank you, James. I'm glad," Alessandra said. "We know what an honor it is to be invited here. It was very kind of you to allow us to be your guests."

James seemed to smirk at that. Despite his European tailoring, he suddenly didn't strike Lou as being German at all. He seemed like an American, Lou thought, peering at him. He reminded him of the preppy white boys he'd played high school football with. One of the quarterbacks daddy whisked off to Switzerland for some skiing when the date rape charges started to pile up.

"Don't mention it. It's nice to see some new faces," James continued as he turned to her. "Especially one as pleasant as yours, senorita."

When Lou glanced at Alessandra, she was all but blushing.

James really must have had some major juice, Lou thought. He was almost waiting for his iron butterfly partner to curtsy. Or to pass out.

"As the Concurso is about to start, would it be okay if we talked business a little bit later?" Alberto, the lawyerly stiff, suggested.

"Oh, of course, that would be fine," Alessandra said, somehow managing not to faint. "And again, thank you so much for inviting us."

Supple as a dancer, James, the mysterious elegant global coke dealer, suddenly bowed full-on gracefully from his tapered waist.

"Not at all, senorita," he said as he gave her hand a soft kiss. "It is I who must thank you for accepting."

31

Gannon's aching head was still ringing and the white soccer jersey was stuck fast to his back with sweat by the time the lift softly tapped the side of the concrete prison facade.

In the glaring noon sun, he saw that there actually was a very low wall along the perimeter of the field, a painted white wood partition that went up to about shin level.

It might stop a low rolling ball, Gannon thought as he glanced down at the yellow dust of the prison yard forty feet below. But it would only serve to trip a running person who was crazy enough to go near it.

"That's not to code," Gannon complained as he carefully swung himself over the lift gate and then over the little wooden wall onto the roof.

Safely on the Astroturf, Gannon, not knowing what else to do, turned and headed toward the center line. As he walked, he noticed that the goals weren't completely open. From the top post of both hung a sheet of plexiglass that left only a narrow opening at the bottom of about two feet high.

Was it to stop long shots? he wondered as he halted beside the center circle.

At the opposite edge of the rooftop field, he saw that several people were standing beside a small shed.

There was a referee in a black-and-white-striped shirt with another guy dressed in a black soccer uniform. Through a window-like opening in the booth itself, he saw two older men in suits sitting at a table with microphones on it. One of them started speaking, and his quick rolling Spanish voice came booming out of the surrounding loudspeakers as everyone hollered and clapped.

They were damn commentators, Gannon realized.

Besides these two clowns, on the outside of the booth stood half a dozen men in black tactical wear, strapping carbine rifles. Gannon shook his head as he looked at their guns and saw that they were FN FALs.

"Of course," he mumbled. "Of course."

He'd been shot with an FN FAL in Iraq. He'd been standing at the time, and the distinctive-looking Belgian rifle's big .308 round traveling at 3000 feet per second had face-planted him down into the dirt like he'd been kicked by a Clydesdale when it struck him in his back.

The bruise it had left from shoulder to shoulder had looked like a rainbow tattoo and if the round hadn't hit the ceramic plate he'd been wearing dead center, he would have headed home early from America's war on terror in an aluminum box.

Sweltering under the blazing sun, Gannon, perhaps lingering a beat too long on this terrible memory, felt the grip he was trying to keep on his mental strength suddenly waver.

You're not making it home, said an evil little voice in his head.

It was true, he thought as a nauseating swimming sensation

began to form in his still-sore head. Like it or not, fair or not, crazy or not, all of it—all the things he had done and not done, everything he was, his life and now his probable death—was being pushed out now onto this strip of cheap Mexican Astroturf like so many chips across the green felt of a poker table.

As he tried to absorb all the stress and absurdity and fear of it in the blistering heat, black spots started dotting his vision. For a second, he thought he might actually pass out.

That's when he suddenly remembered it. What he had felt with the tattooed doctor.

The way out of this.

He lifted his head and stared at the gunmen across the elevated field, at the commentators, at the rapt smiling evil people watching along the walls.

Then as the cauldron of their hatred and disdain and palpable ill will toward him washed over him in rolling waves, another voice was there, cooing to him.

Look! See there? They want you dead. And you're going to give them what they want, aren't you? Because you're tired. And it hurts. Right? And it's so hot. And it's so not fair.

"No," Gannon said, bowing his head.

Give up. C'mon, you know you just need to lie down. On the grass here. It's so soft and cool. Just for a second. Just kneel then lie down. All the way down and close your eyes and—

"No!" he heard himself scream.

When he looked up again, Gannon felt much better, revived, like somebody had thrown a bucket of water in his face. And when he looked along the parapet, he didn't see too many smiles anymore.

He smiled then.

He reached down and lifted up the hem of the jersey, and after he swiped his face, he saw that the referee and the other guy in a black soccer uniform were approaching.

"Bring it, you savage scum," Gannon said quietly through his gritted teeth as he pulled himself up to his full height.

He rolled his neck and spit down between his cleats.

"Let's get it on," he said.

32

"How'd we do?" Manny said as they went back inside to the air-conditioned skybox of the watchtower.

"Very well, Manny," Alessandra said, patting him on the shoulder. "You restrained yourself as I asked. Thank you. You came across as quite professional."

"Yeah, you did a real good job keeping your mouth shut for five seconds, Manny. I'm really impressed," Lou said.

"I see someone I know," Alessandra said, breaking off. "Wait for me at the bar, all right?"

At the bar, the very tall attractive blonde white female bartender who served them wore a shiny iridescent pink leather dress that clung to her remarkable curves like liquid on glass.

"Hey, guys. There you are," said a voice.

Lou turned to see Alessandra's contact, Alberto, suddenly standing beside them, smiling.

"Louis, right?" the lawyer said as he adjusted his eyeglasses with a long forefinger.

"That's right, Alberto," Lou said, lifting his drink. "Thanks again for inviting us."

"Please," Alberto said, clicking his champagne flute to Lou's fresh beer bottle. "To a new happy relationship."

"Salud," Lou said, smiling as he sipped.

"So, first time, huh, Louis?" Alberto said, staring at him closely.

Lou looked at him. It wasn't easy. Behind his rimless glasses, there was a bit of a lizard-like thing going on with his slightly protruding eyes.

"Come again?"

"To the Concurso. First time?"

Lou nodded.

"Uh-huh. The very first," he said.

"Ah, a virgin, excellent. I love virgins," Alberto said, swirling his flute.

The lewd way he said this made Lou want to hit him in the mouth. Instead, he looked out through the window beside them. James was standing now by the guard tower battlement with a pair of binoculars.

How was the guy not sweating in this heat? Lou thought, looking at the mysterious white dude. He looked fresh and cool as an ice cube, like he'd just gotten out of the shower.

"Do you know what this place is?" Alberto said.

"A former presidio? One of Cortez's forts, I heard," Lou said.

"True. But there was something here even before that."

Lou looked at him.

"Was there?" he said.

"Have you ever heard of Pelota Maya?" Alberto said.

"Maya ball!" Manny said, suddenly joining in. "Of course. They taught us at grade school. The Mayans played it. Some crazy primitive ball game. They hit a rubber ball with like their butt or something, right?"

"Yes," Alberto said, his bug eyes widening behind his glasses. "Exactly. It was played at this site. There was a Mayan city right here, you see. And on this prison's very grounds was the largest Pelota Maya court ever found."

"No way," Manny said.

"Yes, but you must understand there was more to Pelota Maya than just ball playing. Much more. Pelota Maya was more like a religious ritual. It was a kind of festival. A great event with feasts. Everyone from the surrounding area—tens and tens of thousands of people—would gather right here."

Alberto took a heavy gold cigarette case from his pocket and opened it and offered it to them. After they shook their heads no, they watched as he tongued one out like a lizard. The lighter that he lit it with was also made of heavy gold.

"First, there would be the games," Alberto said, blowing a smoke ring.

He fingered back his eyeglasses again.

"Then at night came the blood sacrifices of the defeated," he said.

"What?" Lou said.

"I understand that many might see this as barbaric, but is it? What you have to understand is the human necessity for war. It is war that brings men together, not peace. Times of peace threaten the fellowship and brotherhood of warriors so blood-letting rituals allow this unifying need for war to be slaked and preserved in times of peace. In this way, blood rituals actually stabilize and protect societies."

Lou looked at him with a raised eyebrow to see if he was pulling his leg. He wasn't.

I'm looking at one crazy son of a bitch, Lou thought.

"So, you see," Alberto said with a wave of his hand. "This is a very special place. All night, the losers would be sacrificed.

Hundreds, they said. Sometimes thousands. Who knows how long this happened for? Hundreds of years. This happened right here. Right where we are standing. On this very day every year. That's why we come back every year. To...well...you will see. I won't spoil it for you. Especially virgins. This site has incredible power."

"*Had* you mean," Lou said looking him in the eye.

Alberto laughed.

"No," Alberto said, chuckling as he lay a gentle creepy hand across Lou's back, leading them back for the stands.

"I said *has*, Louis. Watch with me, won't you? You will feel it with the first one. You will soon see."

33

Atop the prison roof field, Gannon sized up his opponent in whatever this screw-loose bullshit was as he arrived with the referee.

Like the ref, he looked Mexican and was about six feet tall and in his late twenties. He had a scraggly dark beard but no mustache and despite his height was baby faced and slim shouldered.

Gannon wondered what the doughy and sort of pear-shaped kid had done to get himself into this amount of trouble. Found a bag of dirty money like him? Maybe lost one? Fell asleep in a getaway car?

The ref with him, holding a canary yellow soccer ball under his arm, was a middle-aged wiry-looking dude who would have been somewhat handsome except for a pair of comically thick black eyebrows. When Gannon was a kid, they had Halloween prank glasses that had eyebrows on them like his. Despite this quirk, the man had a stern, alert expression that made Gannon believe he was probably a real referee.

Yeah, Gannon thought, shaking his head some more at the lunatic asylum proceedings. *But a referee of what?*

As they stood there, Gannon's young opponent gave him a hard look like boxers do before a bout. But it looked forced, almost as comical as the ref's eyebrows.

Restraining himself from laughing, Gannon would have said it was all a dream except he'd never had a dream where his heart rate was redlining and his hands were trembling and he was sweating like a pig in a hot tub.

"You are American, yes?" said the hard little ref in not very good English.

Gannon nodded.

He pointed to the far goal Gannon was already facing.

"That is your goal there. We begin."

"Whoa! No, wait," Gannon said. "What are the rules?"

The referee laughed curtly.

"Rules?"

"What if the ball goes over the side?"

"If you put the ball out of play once, okay," he said, making a speculative face. "Twice, there will be consequences."

"Such as?" Gannon said.

The ref suddenly twirled the yellow ball in his hand on one finger.

"You see those men with the rifles there, yes?" he said. "Keep the ball in play."

"What do we play until?" Gannon said. "How many goals to win?"

"That is up to you," the referee said, expertly passing the spinning ball to the finger of his other hand like a Harlem Globetrotter.

"What the hell does that mean?" Gannon said.

The ref suddenly caught the spinning ball in his two hands.

"It is up to you and chance," the ref said.

"Chance? *Chance?*" Gannon said.

"No more questions, gringo," the ref said angrily. "You do not need to understand."

The referee held up the ball over the center circle.

"You only need to survive. On three. One... Two..."

Gannon tensed, got in a running position.

"Three!" the ref said and the yellow soccer ball dropped.

The young Mexican was already moving before it hit the ground. He was faster than he looked. And more nimble. Just as the ball hit, he flicked it at himself with the toe of his cleat and did a kind of pirouette with it, sending it spinning in a whistling curve behind him.

As Gannon ran with him to get the ball, the young guy suddenly stopped short and boxed out Gannon as he sent it in another long curving spin to their right.

The crafty pear-shaped bastard put the jets on then. He bolted powerfully for the ball that was heading back toward the center-half line.

"Dammit!" Gannon yelled as he was left two steps behind.

As the young Mexican arrived at the ball, he just went for it. He drilled a kick on it just before Gannon arrived in a slide to block it.

The announcer in the booth shouted out a loud exclamation in Spanish as Gannon turned and watched, wincing.

The ball bounced once and then again and began to roll quickly toward the goal's low opening under the plexiglass.

"No!" Gannon said as there was a hush in the crowd.

Gannon felt it in his chest when it hit the right goal post.

But it didn't go in. It bounced right into the low board out of bounds.

34

"Alberto?" Lou said from where they stood at the watchtower parapet beside the stands, watching the referee cross the roof field.

"Yes, Louis?" Alberto said, watching with his binoculars.

"Who are the, um—"

"The players?" Alberto said, lowering his binoculars. "Some are prisoners. Others very desperate people who perhaps owe money. Others are cartel underlings who are very good at soccer and wish to please their bosses, if you can believe it. There are eight players at this Concurso. Two per organization. My boss, James, over there is quite excited as one of ours is going right now in the first round."

"The white guy?" Manny said, watching with another pair of binoculars that a waiter had brought.

"Yes. The gringo in white. How'd you know?"

"A guess," Manny said with a shrug.

"What's his story?" Lou said.

"I don't know," Alberto said, glancing away. "And don't want to. One thing I have learned in this business is that you don't need to know everything."

"What the eyes don't see, the heart doesn't grieve," Manny said, still watching the field.

"Exactly, Manny," Alberto said. "Well put. You are a wise man."

"They just play head-to-head?" Lou said.

"Yes. First, there are eight. Then four. Then two. Until there is one survivor."

"Is there betting?" Manny said.

"What do you think? Of course! I have a hundred grand riding against this gringo right now. I've seen gringos before. They are usually terrible."

"What happens to him?" Lou said.

"Who? The gringo?"

"No, the last survivor," Lou said.

"He becomes cherished," Alberto said. "There is an elaborate dinner and dancing tonight under the stars."

"Then he gets killed, too?" Manny said, still watching.

"No. Then he gets his freedom and a great sum of cash and a plane ticket to anywhere he wants," Alberto said.

"Really?" Manny said, a confused look on his face as he finally lowered the binoculars.

Alberto laughed.

"Yes, Manny, really. What do you think we are? Savages?" he said.

35

After the ref retrieved the ball from the low board beside the goal, he placed it down on the half-line center circle and said something in Spanish to Gannon's opponent.

When the guy had backed off to roughly the same distance of a soccer penalty kick, the ref blew his whistle and made a gesture at Gannon to indicate the ball was now his.

Gannon walked up to the ball slowly like he was going to start fancy foot kicking it around like the way the Mexican had done. Instead, he suddenly reared back and punted it as hard as he could at his goal.

He thought he had gotten it past but at the very last second, the Mexican did a lunging, sliding kick save that sent the ball off to the right like a spinning top.

They both bolted into full run as it spun toward the roof's edge on Gannon's right. The ball rolled to a stop about three feet from the edge, and it was only as Gannon got to it a step before the running Mexican that he realized the young guy wasn't going for the ball.

Their shoulders collided, sending Gannon—still running—off balance right at the edge.

The announcer called out some exclamation in Spanish as Gannon screamed and let himself drop face first onto the Astroturf. Gannon felt the rug burn as he bounced and slid and a split second later, there was a loud crack like a puck off the boards in a hockey game as the whole right side of him slammed to a stop against the low plywood partition.

Before he could thank God that it had actually held him, he watched as the off-balance Mexican fell down to the Astroturf as well. As he landed, his shoulder impacted against the ball and shot it hard off the partition and back out across the field like a pinball hit with a flipper.

Gannon and the Mexican got to their feet simultaneously. His opponent was a little bit ahead at first but with white-hot anger now fueling his speed and the son of a bitch's murder attempt, Gannon quickly caught up.

At the other end of the field by the still-rolling ball, the Mexican was trying one of his patented pirouette moves again when Gannon caught him flush in the chest with his shoulder. They were approaching the commentator booth when this happened, and there was an incredibly satisfying loudspeaker squawk as he sent the young man in through the booth's open window and across the desk, knocking over both announcers and all their microphones to the turf.

Gannon thought the ref would blow his whistle for a foul or something, but when he looked at him, he just looked back blankly. Taking this as a sign that the ball was still in play, Gannon ran up to the now-stilled ball and turned and kicked.

With the tip of his cleat, he kicked it, sending it low and hard at his goal.

Gannon waited and watched as it hit the goalpost to the right a moment later.

Then bounced in.

"Goalllll!" Gannon cried out triumphantly as he pumped his fist.

He began hopping up and down as he ran along the edge of the roof like a fool on meth.

"Goalllll!" he cried at the ghoulish spectators as he ran and waved and gave them all the finger.

36

Elated and still laughing to himself, Gannon arrived back at the center line where the young Mexican was now standing. The young man glared at him angrily, his face beet red.

"You just see what I did there?" Gannon said, taunting him with a wink. "That's what you call old-school Neuvo York boogie-down-style, son. Something else, huh?"

The kid gave him the finger.

"Right back at you. Believe it or not, I was willing to work with you. But then you had to go and try to knock me into the graveyard, didn't you? So, no more Mr. Nice Guy."

Gannon's grin evaporated as he turned.

The referee was walking out of the booth. He was flanked by two of the black-clad soldiers. One of the soldiers was holding something metal that flashed in the strong noon light. It was a silver tray.

"What the hell now?" Gannon said, shaking his head.

Then Gannon saw what. He took a huge step back.

"Screw you!" he said. "What are you people crazy? You're all damn crazy!"

The soldier who wasn't holding the tray raised his rifle and motioned Gannon even farther back as they arrived. The young Mexican, still standing at the center line, began to backpedal as well. He held his hands out before him, shaking them back and forth, fear in his eyes.

The ref lifted the pistol from the tray. It was a stainless-steel snub-nosed .38 Special with a stippled wood grip. He held it up high above his head with his right hand as he removed a single bullet from the breast pocket of his shirt with his left. It was a metal-jacketed hollow point.

Up to you and chance, Gannon thought, remembering what the ref had said.

He walked in a wide circle with a ceremonious slowness, presenting both gun and bullet to the people around. The two hundred or so spectators along the old stone walls stared back. Silent and motionless in their fine clothes, they could have been posing for a photograph.

The referee stopped back before the young Mexican player and slipped the bullet into one of the six chambers and spun it. The whirring clicks sounded trivial, like the spinning wheel in a board game. Then the chambers of the revolver stopped their spin, and the ref slapped it back to true and placed it carefully back onto the tray.

Gannon's face and whole body felt numb as the ref lifted the tray and walked back to the young Mexican.

He said something in Spanish as he offered it.

The young man shook his head. His eyes were moist now, his hands trembling.

"Hazlo. Ahora," the ref said.

The Mexican averted his eyes. He just kept shaking his head

no. He looked so young, Gannon suddenly noticed. He was hardly a college kid.

The ref leaned in quickly and slapped him hard across the face. His big raised eyebrows not so comical now.

"Leave him alone!" Gannon yelled.

"¡Hazlo. Ahora!" the ref yelled louder.

The young man, with his hands up beside his head now, only shook his head some more. The soldier beside the ref suddenly blasted the butt of his FN into the young man's chest, knocking him down.

"You rotten sons of bitches!" Gannon yelled as the rifle's muzzle was nudged into the baby fat of the now-crying player's cheek.

"¡Hazlo. Ahora!" the ref yelled again.

The Mexican struggled to his feet.

"No, don't do it. Don't do it," Gannon pleaded weakly as the ref offered the platter again.

The young man didn't listen. It was like he was in a trance as he placed the shining barrel to his temple.

Gannon watched. He couldn't look away. It was like something in a dream.

The young man's finger clenched at the trigger and then the hammer slowly began to draw back.

37

The distinct click of the hammer striking on an empty chamber sounded loud even from where Lou stood along the hot stone parapet.

Then everyone let out their breath. The hiss of it around him sounded like a suddenly rent tire, like someone had pressed a release valve.

On the field, the young Mexican player was handing back the gun. He was smiling.

Lou wasn't.

He shook his head as he thought about his grandmother and Our Lady of Guadalupe and his mortal soul.

I shouldn't have done this, he thought. *Man, oh, man, I should not have come here.*

Lou felt a sudden dull ache behind his skull as he stood there in the heat among his new psychopathically evil pals. He folded his arms as he looked around for Manny and Alessandra. But they had both gone off somewhere. He was all alone now.

"Exceptional," Alberto said with a little fist pump beside him. "I'm still in the game."

Lou stared at Alberto. His ugly face was lit up, rapt, like a horndog along a strip club runway. The runt looked especially excited to be wagering on a man's life like he was betting on a golf putt or a game of pop-a-shot basketball.

Lou could practically feel the psycho killer energy pulsing off him, pulsing off all of them.

He could practically feel it seeping now in through the pores of his own skin, poisoning his soul.

"Very lucky, Alberto," James called merrily over from the parapet beside them as he lowered his binoculars. "Very, very lucky. You're safe for now, but I'll take that hundred thousand from you yet. I told you this gringo of mine is special, but you didn't believe me."

A waiter came by with the champagne tray. Lou shook his head.

"But wait a second, are you really sure you can afford a hundred thousand loss?" James suddenly called out. "Choose your answer wisely, counselor. If you say yes, perhaps I'm paying my attorney far too much."

Alberto nodded good-naturedly as some of the others laughed.

Why aren't you laughing, too, now, Lou? said a voice in Lou's head as he stood there. *Go ahead. Laugh it up with your new friends. You know you want to. You're going to hell now, too, so why not go laughing all the way down?*

"Excuse me," said one of the women on the bench behind him as she stood. She actually used Lou's shoulder to steady herself and gave him the eye as she went past in her stiletto heels.

And why not go for it with another whore while you're at it, Louie baby? Your wife won't know. Come on down here to hell, Lou. The devil's not so bad. Look how cool he is with his silk clothes and all his fake-booby porno sluts. Come on down where it's nice and warm.

"Alberto, truly," James continued. "You can back out now, if you wish. Don't let your regional sympathies bankrupt you."

"No, boss. I'm good," Alberto said, rubbing his hands together. "That gringo got lucky. It won't happen again."

"But are you sure?" James said after a moment.

Alberto bit his lip with a sudden uncertain look on his face. When the little lizard-like creep grabbed Lou's elbow, it took every scintilla of restraint he possessed not to smash him across the face with his beer bottle.

"What do you think, Louis?" he said.

I think I'm going straight to hell, Lou thought.

Lou shrugged.

"No, it's okay," the little bespectacled loser suddenly decided as he let Lou go. "I'm going to let it ride."

"Hey, look," one of the women said. "What is the gringo doing?"

38

As the ref got the ball and went to put it at the center circle again, Gannon peeled off his shirt.

"What are you doing?" he said.

Gannon ignored him as he tossed the shirt down and pulled off his right cleat.

"What are you doing?" the ref repeated. "You don't think you will be killed?"

Gannon pulled off his left cleat and started on the sock.

"Fine," the referee said, dropping the ball. "Begin."

Gannon was sitting shirtless and cross-legged with just his shorts on at the center line when he heard the ball go into the goal behind him.

He stared down at nothing, putting all his concentration into his breathing. He thought at the moment of his death that he would have to wrestle within himself to hold back his fear. But here he was and he actually felt incredible.

The fear was gone and he felt completely serene.

Pray, said a voice. *Pray, Michael.*

It was a woman's voice. His mother's, he thought for a second. But no. No, it was his wife, Annette's.

Hail Mary, full of grace, Gannon mouthed silently. *The Lord is with thee.*

He stood obediently when he was done to see the soldiers and the ref coming with the tray.

Keeping his head down, he swallowed as he listened to the purring spin of the revolver's well-oiled chamber.

He heard a click, and between his face and where he looked down at the Astroturf, the tray appeared in front of him, the shining steel of the revolver gleaming against the old silver.

Gannon lifted the heavy pistol off the tray. He stood looking down at it in his big hand. One beat then two.

He smiled then at a sudden silver joy at the center of himself as he realized that he was about to see his wife again. He could feel her there right there beside him, her arms were open, her hands were reaching out.

Then he turned and threw the gun as hard as he could off the roof to his left.

When the ref turned, jaw dropped, back from where the gun had disappeared, Gannon was sitting again, staring down at the Astroturf, silent and still.

One of the soldiers stepped forward in the dead silence. As the ref stepped back, the soldier worked the FN's charging handle, stripping a .308 cartridge from the box magazine into the bolt with a crisp and loud metal clack. Beside his ear, Gannon heard the metal reverberation of the struck brass toll slightly in the roasting air like the ringing of a tiny bell.

Eyes open or closed? Gannon thought.

Open, he decided as the shot came.

He convulsed as if electrocuted then fell over. When he realized he was still alive, his hands went to his skull, probing. He stared at his fingers, looking for blood.

But there was none.

The hot Astroturf was stiff against his knees then against his bare feet as he slowly stood. He scanned his body for blood. Then looked to his left in abject confusion.

Ten feet away, the young Mexican he'd been playing lay face down, unmoving in a slowly growing pool of blood.

"What the?" Gannon said.

He thought one of the soldiers had shot the Mexican, but they were also looking down at the dead young man with Gannon's same look of shock. The ref, standing above the young Mexican, turned and stared at Gannon with a kind of terrible wonderment. As if Gannon were somehow responsible.

Then they all turned toward where everyone was looking at one of the watchtowers.

A man, some blond man in a navy blazer, was standing atop its battlement. There was a pistol in one of his hands and a phone in the other. He lifted the phone and began speaking into it.

"¿Quien?" the ref said to Gannon in the silence. "¿Quien es ese?"

But Gannon couldn't have answered him had he spoken in English.

He was already sitting and looking down at the Astroturf again, already somewhere else.

39

"What in blazing hell was that?" Lou said to Alessandra as she finally arrived in their Escalade out in front of the compound ten crazy hectic minutes later.

"Driver, back to the village, please. Quickly," Alessandra said as she clipped her seat belt.

"Alessandra, talk to me," Lou said as they rumbled out.

"It's okay," she said. "It's going to be fine."

No, Lou thought, glaring at her. It wasn't okay.

After their new business partner, James, had inexplicably blown away the young Mexican player with a pistol from the parapet, there had been quite the commotion.

Some of the other partygoers, members of the rival cartel, who had been sponsoring the young Mexican no doubt, had tried to enter their skybox from the outside wall. As some angry words and then some flying glasses were exchanged, Alessandra—assessing the situation—had grabbed Lou by his sleeve and told him and Manny to get going to the stairs and to head straight to the car.

"Fine," Lou said.

"We're all leaving now," she said. "James and his people. All of us. We're to go to James's place at the beach now for our meeting. We're still good. Still good."

"Good?" Lou cried. "Was I seeing things a second ago? I know I'm not up on all this like you are, but didn't our new partner, James, just murder some other cartel guy in cold blood in broad fricking daylight?"

"Exactly," Manny said as he took off his sunglasses. "This don't seem good to me either! What the hell are we in the middle of? I didn't come down here to get my ass shot off in the middle of some crazy cartel war. What is your white boy on?"

Alessandra rifled through the center console and removed a water bottle as they reentered the jungle path.

"Relax. The both of you," she said. "Here's the story Alberto told me. One of the Concurso rules is that you can kill your own player at any time, okay. It doesn't have to be through Russian roulette. It's like an option to forfeit."

She cracked the lid of the bottle.

"James just missed his gringo and shot the other guy by accident."

"What? An accident?" Lou said.

Alessandra shrugged.

"So he's claiming."

She took a sip of the water.

"A stretch, I know. Obviously, everyone is pissed. But money is being shifted around to unruffle any and all ruffled feathers. It's not our concern."

"What if that doesn't do it though?" Lou said. "The stone-cold cartel killers I know don't take a diss like this lightly."

"Right!" Manny said. "This James lunatic just pissed in the face of the devil."

"You don't understand. James is…not a man to trifle with. Also, he is very valuable to everyone. His value to the rest of the organizations supersedes his…eccentric nature. No retaliation will happen. It's not possible."

"Even so. Is a man with such an eccentric nature wise to be in business with?" Lou said. "Vicious, I can deal with. Mad dog lunatics who randomly shoot people are another."

"Exactly," Manny said. "What if he decides in the middle of our meeting to take some more sudden eccentric target practice and also 'miss' again?"

"Get off my case, the both of you," Alessandra said, wheeling around and glaring at them. "Did you not think this business requires a great appetite for risk? You agreed to come here. The connection has been made. You act like there is a choice to get out of it. There is none. Not now. We are in this. Now grow up."

When Lou looked out the window, they were back at the pyramid. Not only that, there was some kind of large black bird at the apex of it now. Some ominous-looking black crow or something perched there motionless. An emissary of the devil, no doubt sent to collect Lou's soul.

He didn't even look at Our Lady this time. He couldn't.

"And I thought this was going to be fun," Manny said with disappointment.

40

Ten miles north up the beach from their hotel in La Crucecita, James's place was a white box beach house that was large and modern with a lot of glass.

Even after they got buzzed through the gate, Lou was still watching out the back window for an ambush.

"Alberto told me they're about to leave to their plane now," Alessandra said as she bagged her phone. "That's actually a good thing. That's good for us."

"Why's that?" Lou said.

"James will be in the mood for deal making. One of my husband's rules to live by was to always wait to ask for something when the boss was hurrying out the door."

Lou opened his mouth. Then he closed it, not wanting to remind her that her husband's rules to live by hadn't really served him all that well, had they? Since he recalled that the drug dealer had died a horrible violent death several years ago in a Medellín cartel car bombing.

Lou patted at the sweat on his face with a jacket sleeve as they stopped in the circular driveway. When the driver got out for a second, Lou, still in a bewildered state bordering on panic, thought very seriously about hopping into the front and slipping it into Reverse and just slamming down the accelerator.

Alberto greeted them at the door and just inside it there was a large man in camo wearing a ski mask and a .45 in a belt holster.

"It is okay. These are friends," Alberto said as the meaty guy held up a metal detector wand. But the guard completely ignored him as he wanded them anyway.

The living room Alberto led them into was the size of a hotel ballroom. Beyond the soaring window at the other end of it, James, with his shirt off, was on the covered patio before the water view infinity pool sipping at a drink while he talked on the phone.

"James will be with you in a moment," Alberto said as they were led to a white sectional couch the length of a limousine. "Drinks?"

No one wanted drinks. As they sat, Lou watched shirtless James pace back and forth by the window. He was in great shape. He had stomach muscles like a male model or something. Even with steroids in his midforties he had to work out like what? Three hours a day?

Lou looked down at the Mexican tile, trying to breathe down his anxiety. There was a soundless flat-screen on the wall to the left and when he looked up at it, an Asian female golfer was lining up a putt.

The ball just missed the hole as Alberto returned with his own drink.

"Is there a restroom I can use?" Lou said, standing.

Alberto pointed toward the kitchen to the right. The open door of the powder room was in the corridor just beyond it but Lou, still not liking any of this in the slightest, immediately stepped past it toward a flight of circular stairs at the end of the hallway.

Halfway to the stairs beyond the powder room door on the right side was another door half-open and he peeked inside.

It was the garage. Inside of it was a large van.

And beside the van was the American player from the Concurso, sitting in a wheelchair.

The poor son of a bitch was in a waist chain and handcuffs interlinked with leg shackles and he had a black cloth bag over his head. But Lou could tell it was him because he was still in his soccer shorts.

Whatever his story was, Lou admired him. Dude had king-size balls, the size desperate housewives did Pilates on. Out of all the people here, he was the one person who still seemed sane.

Lou looked up and down the hallway.

He pushed through the door and quickly came down the steps.

As he approached, he could hear the guy's labored breathing.

No wonder, Lou thought. The un-air-conditioned garage was about a hundred degrees.

The guy stiffened and glared up at him as Lou pulled off his hood. It was the crazy gringo all right. He was sweating and red-faced and he had a gag on, a black ninety-nine-cent store bandana. Lou was still working on the knot when he heard the door behind him.

"What in the hell do you think you're doing?" said a voice.

Lou turned as a soldier in camo and a ski mask came down the steps. It was a different one from the one who had wanded them into the house. This one was very tall and had his hand on a .45.

"What am I doing?" Lou said, shifting into immediate outrage. "What the hell are you doing? Get this guy a damn bottle of water, would you? It's a hundred degrees in here. I'm coming out of the bathroom, and I hear this guy gasping his last breath."

"What are you? His nanny? Get lost!" the thug said.

He was half drawing his pistol when Alberto suddenly appeared at the doorway.

"Louis! Where have you been?" Alberto said. "James is ready."

Instead of moving an inch, Lou stood eyeing the tall masked scumbag until he turned and left the garage.

Then he finally undid the knot and let the gag fall to the floor.

"You're all set," Lou said as the American began spitting.

"Louis, now," Alberto said.

Lou paused. Then he shot the cuffs of his sport coat.

"I'm coming," Lou said finally.

"Hey!" called out a voice as he got to the top of the steps.

Lou glanced back at the brass-balled American in the wheelchair. He was smiling widely.

"Thanks, homey," he said.

41

"Please, everyone. Relax, relax," James said, slipping on a white silk shirt as he entered the living room. "Welcome, especially you, senorita. Alessandra, right? I couldn't forget you, now could I? Sorry about that mess up the hill. It was an unavoidable situation I won't bore you with. Anyway, now that we're in a less stressful setting, let's talk. I have an idea of why you are here, but if you could please quickly refresh my memory."

"Alberto said you are in the market for some transportation," Alessandra said. "That's what our firm provides."

"What kind of transportation?" James said as he sat.

Alessandra offered a palm at Lou.

"Air and then ground," Lou said. "I have planes and pilots with the state-of-the-art techniques to avoid detection over the water. Then Lt. Herrera here takes it the rest of the way by armored caravan."

"To where? What's the point of entry?"

"We guarantee delivery into Brownsville, Texas, within seventy-two hours," Alessandra said.

"That is quite the guarantee," James said as he finished buttoning his shirt. "FedEx hardly does better. You take off and land where? Not in Mexico?"

"Honduras. Near the border of Guatemala," Lou said.

"Then?" James said, fastidiously brushing at his slacks as he sat.

"Then I and my federales take it up through Guatemala and straight up along the Gulf," said Manny.

"Honduras," James said, crossing his legs. He looked up in the air above them with an expression of intense concentration. He pursed his lips.

"Honduras," he repeated with a nod.

"There's no issue with the border there, if that's a worry," Lou said.

James glanced at him.

"I do need transportation," he said. "And new routes are always welcome, depending on the price. What do you charge?"

Alessandra gave a number per kilo which was more than twice what they had been charging the Panamanians.

"That's outrageous," James said with a frown. "Where do you get your numbers from?"

"We run a tight operation. It's worth every penny," Alessandra said.

"Fine," James said, rolling his eyes. "I will agree to your outrageous price provided you take care of all the details. A new facility I'm building is almost complete, but a runway nearby will have to be made into the jungle. That's on your end or it's a deal breaker. If you make me tackle that headache, you can forget the whole thing."

Alessandra looked at Lou. He nodded. He'd arranged jungle runways before. It was a pain in the ass getting the proper equipment in but doable.

"We will take care of it," Alessandra said.

"Perfect then," James said as Alberto handed him another drink. "Meet me at my estate in Iquitos in three days."

"Iquitos?" Alessandra said.

Iquitos was damn Peru! Lou thought. Shit.

"Yes, Iquitos. Is there a problem?"

"The planes we use," Lou said. "The range is limited."

"What kind of plane?"

"It's a Cessna 414."

"How much can it carry?"

"One ton. It will go fifteen hundred miles empty. It's the return trip I'm worried about."

"That's your lookout. Give me a break. Can you handle this weight or was all this a waste of my time?"

"Yes, we can handle it," Lou said, not sure if that was true.

James lifted his drink to signal the meeting was over.

"Okay then. It's a deal. Three days. When you get to Iquitos, contact Alberto and we will share all the details with you," he said.

PART TWO

CHANGE OF PLANS

42

After the home run of the Ginny Mickelson Senate campaign announcement, Adrian Bright drove straight back to DC to get a few more things done.

No rest for the weary, he thought as he crossed through the center of the Georgetown University campus carrying a cardboard box.

In the box were books and the last of Claudette's things from her office that she was always forgetting to clear out. His wife was an American literature associate professor. She was taking a sabbatical this semester but come fall, she would be teaching in the Middle Eastern nation of Qatar of all places. Georgetown had built a new campus there along with a few other American colleges like Cornell and Texas A&M.

What a supposedly Catholic institution was doing in a Muslim country with a one hundred percent Muslim student body teaching American literature he had to admit was quite a puzzler. But if Claudette was excited, so be it. The adventure that was their marriage was always taking them somewhere new, wasn't it? he thought.

He smiled. He was all about constantly expanding horizons.

"Sir, is that your dog?" said a security guard coming the other way as he crossed through the center path of the main quadrangle.

Bright glanced down at the obedient Stanley trotting along at his heel as if he were glued to it.

"Yes, of course. It's okay. He's one of the, um, new safe space comfort dogs."

"No dogs on campus," said the security guard as he rolled his eyes.

Two minutes later, Bright arrived at the top floor of the east campus parking garage where he had left the Porsche. He had just deposited the box into the back seat and Stanley back into his co-pilot seat when he thought of something. He took the sat phone from the glovebox and thumbed it on.

"Shit," he said.

There were seventeen missed calls.

"There you are," Bouthier said.

Bright winced at his agent's somber tone as he opened the Porsche's driver's door and sat.

"What is it? What happened? The target is dead. Tell me he's dead."

"The plan has changed."

"What do you mean? Gannon is supposed to be dead."

"That was the old plan. There's a new plan now," Bouthier said.

"What happened?"

Bouthier told him the whole story.

When he was done, Bright closed his eyes and rubbed at his temples as he shook his head.

Because it was shocking.

"You're telling me that James killed Gannon's opponent in front of everyone instead of letting Gannon get killed?"

"Yes."

"You're still in Mexico?"

"Yes. We're about to get on the plane back to the compound. We're at the airport. They're gassing up the plane now."

"Where the hell is Gannon?"

"He's tied up in the van beside me."

"But why?" Bright cried. "He was just supposed to enter Gannon into this thing and walk away."

"Well, he's been un-entered," Bouthier said. "I guess the boss changed his mind."

Bright rubbed at his forehead as he thought about everything.

Changed his mind, he thought. His insane mind.

James Devine had been a personal project from way back, a rare jewel plucked from the nonstop shitstorm of Iraq and Afghanistan. Iron tough, capable, smart, and best of all, blindly obedient. Bright had raised Devine almost like a son, coached him.

Bright wasn't actually surprised. Devine was a loose cannon all right. More of his calls were unreturned these days than returned.

Devine had been his puppet and an excellent one at that. But apparently, he was more of a real boy now as puppets weren't supposed to stray from their strings.

And now Devine was losing it apparently.

Bright looked over at Stanley staring back at him.

"What do you think he's going to do with Gannon back at the base?" Bright said. "Any clue?"

"None," Bouthier said. "We're boarding the plane now."

Not good, Bright thought. The off-the-books jobs were always nail-biters. The blowback on him if things went screwy was not going to be good.

Bright chewed at his lip.

He looked down to see his right leg beginning to shake. His one tic when things got dicey was that his right knee would begin to bounce up and down like a Mexican jumping bean on a trampoline.

"Bouthier, listen to me very closely," Bright said. "I need you to keep me informed morning, noon, and night. Understood?"

There was silence. Bright looked at his phone then threw it into the back seat.

The sat connection was already gone.

43

John Barber got off the plane at Ronald Reagan International Airport in Washington, DC, at nine o'clock at night and walked through the almost deserted terminal to the car rental agency.

After some negotiation, the clerk there ended up giving him a Chevy vehicle Barber had never heard of before called an Equinox, and twenty minutes later he drove it out from the airport's depressing cement parking garage into lightly falling snow.

He found Route 120 and took it to 395 North. Ten minutes and twenty miles north from where he got on, he pulled over onto the shoulder in front of a marked police SUV with its lights spinning.

Or at least it looked like a police SUV. You'd have to squint and look twice to read where it said Pentagon Force Protection Agency beneath the blue stripe on its white door.

He got out of the Equinox and walked through the softly falling snow and pulled open the SUV's rear door.

"You don't have to do that," John Barber's old unit buddy, Eddie Navarro, said from behind the wheel.

Barber shut the door with a thump. Like Mike and himself, Ed had been a veteran of their Task Force Orange unit when it had sneaked into Pakistan and Iran.

Ed had the look of a dumb jock, but looks could be deceiving as he was an electrical engineer and a computer and technical genius. He had been their head computer tech. He was a section chief in the Pentagon's satellite reconnaissance office now.

"Look around. It's dead," Ed said. "Sit up here. It's colder than a well digger's ass back there. Come up here where it's warm."

"Screw it, brother. I'm back here already. How's Caroline?"

"Wouldn't know. We're separated," Ed said with a shrug of his beefy shoulders.

Ed, never svelte, had packed on some more pounds since their glory days, Barber could see. He looked at the back of his head where a bald spot was growing.

"What? No!" Barber said. "That sucks, man."

"Yeah, it's a long story. It's okay. I'll figure it out. At least maybe."

"Sorry to hear that."

"Yeah, I hear a lot of the old crew are taking a beating these days, aren't we? Poor Mike. I loved that lead-balled bastard."

They both turned as a speeding eighteen-wheeler went by in a rushing blaze of lights. It was close enough to shake the car.

"You can still love him, Ed. We just have to find him."

"Okay, so here's what I got for you. First off, you're right. Those two GI Joe types you got off the hotel footage up in Alaska were operators."

"Contractors?"

"What else is there these days?"

"Names? Addresses?"

"C'mon, John. You kidding? You ain't going to get those. You're lucky I was able to just get confirmation that they're in the business. Freelance mercenary outfits very rarely kiss and tell."

"C'mon, Ed. You're a genius computer geek. You couldn't hack into the likely firms?"

"A year ago you could, but the encryption is getting super crazy. So, no. Or not yet at least."

"Shame."

"But here's what I do have," he said as he passed back a stack of printouts.

Barber put on his phone's flashlight and looked at the top sheet. There was a blown-up photo of a plane on it.

"A plane with markings that connect it to some kind of text-book CIA dummy company landed at the Juneau airport six hours before Mike and his kid. Then it took off the evening of the day Mike went missing."

Barber peered down at the plane. Some kind of white jet with blue pinstriping. He remembered he and Mike passing off a prisoner onto a similar-looking jet some years back from the Bagram airport in Afghanistan. He wondered if it was the same one.

"So the Company took him? The CIA?"

Ed nodded.

"Definitely looks like one of their planes."

Barber yawned. Out the window to the right through the snow he could see the Washington Monument. The red lights on the top of the giant obelisk looked like a pair of spider's eyes.

He stared at them. He'd always hated that freaky Ancient Egyptian thing. What the hell did Ancient Egypt have to do with America or George Washington? he always wondered.

"That's what Mike gets for working selflessly for them like a dog after deployments in two theaters of combat. That's his pension? A bag over his head? Now that's loyalty."

"What is going on in this town at this juncture," Ed said as he scratched at his bald spot, "is beyond my ability to comprehend."

"That's it?"

"No. Look at the other sheets."

"What's this other one?"

"A small airport in Oaxaca, Mexico, on the coast. I saw it last week. I couldn't get a perfect read on the markings, but it looks like the same plane so I scoured all the feeds. A day after Mike was snatched I got a partial feed where it looks like a guy in a wheelchair being put on it."

"That's it! That's Mike. Has to be! Where did it go then?"

"South. I was psyched because they left the transponder on. But then it went off as it crossed over the Colombian border. There were no other birds around to track it into Colombia. I lost it."

"So, Mike's in South America somewhere. That nails it down."

"At least if it's him, he's still alive. Dead people go in body bags last time I checked, not wheelchairs."

Barber looked out at the empty gray cold highway as he wondered about that. If that was actually a good thing at this point. If maybe it would be better if he were already dead.

Then he stopped thinking like a loser.

"I appreciate it, Ed. Sticking your neck out."

"How old is Mike's kid?" Ed said.

"Early twenties," he said.

"I got one of those. A twenty-year-old daughter. Off at school. She never calls me ever since... Whatever. I miss her like crazy."

"It's actually Mike's son's birthday today," Barber said.

"Happy birthday. Wow."

A passing plow truck splattered slush against the cruiser's door. They listened to the wipers flop back and forth in the silence.

"At least the weather's picking up," Ed said.

"Yeah," Barber said as he grabbed the cold door handle. "At least we got that."

44

On whatever number day it was since Gannon had been snatched, he woke staring up at a faint light coming in through an eyebrow window at the top of the twenty-foot-high concrete wall beside his bed.

Was it morning? Evening? He didn't know. He thought evening maybe. But that was a guess.

There was a book open on his chest that he'd started reading when he fell asleep and as he sat up, it tumbled and fell loudly to the cement floor.

He looked down at it groggily.

There were plenty of books, but he found himself going back to this one more and more.

"Yeah," he said as he bent and dusted off the leatherbound King James Bible and placed it carefully back on his nightstand. "Go figure."

Beside the Bible, there was a half-full plastic bottle of water, and he lifted it up and unscrewed its blue cap. He drained it on one lukewarm sip and then idly tossed the empty in a long lazy arc toward the wastebasket in the corner of the room. It rang like a bell as it hit off both sides and then dropped in.

"You see that!" he called out excitedly.

He pointed up at the surveillance camera above the steel door.

"Yeah, you know you saw that," he said as he sat up. "Boo-yah, baby. That's what I'm talkin' about. You know this kid's got himself some *real* skills."

Why he was talking to the camera now he wasn't sure, he thought as he inched farther back on the bed to lean his back up against the cell wall.

Then he realized it.

It's because you're slowly going nuts, Mike.

His new accommodations were almost more like a hotel suite than a cell. There was a little kitchen with a sink and a mini-fridge, a bathroom with a shower and a door. Beside the bed on his right, there was a bookcase and beside that was a Bowflex-like resistance workout bench of all things.

Three of the concrete walls were painted a calming light golden mustard while the fourth wall was accented with dark plum, giving his little personal prison some real panache.

In order to be fed and have the sheets changed, his buddy Button Eyes's gruff voice would emit from a speaker beneath the camera on the wall and order him to place his wrist into a remotely controlled handcuff-like restraint that was bolted to the wall in the bathroom.

That the thirty-something Hispanic woman who came in to turn down the sheets wore a ski mask was something out of a low-budget indie horror movie, but it could have been worse.

Maybe.

He still didn't know why he was here or what his captors had in store for him, and that, he had to admit, was a tad mentally taxing.

Perhaps they had nothing in store for him, he thought for the thousandth time. Perhaps this was to be his punishment, a civilized one of living out his days in this dorm-like jail cell, eating fairly nice meals, reading and sleeping in, and working out while talking to himself and inanimate objects.

Or maybe it was something else, he thought as he stared over at the surveillance camera on the plum-colored wall that was protected by a plexiglass shield. It was a white iPhone-looking high-tech thing with multiple lenses.

You almost had to hand it to the freaks. The regular meals and boredom were nearly worse than constant uncertainty as the monotony of it all started to remove fear. Fear at least kept one sharp.

He lowered his gaze and stared forlornly at the inside of the steel door's key insert.

He would have already tried to pick it except the bastards had found the airplane wire he'd been hiding in his mouth.

Just before they'd taken off on the jet out of Mexico, his buddy Button Eyes had unexpectedly shoved a rubber dental dam in his mouth and then rammed one of his stubby gloved fingers in and found it.

No doubt about it. Things weren't looking exactly peachy, were they? They were grinding him down mentally. At this point he thought with a sigh, even he was starting not to give a shit what happened to him.

"Oh, no, you don't, you silly son of a bitch," he said to himself as he suddenly leaped off of the bed.

He crossed the room and grabbed the wastepaper basket and hurled it savagely at the surveillance camera. It went off like a gong as it blasted into the plexiglass dead center, showering the room with water bottles and used Kleenex.

"That's it! Let me out of here, you damn dirty pricks!" Gannon screamed as he smashed at the plexiglass again with the wastebasket. "You hear me? I've had enough of this loony-bin bullshit! Patience officially over! Let me out!"

45

Twenty minutes later after his rather stress-relieving tantrum, Gannon had cleaned up and was lazing back on the bed in the dark, writing a letter to his son in his head when he heard the footsteps coming.

He sat straight up.

Because he could tell immediately by the heaviness of them that it wasn't the ski mask maid.

He swallowed with sudden dry-mouthed panic as all the lights abruptly came on.

"What did I do?" he muttered to himself as he stood, staring at the camera.

"Chain yourself to the wall! Now!" Button Eyes's voice screeched from the speaker.

"Go to hell!" Gannon screamed back at it.

Suddenly, a sound he had never experienced before filled the room. A torturous electric buzzing that drilled through his eardrums like a hot wire. It sounded like a mosquito caught on a rock concert microphone.

"Fine, you win," Gannon said, hurrying into the bathroom.

The bathroom cuff had just clicked when the buzzing stopped and the door swung inward.

When he saw who it was that stepped in, Gannon couldn't hide his surprise.

Because he'd spent so much time speculating as to what would happen next during his stay.

And this wasn't even close to being it.

"Jimmy?" Gannon said.

James Devine smiled.

"Hello, Mike," he said.

Gannon's mouth dropped open. It stayed there. He tried to think of something to say.

But what did you say to a former friend and brother-in-arms fresh back from the grave?

Gannon came up empty.

"You should see your face," Jimmy Devine said, smiling. "Sorry I couldn't have come by sooner to say hi. I've been dealing with some…domestic issues. Won't bore you with the details. Anyway, welcome. You look well. Incredibly well. Your head especially. I see it's almost completely healed. And the color is back in your cheeks. That pleases me. Welcome to my home."

Gannon stared at him in the silence.

Then he remembered the mission.

It was a covert infiltration out of Iraq into Iran to take out a government nuclear scientist. They were flying nap-of-the-earth two miles to the drop zone when a sparkler-like streak suddenly rose from between his combat boots and hit the back rotor. Two or three free-falling spinning, beeping seconds later, a hill smashed in through the Black Hawk's opposite open door.

Gannon was immediately knocked out as his skateboard-helmeted head smashed into the bulwark beside the door. He must have been thrown then and when he woke up, he was on the hillside downrange from the burning wreckage. In a daze, he remembered going up to see what was what. But the aircraft was gone. Just a bolus of flaming metal. When he heard the popping of small arms gunfire a few seconds after that, he immediately chose the direction opposite from it and ran.

It had taken him two days of hiding and moving by night to get back over the border.

Out of the six SEAL operators in his team and two pilots, he was the only one who had made it back.

Or so he had thought.

"You're alive, Jimmy," Gannon finally got out.

"Life's just full of surprises, wouldn't you say?" Jimmy said as he stepped over and lifted the Bible off the bed stand.

46

Gannon sat looking at his old friend.

His dirty blond hair and his insane fitness were about the same, but his style was new. The Jimmy Devine he'd known was a scruffy, laid-back, fun-loving former high school athlete from football country outside of Pittsburgh. A wings-and-beers sort of guy. His call sign was Blondie from the old Clint Eastwood Westerns.

Now he was...stiffer. More elitist or something. The single-breasted suit in dark gray was pinstriped and perfectly tailored, and he wore it with a silk tie that was the color of an apricot. In the fluorescent light, the slight blush of a silk sheen was visible in his bespoke suit's warp and weft.

This new Jimmy was regal as a count, Gannon thought.

"I thought you were...dead," he said.

"You weren't the only one," Jimmy said as he glanced down at the bookmarked passage.

Gannon stared some more.

"What happened?" Gannon said.

"I woke up chained and naked on the floor of a filthy inter-rogation room in Sabzevar is what happened, Mike. When the Iranian Republican Guard captain asked me my name, I spit in his face. Then he crushed my right ball into pulp with the toe of his spit-polished steel-toed boot."

Jimmy closed the Bible and placed it back down where he'd found it.

"Now that was a wake-up call," he said with another smile. "Believe you, me, the first time they go downstairs on you, Mike, is something you never forget."

Gannon watched him walk over to the bookcase and select another book.

"Solzhenitsyn's *Cancer Ward*," Jimmy said, reading the cover. "I love the Russians. Best prison writers of all time. Read this one yet, Mike?"

"Not yet," Gannon said, his mind still spinning. "How did you get out of that wreckage, Jimmy?"

"How did you?" Jimmy said, without looking up from the book.

"I was thrown," Gannon said.

"So was I," Devine said, looking up. "Different direction, I guess."

"Where? Above it?" Gannon said. "I was below and I came up and looked around. All I saw was burning metal."

"Oh, I'm sure you tried to find me, Mike," Jimmy said, look-ing at him as he softly closed the book. "I'm sure. Or did you? I wonder."

Yeah, he really was different, Gannon saw. He had always been jacked but even more so now. Maybe on roids? Despite his new PBS *Masterpiece Theatre* attitude, he'd still been keeping up with the SEAL, Sleep Eat And Lift, lifestyle. That was for damn sure.

Jimmy slipped the book back onto the shelf.

"Don't worry, Mike. Just wanted to pop in and say hi for now. We'll talk later, okay?"

He smoothed his beautiful tie and flicked and fluffed at its matching pocket square.

"We'll talk *all* about it," he said.

"Sounds good," Gannon managed to get out.

"Mike? One last thing. I have a dinner party tonight so I'd appreciate it if you could do me a favor and keep it down with all the hooting and hollering."

"Come again?" Gannon said.

"You know. Your Charlton Heston routine," he said with a grin. "I found it amusing, but the last time I had guests, the previous occupant of this room started screaming obscenities at the top of his lungs right in the middle of dinner."

"Is that right?"

"Yes. My adult guests thought it was whatever but there were children present at the dinner who looked very sad and afraid. I felt bad for them."

"All rightee then," Gannon said. "I'll…just go back to sleep."

"Thanks, Mike. I knew you'd understand," Jimmy Devine said as he left.

47

Many hours later deep in the night, Gannon came awake as his steel cell door shrieked open. Before he could even so much as sit up, a pair of strong hands seized him in an iron grip. Bright stars came out suddenly in the darkness a second later as his head bonked painfully off the concrete from them roughly dragging him out of bed to the floor.

"What the hell!" he said as he was turned over.

As if in reply, a sharp knee was painfully dug into his spine as his hands were cuffed behind him.

"Shut up," said the familiar voice of Button Eyes in his ear.

A sack was popped over his head as he was lifted to his feet. Barefoot and shirtless with just his boxer briefs on, he was half dragged down a concrete corridor and up some stairs.

Past a doorway at the top of them, he was hurried through another concrete area that seemed more open. After some distance through this space, another set of cement stairs crashed into his shins. His toes were stubbed hard enough to bring tears to his eyes as he was mercilessly shoved and pulled and dragged upward again.

Atop this next flight, there was suddenly a wood floor under his scrambling bare feet. He was shoved to his left almost off his feet through what seemed like a creaky swinging door.

When he was violently seated, he was thinking they were about to waterboard him or something.

But he was wrong.

The hood was removed and he sat blinking out at a massive elaborately set dining room table, the china and silver glittering in the flickering light of a half dozen or so candles.

As Gannon tried to absorb this patent absurdity, his old buddy Button Eyes appeared and undid his left cuff. Then he re-cuffed it to a steel eyebolt embedded into a massive concrete block that sat, Gannon suddenly noticed, beside the left elbow of his tufted chair.

"I, repeat, what in the hell?" Gannon said as Button Eyes retreated.

If his cell had a Tuscan theme, this one was French, Gannon thought. Decorating the wallpaper were old oil paintings, landscapes, portraits.

Ugly portraits, Gannon thought, staring up at the deathly pale and wigged European faces.

He looked at the wallpaper. On it, old-timey Three Musketeer-looking dudes on horseback were deer hunting. What was it called again? Toile? His wife, Annette—pregnant with Declan and nesting—had done their powder room in it. Annette had minored in French in college.

The door flew open a moment later, and Button Eyes was wrestling another prisoner.

As he was sat and cuffed at another concrete block, Gannon could see he was a barrel-chested guy with longish curly dark hair and a dark beard. His dark button-down shirt had some embroidered cowboy stuff on the front of it. He looked like a country Western singer or something.

"Hey," the man said, smiling broadly as Button Eyes left. "You're new, huh?"

He had a Spanish accent.

"Me? No, I'm a regular," Gannon said. "Try the soup. You'll thank me later."

The guy laughed merrily. Gannon laughed himself. He didn't know if the guy was a plant or something but liked him immediately. There was a good vibe off him, a happy upbeat energy. And heaven knows, that was in short supply here.

"What are you in for?" Gannon said.

"Political wrong think. Or do, in my case. Same as you, I bet. They don't bring you here for slight offenses."

Gannon nodded.

"Oh, yeah. I've been a bad boy, all right. Where you from? Spain? Portugal?"

"Brazil. And you are American. From New York?"

"I am," Gannon said. "How'd you know?"

"I love American movies. *Die Hard* is my favorite and you sound like John McClane. You know John McClane from *Die Hard*?"

As he said this, he flicked something at Gannon across the table. It ricocheted off one of the silver sticks and landed before him on the linen. It was folded-up paper like one of those little footballs from grammar school.

"Know him?" Gannon said as he knocked the paper off the table and bent and tucked it into his waistband.

"John McClane is my spirit animal," he said.

"You are very funny," the guy said with another goofy laugh. "I am Paolo."

"Mike," Gannon said.

"Miguel, a pleasure."

"Now, now. No talking in class when teacher isn't around," Jimmy Devine said as he came in through the door behind Gannon a second later.

48

As Jimmy Devine sat at the other end of the runway of china and silver, Gannon saw that he was wearing the same pin-striped gray suit but the tie was gone. He also noticed that his face had a flush to it. Gannon eyed him in the candlelight. Jimmy seemed very drunk.

Just as he noted this, a formally attired waiter, a morose-looking middle-aged Hispanic man with a mustache, came in through the swinging door. He held a silver tray before Gannon. There were little toothpicked cubes of food on it.

At least it isn't a .38, Gannon thought, eyeing the tray suspiciously.

"Don't worry," Jimmy Devine said. "My chef is quite playful. This is just an appetizer. Don't look. You're supposed to select one at random and eat it. Paolo, show him."

"My pleasure," Paolo said as he selected one with his free hand. Gannon followed suit.

"What did you get?" Jimmy Devine said after he had selected his own and popped it into his mouth.

"A tangerine," Paolo said. "A very tasty one."

"And you, Mike?" Jimmy said.

"Potato, I think," Gannon said, chewing.

"Ha! How ironic. Bless your Irish heart," Jimmy said.

"Yeah, all I need is a six-pack for my seven-course meal, and I'll be good to go," Gannon said good-naturedly. "What did you get, buddy?"

"A jalapeño," Jimmy said with an almost girlish giggle.

"Is that right?" Gannon said, nodding at Paolo and then smiling despite all the insanity. "Got some of the hot stuff, huh?"

"How do you like my table here?" Jimmy said.

Gannon studied it. It actually was very nice. In all the flickering light, the highly shellacked inlaid top of it gleamed like a sheet of volcanic glass.

"It's beautiful. What is it? Maple?" Gannon said.

"Pollard oak. Notice the tiger's-eye effect in the grain. It's an actual Chippendale."

Gannon smiled politely as he looked down at it some more.

"Gorgeous," he said.

"As you can see, I've come to like beautiful things, Mike," Jimmy Devine said as he swept a hand at the room.

"Oh, so you two know each other?" Paolo said. "Some history, yes?"

Jimmy looked at him, assessing.

"You know, Paolo, I apologize," he said as he pressed a button. Button Eyes came in.

"This was a bit premature. As much as I love dining with you and wanted you guys to meet, I actually have some personal things to discuss with my old friend here. This is a reunion of sorts."

"Of course, James," Paolo said, standing and offering his hand to be cuffed. "Old friends do not need a third wheel. I understand perfectly. Miguel, again a pleasure."

"Same here," Gannon said.

"And please try the soup," Paolo called on his way out. "You will thank me later."

After Paolo was led away, Gannon turned to see Jimmy lovingly staring up at the portraits behind him, which somehow, despite their rodent-like ugliness and moles, managed to gaze arrogantly back.

"Do you see Paolo's manners, Mike?" he said as the door swung closed. "That's pure old-world charm. We miss so much being American. How to live elegantly. You know how well read he is? He gardens, too. He gave me advice about my tomatoes."

"Jimmy, that's, um…cool," Gannon said with a hopefully calming smile. "Your whole setup here. It's ah, really…um… really cool."

Jimmy popped a button on his shirt to show his bare muscular chest.

"Yes," Jimmy said. "Things change, you know. People, too. I've grown so much."

49

Gannon looked up to see the morose waiter was back. He had a decanter in his hands. The soft yellow light flickered off its faceted crystal surface as he made an inquisitive gesture with it at Gannon's glass. Gannon nodded heartily. Boy, could he use a drink.

The filled wineglass was heavier than he expected. He put it to his lips. Holy smokes, he thought, blinking rapidly. It was ridiculously good. It was blackberry fruity yet…something rich and complexly satisfying. Something silky…expensive.

"Wow, this wine is incredible," he said, looking at it.

"Oh, yes, isn't it? Bordeaux," Jimmy said with a proud look. "I had them select something special from my wine cellar to welcome you. For you, Mike. Seulement le meilleur. Only the best."

"That was nice of you, Jimmy. Thanks," Gannon said, taking a very long sip.

"You do like it," Jimmy said, chuckling.

"It's about the tastiest wine I think I've ever had," Gannon said, wiping his mouth with the back of his only free hand.

The waiter, standing at attention behind him in the corner, took up his empty glass and expertly filled it again. Then he returned to the corner and stood there still as a piece of furniture.

"Oh, you'll like it here then, Mike. Tasty wine is a priority around here. I have vintages of claret that date back to the turn of the previous century."

Gannon studied the new Jimmy across the table as he took a dainty sip of his vino.

Things change all right, he thought. The last time they drank together in their FOB hootch in Iraq, he remembered Jimmy shotgunning a full PBR tallboy with a Bic ballpoint pen before letting out a Jurassic belch.

Gannon smiled, already feeling a bit of a buzz.

"Can I ask you a question, Jimmy?" Gannon said.

"Yes, Mike. Sure."

"How the hell did you get out of Iran?"

Jimmy's goofy expression evaporated instantly as he stared down.

"They did experiments on me," he said.

"What?"

He nodded.

"For years," he said. "One of them screwed me up so bad, I got sepsis. I was on death's door, so they transferred me to some shithole hospital somewhere. I think it was in Pakistan. When I woke up a few days later, I was in another hospital in Turkey. The Company had negotiated a secret deal where they sent back a top guy from Hamas for me."

Gannon wondered about that.

"Whoa," he said. "That had to have been a happy surprise. You just woke up and you were free. A miracle."

"Yes. That's exactly what it was. I owe the Company so much. They brought me back. They took me to a hospital in Belarus.

It took me a year to fully recover. They said I could just go home or I could get another identity. I would have chosen to go home, of course, but it was almost five years later, and Joyce had remarried by then. She married a doctor. They had just had twin girls. With my two boys that made four. They showed me pictures. They all looked really happy."

Despite the pickle he was in, Gannon suddenly looked over at his former friend with genuine pity, unable to fathom the incredible hurt of that.

"That's why I started working with the Company. I needed a new life, too," Jimmy said.

They sat in the flickering light.

"Got sheep-dipped, huh?" Gannon said after a while.

Jimmy, still looking down, drew a finger across the shiny tabletop.

"Yep. I owe them my life," he said quietly as the waiter brought in plates.

"Steak! All right, that's what I'm talking about," Gannon said, trying to restore the mood.

"Chateaubriand," Jimmy said sitting up a little, brighter now. "I insisted. For you, Mike, we kill the fatted calf."

"You're the best, bro," Gannon said with a hopefully natural-sounding laugh as he took an awkward bite at his presliced meat with only his fork.

"How is it?"

"You kidding me?" Gannon said after another hit of Bordeaux. "What do the French say? Ooo-la-la? A total home run."

"Good. What else do you want to know, Mike? I'm sure you must have many questions."

"I do actually," Gannon said, finishing his wine and waving his glass at the waiter in the corner to keep it coming.

"Why am I here, Jimmy?" he said as he lifted his refilled glass.

Jimmy, slicing his meat, peered over at him.

"Do you know the Greek legend of Prometheus?" he said.

"The guy who gets his liver eaten," Gannon said.

He nodded.

"Prometheus was a Titan who defied the gods by giving man the fire of the gods. For this he was punished."

"You're not saying I'm here to have my liver eaten, are you?" Gannon said, laughing awkwardly.

Jimmy gave a funny laugh himself as he cut his meat some more.

"Some would love that very thing, Mike. That *very* thing, believe me. But no. I intervened on your behalf."

"Sooo, you're…going to let me go?" Gannon said hopefully.

Jimmy looked up from his plate.

"I'm going to give you…a chance," he finally said.

50

Whatever that meant, Gannon thought.

He had a feeling it was probably best for the moment to leave it unexplored.

"Who are the gods?" Gannon said.

"The gods?"

"That I pissed off," Gannon said after another sip. "The Company? The CIA?"

"Obviously," Devine said, swirling his wine.

"Okay. A quick follow-up question. Who does the Central Intelligence Agency work for?"

Jimmy looked over at him with an amused look.

"How do you mean?"

"Well, technically the CIA is supposed to work for the citizens of the United States, right? They're supposed to protect and to defend the Constitution and United States citizens from foreign threats. Well, I'm an American citizen, a patriotic law-abiding one. A decorated war veteran. If I committed a crime, by law I should be arrested. Yet, here I am renditioned. Plus, that was all drug cartel people at the prison soccer thing, right? Aren't we supposed to be, um, stopping the drug cartels? Looks like the Company is sort of running them."

"Being only a mortal myself, I do not know exactly the who, what, and why of things," Jimmy said as he cut another slice, "but like many, I have an opinion. Though I guess mine is what you might call an informed opinion. It has helped me to explore and to devise what you might call an alternative history of things. Would you like to hear what I came up with?"

"Very much," Gannon said, sipping.

"Again, this is just a theory."

"Theory, got it. Let's hear it," Gannon said.

"A smart man once said that the characteristic danger of great nations which have a long history of continuous creation is that they may, at last, fail from comprehending the great institutions which they have created. This seems to be the case with our own, Mike."

"So," Gannon said, "you're saying the US got too big or something? The right hand doesn't know what the left is doing."

Jimmy nodded.

"Though it's actually bigger than that. You have to look at things in a different light from the way you are used to. From a higher position and longer time frame. When you think of a country, you think of a place with a bunch of people who do things a certain way, right? For example, take the country of Colombia. There's a certain style of dress, a certain attitude, a certain music, regional dishes, a citizenry that considers themselves connected in an almost sibling-like fashion."

He popped another piece of meat in his mouth, chewed, swallowed.

"Colombian climate, Colombian culture, Colombian people. That's Colombia," he said.

"Are we in Colombia right now?" Gannon said.

"Wouldn't you like to know?" Jimmy said, smiling as he took a sip of wine. "Are you following me?"

"Yes, keep going," Gannon said.

"Now the tippity-top people who I think that I work for," he said, cutting another slice, "see a country as something else. They see every country as nothing, just a pile of dirt to place a bank on."

"Why a bank?"

"Because as soon as a bank is set up, they can start sending the wealth in that area of the world out of that area and into the pockets of the bank's owners in Europe."

"The CIA works for the Europeans?"

"Sort of. See the Europe part doesn't matter, places don't matter. Or names. Europe, too, is just a pile of dirt. Bear with me. The word *bank* comes from its nautical connotation. The bank of a river controls the current, right? Well, a human bank controls another kind of current, otherwise known as currency. The currency flows between the banks, and the bankers who control this flow busily siphon it off into their pockets as they suck it out of various parts of the globe."

"Banks, huh?" Gannon said, puzzled. "Bankers are the gods? I thought they were a business. Like a hardware store. But instead of selling hammers, they helpfully lend out money like mortgages and pay out interest for savers, right?"

Jimmy laughed.

"You really don't know anything, do you? You've never heard of our fractional reserve central banking system. When you deposit money into a local bank, they go to the central bank, who gives them a near zero percent loan of nine times what you put in for them to lend out. If you put in a hundred thousand at one percent interest, they get their hands on another nine hundred thousand from a central bank and immediately loan out a million at three percent per year. At the end of the first year, you've made a thousand on the hundred thousand you actually did something to earn. They've made thirty K on it for doing nothing at all."

"That doesn't sound very fair. Or even legal."

"It's not fair," Jimmy said, laughing. "Though it is extremely legal. The bankers work diligently with their lawyers and bribed politicians to ensure that."

"Where does the European central bank get its money to loan out?" Gannon said. "No, wait. Let me guess."

He pointed at the portraits above Jimmy's head.

"From the Euro royal dudes, right? They get it from the royal jewels?"

Jimmy laughed for quite some time. He dabbed at the corner of an eye with his napkin.

"You're right!" he said. "You are smarter than you realize. In the beginning, the banks did use royal gold as reserves for the currency. But that was only in the beginning. Now the banks— get this, Mike—this is the best part. Now the banks don't back the money with anything! They conjure it up from thin air, from nowhere. How's that for a racket? They just go to a keyboard and type a number and hit Send and voilà! A bank account has that much money in it. The real wealth flows in. The fake bank money flows out. That's fractional reserve banking."

"That's how the world actually works?" Gannon said. "That sounds like a Ponzi scheme."

"Oh, yes. It is."

Jimmy laughed again.

"You are totally getting this, Mike. That's exactly what it is."

51

"So, you're saying the whole thing, the way the world is set up as we know it with countries and stuff, isn't real? It's like a movie set and that behind all of it are connected royal bankers out of Europe robbing everybody blind?"

"Yes."

"What about democracy?" Gannon said. "It's a trick? The royals bribe all the politicians?"

Jimmy nodded.

"So, the sun never set on the British Empire," Gannon said, remembering what an SAS soldier friend once told him. "Because God couldn't trust an Englishman in the dark."

"Not quite," Jimmy said. "The sun did set on the British Empire. But then they just started working the night shift with the intel services and the royal-owned banking system offshore. It's all about secrecy, Mike. Secrets, secrets, secrets. It's all about those secrets. Those who know them are the rulers of the world and those who don't are the ruled."

"But no matter what they think, justice is bigger than any government. It's older than America, it's older than recorded history. It's in my human DNA, Jimmy. Nothing on earth can make it stop. You can even take me out, but guess what? Too late! I already put it in my son! It's in every good person. It's in you too, Jimmy.

"Unclick my cuffs, Jimmy. Let's blow this clambake. Come home with me. Let me take you home to your family, man. Do you have any idea how many people came to your memorial? Your whole county and every damn SEAL whoever was was there, saluting. Do you have any idea how much people love and miss you? Come home, Jimmy! It's not too late."

The crowds of portraits behind and around suddenly didn't seem to be looking at Gannon anymore. They seemed to be looking down at Jimmy as if awaiting his response.

The last candle finally went out as Jimmy Devine blew on it.

"Oh, grow up," he said from the dark.

52

Back in his cell, Gannon unfolded the piece of paper he took from his waistband.

"I'm in the cell beneath you. Go into the bathroom and unscrew the trap of the sink and tap on it softly so we can talk through the pipe."

Gannon remembered Paolo's goofy grin.

Could be a trick but what the hell? he thought as he walked for the bathroom. What if it wasn't? And what other choices did he have?

"Hello," came a whisper out of the water pipe after he crawled down on the cold tile and followed the instructions.

"Hey," Gannon whispered back.

"I can't hear you clearly. You must come closer."

Gannon, still drunk, laughed as he stuck his head down deeper between the sink and the wall.

"Hey," he said again.

"Much better. How was your dinner?"

"Delicious," Gannon said.

"Devine is completely insane. How do you know him?"

"He was in my navy SEAL unit."

"A former brother-in-arms, I see. What did you do to him?"

"Nothing. I did something to the people he works for. I think they pawned me off on him to take care of me. I'm not sure. Where the hell are we?"

"We are in Peru in the Amazon near a town called Iquitos." Peru, Gannon thought. Wow.

"Iquitos is to the southeast of here. There is a railhead there. Also boat traffic on the Amazon. It is a lumber town and they float the logs down it. If you come to a river, go with the flow."

"Come to a river? I can't get out of my cell."

"You will be brought out of your cell like the others."

"The others?"

"Yes. There were two other men in your cell since I have been here. A Finn and a Japanese. The Finn, Aku, was the one who told me about this pipe phone, but they were both taken somewhere. Driven away never to return. I think Devine hunts them."

Gannon tried to process that but failed. Better to forget that for now, he thought.

"How many people are here? How many guards?" he asked.

"Possibly half a dozen security men plus the butler, and there's also a chef who lives here."

"Good," Gannon said. "Not as bad as I thought."

Paolo laughed.

"You are quite an optimist," he said. "Wait! I hear something. Restore the trap and leave the bathroom. We will talk in the morning."

"One other thing."

"Yes, Miguel?"

"Why are you helping me?"

There was a pause.

"Why do you think?" Paolo said with another laugh.

"I don't know," Gannon said.

"Because I believe in God, you fool," Paolo said. "And because I hate these people. How dare they take me from my parish and lock me up!"

"Your parish?"

"Yes Miguel. I am a priest."

53

The Toyota Land Cruiser's back end began to fishtail yet again in the loose mud of the jungle road, and Lou was jamming on the brakes.

"Shit," he said as he countersteered like he was in last place on *Wheel of Fortune* and it was the prize puzzle round.

The left front side bumper of the rental truck, tapping a palm tree, finally brought him to a jarring halt.

Again.

"Dammit," he yelled as he turned the wipers up to eleven. When the hellish jungle road's Mexican-chocolate-colored splatter cleared off the windshield a little, he saw that the logging truck he was following had also come to an abrupt stop.

After a moment, his logging contractor, Julio, was high-stepping along the muddy side of the flatbed in his Wellington boots. Weather-beaten and mustached with a Cincinnati Reds ball cap of all things perched atop his shaggy head, he waved over with one of the biggest hands Lou had ever laid eyes on.

And unlike the first couple of logging contractors he'd interviewed back in Iquitos, Julio even had all of his fingers.

Strapped down to Julio's flatbed was a jungle-clearing Cat grader and a couple of beat-up Cat tracked skidders. Four hours outside of Iquitos north into the Amazon, they were still searching for the river crossing where they needed to get the logging equipment across.

It was like turning up the volume on a nature soundtrack when Lou opened his door.

"What's up? This isn't a river," Lou said as Julio arrived.

"I know. The road down to the river ahead is still too wet," Julio said. "I don't want to flip it. It will be firmer in an hour or two as it gets hotter."

"Hotter. Oh, goodie," Lou said, wiping at the sweat already beading on his brow. "What do we do now?"

Julio shrugged.

"We wait," he said.

"Where's the river? Far?"

"Not really. There's a trail. Follow me," Julio said, splatting mud as he turned.

Lou frowned as he climbed out. In contrast to Julio, he was wearing a nice loose cotton jungle shirt and new trail pants. Back at the rancid Iquitos hotel, Alessandra had laughed at his crisp Hemingway-esque safari getup before she wished him good luck. Alessandra, Duchess of Venezuela, didn't do jungles, of course.

Neither did his city-boy ass, Lou thought, scanning the lush humid greenery for jaguars. Yet here he was for some odd reason.

As they arrived on the other side of the flatbed and came to a trail, he could suddenly smell the river. Most of the trees within the triple canopy jungle were thin but here and there were massive primordial trunks that soared skyward wrapped in helix-like vines.

There was a sudden flapping above in the trees and instantly, from all around, bugs, frogs, birds, and who-knew-what-else could kill or poison you or bite your face off suddenly began chittering and chirping and ye-ye-yowing like someone just poured LSD into a zoo's water supply.

Lou stopped in shock but Julio, still walking ahead, didn't even seem to notice.

Lou followed as the trail skirted a pond with a thick froth of green scum riding its surface then went down a rocky little hill split by a jet of cascading green water. Grabbing at a vine to steady himself on a slick rock, a big rubbery leaf brushed Lou's cheek and left some kind of horrid sticky sap on his chin.

"Give me a break already," he said, spitting and swiping at it with his sleeve.

The river that appeared a moment later wasn't wide but the current seemed strong. They came to the edge of its low-cut mud bank and stood, looking. It was a tributary of the Amazon River itself and under the overcast sky, its water looked gray and thick as mushroom gravy.

In the hundred-degree humid heat, Lou looked around the bank of mud for a place to sit, but there was nothing. No sitting here. No human peace or help.

It was a place where poisonous things lived, he thought, unrolling his sleeves and buttoning them. It was where people came to go insane and die.

You unbelievable idiot, Lou thought to himself. A trip to the actual freaking Amazon jungle to do a deal with a pack of throat-cutting maniacal murderers that, even if it comes off, will most likely get you sent to the slammer.

All this because you don't want to tell your wife that you were only human one night fourteen years ago and went behind her back?

Light-headed in the heat, Lou stood there, thinking about it.

"Yes," he said finally nodding to himself.

That really was the reason why and he decided it was a pretty damn good one.

"Now grow a set," he said as his foreman suddenly whistled out across the water.

When he pointed, Lou turned and suddenly noticed the ropes strung across the racing water a hundred feet to their right. Across on the other bank where the ropes went into the trees, two shirtless young men appeared. Lou watched as they walked farther away up the bank and started untying something in the brush there. It was a primitive flatbed barge made of wood that they began pushing out into the stream.

Lou gaped in awe as they hooked the crazy-looking contraption to the ropes and began poling it across.

"You have to be kidding me," he said to Julio with a genuine laugh. "That dugout-canoe-looking thing is supposed to bring across the heavy equipment?"

Julio laughed himself as he slapped his big hand hard on Lou's back.

"Welcome to the jungle, amigo," he said.

54

The meticulous grounds of Devine's compound had high green hedges that gave it a look somewhere between a country club and a botanical garden.

"This backyard, wow," Gannon said.

Devine, on the other side of the patio dining table, smiled as the morose waiter expertly whisked away their breakfast plates.

"It is pleasant, isn't it, Mike?" Devine said. "I like eating outside here when it's still cool."

After their midnight supper, Gannon had woken incredibly hungover to find a pastel sky-blue polo and a pair of stone-colored chinos laid out for him. He was just slipping on the Sperry docksiders that came with the preppy outfit when Two Tall and Button Eyes buzzed in a few seconds later and cuffed him and popped another bag over his head. He didn't know what he was in for as he was dragged outside until they unhooded him and re-cuffed him to a stone block.

The weird was not letting up apparently, was it? he thought, looking over at his personal Mad Hatter, Devine, who also looked like he was dressed for a tea party in tennis whites.

Gannon patted some poached egg off his cheek with his linen napkin.

Did they serve poached eggs before firing squads? he thought.

A sparkling water glass gave off a chiming sound in the passing breeze. As it died down, Gannon noticed from somewhere behind them there was the sound of trickling water, soft and pleasant, like spa music. He turned around. It was a fountain.

"What are those purple flowers beside the fountain there?" Gannon said earnestly as if he really gave a shit.

"Blue irises, I think," Devine said.

"Amazing. Like a French painting or something. How do you get anything done?" Gannon said.

"It's a challenge," Devine said, suddenly reaching into his pants pocket.

"My stupid phone always buzzing. Give me a second to turn off my alerts."

"Sure thing," Gannon said, "but could I borrow your phone after you're done? I seem to have misplaced mine."

They both laughed at that. Almost genuinely. Like normal people just goofing around.

Yeah, Gannon thought. I'm not always a captive in the clutches of a homicidal lunatic but when I am, I like to keep things light.

"There we go. Done," Devine said, standing and snapping his fingers over at Button Eyes. "Feel like a walk, Mike? Let me show you where I like to have my coffee. You'll like it. There's a view. We can even dispense with the cuffs if you promise to behave."

"Scout's honor," Gannon said, holding up two fingers.

Gannon was uncuffed, and they walked out toward the fountain followed closely by the guards. Down a white gravel path on the other side of it, there was an arched opening in the high hedge wall and when they came through it, Gannon suddenly stopped and stood gaping.

On a fall-off five or six stories below, there was a vast flat clearing with rows of barracks and a shooting range and athletic fields. A high concrete wall ran along the far side of these structures, and it was rimmed with what looked like high-density anti-climb steel prison fencing. Behind this fencing in every direction was some of the densest jungle Gannon had ever seen. He figured they must be up on the top of some elevation as the only other bit of higher ground was a ridgeline in the hazy distance about two miles away.

The distance from the chateau to the razored fence line was what? Gannon thought, squinting. About a klick and a half. He stared at the heavy foliage, the overcast sky.

"Hey," Gannon said, spotting a square of blue on the other side of the shooting range. "Is that a pool?"

"Why, yes, that is a pool, Mike. And there are tennis courts as well and even a bowling alley."

"No shit! For real? After coffee do you think we could we go for a swim to cool off?"

"No," Devine said, yawning. "No way."

"Why not?" Gannon said.

"Oh, I don't know," Devine said, smirking as Two Tall snapped out some camp chairs for them. "I remember you're a pretty good swimmer and I've got a funny feeling that if we go swimming, only one of us will be getting out of the pool."

"This really is a cool view," Gannon said as the waiter arrived with the silver coffee service. "Are those barracks or something? This is a military compound?"

"Something like that," Devine said as they sat.

"Where is everybody? I don't see anyone," Gannon said as he was handed his little coffee cup.

"Enough with the twenty questions, Mike. Relax. You're like

a three-year-old," Devine said annoyed. "Here's a question for you. Do you notice my attire?"

Gannon looked at him. The white tennis sweater he was wearing despite the heat looked like something out of *The Great Gatsby*.

"Quite, um, fetching and classy. Only the best, right? Is it French too? No. Italian?"

"Besides its style and quality," Jimmy said, "notice anything else?"

"You're wearing a sweater though it's pretty hot?" Gannon said.

"Finally," Devine said. "Your powers of observation are still as trenchant as ever, I see."

Trenchant, is it? Gannon thought, struggling to not roll his eyes. He must have skipped that page in his SAT prep book.

You like trenchant observations, Devine? Here's another, Gannon thought as they stood there looking out on the nut job's little jungle kingdom. You seem to have lost your one-way ticket to the funny farm, buddy.

"So, why aren't you sweating?" Gannon said.

"I have the Iranians to thank for that. I told you they did experiments on me while I was in captivity. Well, they pretty much destroyed my thyroid. Now no matter how hot it gets, I always feel cold."

"That's crazy," Gannon said truthfully. "That's so screwed up. What a pack of scumbags."

"I know. They deregulated my very perception of reality. Who could imagine such a thing was possible."

"The things men do to each other," Gannon said, smiling at Button Eyes over the rim of his cup.

55

Gannon craned around to look at the barracks again. No. There didn't seem to be any training going on at the moment. The whole place had the quiet off-season vibe, like a college between semesters.

"What is this place, Jimmy? I mean, you didn't build it, right? It seems too old, especially the castle."

"Chateau, Mike. It's a chateau. Please be more precise. Words matter. To answer your question, I have my German predecessor to thank for this impressive spread. This was his home. I inherited it, you could say, with the job."

"Uh. What is your job again?"

"That's a good question. After I decided to stay on with the CIA, I started out as a military adviser at a place in Brazil. But then I was soon sent to work here with a German military expert to aid with weapons training and other military techniques."

"A German?"

"Yes. El Aleman, they called him. That's 'the German' in Spanish. When I arrived, we became very good friends. He was like a mentor to me. I was led to believe that he was just the Peruvian cartel's military advisor but then soon he let me know that it was he who was in charge and that the Peruvians worked for him. When he died, I became his successor and I kept the name. Now I am El Aleman."

"This Peruvian cartel is a major player in the drug trade, I take it?"

Devine gestured out at his fields and jungle.

"This is the wholesale facility where half of the South American cartels get their cocaine. About twenty-five percent of the world's cocaine is grown here."

He tapped at his coffee saucer.

"Right here in my domain."

"Wow," Gannon said. "So, what you're telling me, Jimmy, is that you're like the new Pablo Escobar or something?"

He laughed.

"Pablo Escobar." He spat. "The television shows make me laugh so hard. Pablo Escobar was a stock boy. He was nothing. He was just a front man. A minor employee of my predecessor. One of many."

Devine sipped at his coffee as Gannon absorbed that.

"So, your old boss was a Nazi, right?" Gannon said, turning to him. "A German in South America? I've heard of this on the History Channel. It wasn't Hitler, was it? Some say Hitler's suicide was faked. Don't tell me you and the CIA worked for Hitler."

Devine snorted as he took another sip.

"Must you really be so obtuse, Mike? No, I didn't work for Hitler."

"But El Aleman was a Nazi, right?"

"Yes. Okay, yes. Technically. If you must know, he was a former Nazi general who got out at the end of the war, which is all I will say as the history lesson was last night and my head aches and it bores me right now. His politics aren't the point, Mike. This German was…a cultured man. Even though he was in his nineties, his mind was one of the sharpest I have ever encountered. He became a mentor to me, taught me the treasures to be found in his extensive library. He was especially fond of philosophy. Do you know Wittgenstein?"

"No."

"Pity. A brilliant man. He said that when you come across that which you find superior to yourself you have two choices: to admire it or to envy it. Wittgenstein thought admiration was your only hope because the only way to stop the agony of envying—the unacceptable knowledge that there is someone who exists who stands above you—is to destroy them, to erase them, to make them not be there anymore."

"Is that right?" Gannon said.

"Yes. You pander to me while you should be listening, Mike. That's actually the reason why you are here."

"What are you talking about?"

"I admired you," Jimmy Devine said. "Who didn't? You were the best out of all of us. You were a five-tool player. Great hands. Nimble. A quick study. So very calm. You could flick your berserker fury on and off like a switch. And you were funny. Hilariously so sometimes. Everyone liked you. It was hard not to. Few men are such natural leaders. You could have risen up the ranks. But you chose not to. Because you were content to just be helpful and good at your job and a friend. A very talented and humble unambitious Mr. Nice Guy."

"Why thanks, Jimmy. That's nice of you to say. Like I said, I liked you, too."

"And your wife. Annette," Devine said, ignoring him. "That time she came by with cupcakes before we were deployed. My. She was so very beautiful. Those eyes she had. The life in them. What color were they? Blue? Green? Bit of both? And her smile. And that shape. So tall and slender. Simply bewitching. I wasn't the only one of the men who thought so either, who imagined what it might—"

"Um, Jimmy," Gannon said, smiling. "Don't mean to interrupt, but if we're going to be going down memory lane here for much longer, could I maybe have a real drink? I know it's early, but a beer or two would go down mighty dang smooth right around now. Especially with this great view. I remember you had a taste for PBR."

Devine smiled.

"I'm not sure about that," he said, squinting at him. "I might drop my guard. Then I'd have to worry about you getting those strong hands of yours around my neck."

"You're afraid of me? You're the one with the insane workout regimen."

"No. Final answer," Jimmy said. "Anyway, where was I? What was I just saying?"

Gibberish, Gannon thought.

"Admiration?" Gannon tried.

"Ah, yes, envy. Bottom line, Mike. You are here because I have to work out my envy of you. I have everything. Money. My goodness. You would be simply astounded by the amount. Power. These men are deeply, deeply under my control. Romance whenever I wish it. Or close to it at least. I pay my whores enough to fake it, believe you me. Even culture. My charming dinner parties are legendary among a certain darker segment of the jet set. I should be happy. And yet. There's you. Every night as I lay down to sleep, my envy of you settles in behind my skull like an unscratchable itch."

"But what the hell did I do?" Gannon cried. "We were friends, brothers."

"You didn't kill me, brother," Jimmy said calmly. "That was the deal, remember? In my time of need you left me hanging in the breeze."

56

Gannon remembered. It was true. They'd all said they'd kill each other as a last resort not to be captured by the jihadi torturers.

"But Jimmy, I didn't get a chance! I fell out of the damn helicopter. That I didn't die along with everyone else was a freaking miracle!"

"Excuses bore me!" Devine yelled, leaping to his feet with a sudden fury. "You fled from the gates of hell while I fell in backward. As you sit there before me, pink and healthy, every beat of your vibrant heart makes my blood boil. Every laugh of yours over the last two decades was mirrored by a scream from myself in a shithole dungeon where unspeakable things were done to me. Nights like decades where I had to endure the unendurable.

"Why me and not you? I lost my wife. She sleeps beside another man. Her children are not my children. My entire life was tossed into a wood chipper. But not yours. Oh, no. You went home. You had a son. A life. It's…difficult for me to describe how much your continued existence is a misery to me!"

"Difficult?" Gannon said after a long beat of ringing silence. "No, Jimmy, don't worry about that. I'm getting it. You're doing a real good job of explaining."

"And I have heard other things, Mike. How only a few of us knew about our Iranian destination. How you were one of them."

"What?"

"Keep playing stupid. It will do you no good."

"Wait. You think…" Gannon said, sitting up. "That I sold you out? Betrayed you? And the others? My brothers? To the freaking Iranians?"

"How did you get out? Twenty miles of enemy territory. How? Plus, the money you have now. Alaskan trips are for the super wealthy. Thirty silver coins go further these days, I guess."

"I see," Gannon said. "Now we're getting somewhere. I'll say it once, Jimmy. You're being played. Somebody might have set us up. But it wasn't me. You're so smart now, it ever occur to you that maybe it's the guy who sicced you on me set the both of us up?"

Devine laughed then, cackled like an actual madman as he dropped back down into the lawn chair.

He said something under his breath that Gannon couldn't catch, then he bent and put his head in his hands and started giggling.

"Maybe, Mike," he finally said. "Or maybe I'm just bored. No one ever really thinks that they will wake up one day middle-aged, do they? I guess I desire a contest, Mike. A real no-bullshit contest. Your name came up and I thought, wait a second. He was one formidable son of a bitch. Send him my way. He might give me a run for my money. I guess that's what this mostly is. I miss the action, Mike. The juice. The real stuff. Like that time the truck came in Tikrit. Do you remember when we were on that roof?"

Gannon did remember. Pulling guard duty together. One second, they were playing hearts and the next they were pouring a box of .50 caliber in through the windshield of a large dump truck that had breached the fence. It exploded spectacularly a split second later, and the blast wave knocked them off their feet onto their asses. He never forgot that surreal moment after, where they sat there coughing sand with the playing cards softly falling and landing all around them like confetti in a ticker tape parade.

"What roof?" Gannon said.

"You do remember, you liar. I see it in your eyes. It's still there. The exuberance."

"Exuberance?"

"For destruction. Anyway, enough, Mike. Tonight, you must sleep soundly. For tomorrow there is going to be a contest. Me versus you. When it is over, one of us will no longer exist. Either outcome at this point, believe me, I welcome with open arms."

The others, Gannon thought, remembering what Paolo had said.

Gannon looked at him. Sitting there tan and well dressed with a razor part in his pretty boy hair. First flexing to let him know that he was Pablo Escobar 2.0. Now telling him he was going to hunt him down like an animal.

He was gone. The friend he knew wasn't there anymore. This Jimmy Devine was… He didn't know what it was.

"Amor fati," Gannon said.

Mad Jimmy Devine giggled again, a high off-putting sound.

"Precisely! The love of fate even if it is death! You know your Nietzsche," he said.

Gannon stood and put his wrists out.

"Let the games begin."

57

The room off the front hall in the castle-like building on James's compound looked like a high-end home office on massive steroids.

Across from where Lou sat was a fireplace the size of a door-way, twenty-foot-high ceilings with wood beams, heavy red curtains bookending arched cathedral-like windows.

Drumming his fingers atop a gilt antique desk at the center of it, Lou thought it might have had the dimensions of his grammar school basketball gym. Or maybe even the church he was married in.

This place was a trip all right, he thought as he crossed his feet on the Persian rug. An actual damn castle would have been over-the-top in NYC let alone literally in the middle of the jungle.

And what a hellish damn jungle it truly was, Lou thought angrily, glancing out the cathedral window. Just now as he and Alessandra were coming in from the car through the twilight something indistinct and large flew past in front of them. They both thought it was a bat before they registered the buzzing insect sound of it, and he had to race Alessandra for the front door.

They were there coming on a quarter of an hour of waiting when they heard footsteps and two women went by in the open doorway of the hall. They were nice-looking white girls in bathing suits, laughing together. One was in a flaming orange one-piece that did a thong thing at the back and the other was wearing a flowered beach towel in such a way as to make Lou think that was all she was wearing. Late twenties. Hard-eyed. They didn't even so much as glance in at them.

They were call girls, had to be, Lou thought. Pricey ones.

Lou exchanged a WTF look with Alessandra but neither said anything as the room was no doubt bugged up the wazoo.

After another minute, techno began thumping from somewhere within the huge building. Lou walked to the window and looked out. Beyond their car above the jungle fronds, there was a mellow blue light in the sky now after the setting of the sun.

As they continued to wait, Lou noticed that his cool-as-a-cucumber partner, Alessandra, actually had a nervous habit of grabbing at her earlobe.

His daughter had done that as well when she was like three, Lou remembered. It was usually accompanied by sucking her thumb. He and his wife used to laugh that she was a little air traffic controller talking into a microphone.

Lou suddenly wondered if his other daughter had done it as well.

His forgotten daughter, he thought. The one he was now here risking his ass in the middle of the Amazon jungle so that she would remain gloriously forgotten forever.

Gee, Lou. What a guy you are. You need to apply for father-of-the-year.

When James came in through the front door into the hallway five minutes later, he was wearing midnight blue jeans and a crisp white shirt the color of starlight. There were three other men with him. Two large white guys and one shorter, younger

Hispanic. James said something, and they all laughed. The three soldiers kept going as James stuck his head in the doorway.

"Hey, guys. Sorry I'm late," he said as they got the handshakes out of the way.

Lou looked at him. His hair was slicked back now. He looked like a guy about to go out clubbing.

"How do you like my place?" James said.

"It's wondrous," Alessandra said.

"Isn't it?" James said, looking up at the beamed ceiling. "It's a French manor house from the 1400s. It was brought here in the forties. This room, found in all manor houses in the Middle Ages, stood in for the town hall. Here, they would make decisions, hold trials, count the taxes that were paid to the marquis. I love this room."

"It's incredible," Alessandra said.

"So, what do you have for me?" James said.

Lou already had the marked map and photographs open on the desk's tooled leather top.

"The runway is done. Right here where you wanted it," Lou said. "I even had my guys improve the drive down from this logging road for better access."

"What's this opening here in the photo for?"

"The space to get tanks in for fuel storage that are on order."

"On order?" James said with frown. "I thought you were done."

"I am. It's fine. We are ready to go. While we wait for the order, I brought barrels out and a pump you plug into a truck. A fuel truck from Iquitos is on standby for the first refuel. We are ready to go as soon as you want."

"Excellent," James said, nodding as he looked at the papers again. "You guys really are the real deal. Very professional. Nice job. I love it. Efficiency and speed are two of the three things I love most in a partner."

"And the third?" Lou said, smiling.

James gazed coldly into his eyes as he gave Lou's shoulder a slap.

"Undying loyalty, of course," he said.

58

"You have all three then," Alessandra said with a nervous little laugh.

"Exactly," Lou said, clearing his throat. "So, when can we get started?"

James shrugged, put out his palms and then closed them together in a praying gesture.

"You tell me," he said.

Lou checked his watch.

"I can have my guy take off in…six hours. Be here, say, noon tomorrow. How many kilos should we expect?"

"Five hundred."

Lou blinked. That was five times what he had expected.

"Let Alberto know the ETA of your guy, and it will be sitting right at the new runway you built. Things works out, you keep sending your guys as quickly as you can."

"For five hundred a trip?"

"Yes."

"Every week?"

"Sure. Twice a week, if you want. As fast as you can get it out. Please, by all means, we are way behind schedule with the last seizures. My product is worthless sitting in the jungle."

"Okay then," Lou said, standing. "We'll nail down the scheduling tighter once we get the first trip out of the way. We'll keep Alberto posted."

"Well, there is just one thing," James said.

He suddenly grasped Alessandra by her wrist.

"Yes?" Alessandra said, looking startled.

"I have one open seat left at my dinner party tonight," James said as he began to tug her toward the doorway. "And Alessandra, I insist you must honor me with your presence. We have to toast our new partnership. And my other delightful guests will be very happy to meet you, I promise. I will have my driver return you to your hotel straight after."

As James said this, he began tugging Alessandra with him toward the hallway.

When Lou glanced at Alessandra, she was looking a way Lou had never seen before.

Scared out of her mind.

"But," she said. "I'm...not dressed."

"Alessandra, you're in luck," he said, really bum-rushing her now. "I have closets full of dresses. Please do not worry. I don't bite. We must celebrate our new partnership. I insist."

"Enjoy," Lou said. "I'll see you back at the hotel."

Lou watched her fear turned to white-faced panic as she was pulled to the doorway.

"Oh, shoot. What am I saying?" Lou said, snapping his finger.

"What is it now?" James said as he stopped, annoyed.

"I forgot. Alessandra has to come with me," he said.

"Why?" James said.

Lou smiled calmly.

"I can't drive stick," he said.

"You can't drive stick."

"No. Never learned. I only know how to drive automatic. Stupid me. The rental is stick. Alessandra was the one who drove us up here."

"That is rather stupid of you," James said, squinting at him. "I agree with you there."

He finally sighed as he let Alessandra go.

"Oh, well. Next time, Alessandra," he called without turning around. "Don't forget to get Alberto the details about tomorrow."

"Of course," Lou said as he quickly waved Alessandra the opposite way into the hallway before him.

"Lou, I..." Alessandra said, squeezing his hand as they all but ran down the lunatic drug dealer's stone steps and jumped into the car.

"Owe me big time," Lou said as he started the car and put the fully automatic transmission into Drive.

59

Bright lay wet and naked on the hotel bed after his shower. On the big flat-screen before him, the next senator from the great state of Maryland, Ginny Mickelson, was killing it.

"Can you hear me, Mr. President?" she said.

There were two loud thumps as she knocked on the mike.

"Knock, knock. Anyone home?" she said.

Wow, she was funny, too, wasn't she? he thought, watching. What couldn't this lady do? Her likeability was in red-zone territory now.

The packed-to-the-rafters Orlando PAC conference around her seemed to think so. They were actually hooting now, literally going nuts. There was no better way to get them going than to refer to the opposite party's sitting president's obvious room for improvement in the intellect department. The pink-faced conventioneers laughed on and on. They had had their fat sides split, and now it was time for their made-by-Crisco thunder thighs to be slapped silly.

The conference was at the Orlando Marriott, but Bright was staying down the street at the Waldorf Astoria.

Good thing, too, he thought as he turned off the sound and put his hands behind his wet hair. He was good with hicks but wow, did they tire him out.

"Or as they would say, 'tar,'" he said as his phone jingled.

He leaned over. It was Admiral Mickelson. Of course, it was. Who else would it be?

Are you seeing this? he had texted.

Me and the rest of the country, he texted back as Ginny left the stage.

Goosebumps, Bright added.

Mickelson sent back a fire emoji then a thumbs-up.

Bright smiled.

He had done it. He and the admiral, who was a DC player to truly be reckoned with, had achieved emoji level now.

"I love it when a plan comes together," Bright said as he stood and found his bag with the coke.

Oh, yeah. He knew him some hicks, he thought as he laid out a fat line of top-shelf yayo on his iPhone screen.

His eyes rolled up into his head after he drilled his first rail of the night.

Then he lay back on the bed and smiled as the happy, happy joy, joy began to sing through his bloodstream.

He knew all about them hillbilly folk from the inside out.

Bright gave off the air of being just another overgrown DC prep school boy, but he was originally the hick son of a hick county sheriff in hardscrabble rural Missouri. The other members of his family included his obese Bible-thumping mother (Chief liked 'em big, it was whispered in town) and three older, equally obese sisters. So, almost from when he was born, the Chief doted over Adrian, his only son.

Go-with-Daddy-to-work day in his cruiser was pretty much every day, and Bright was a quick study. There was much to study since the Chief's justice of the peace boss had a wild family who kept his services at cover-up in high demand. Though his father had never been in the military, he affected a military bearing, a stately pushiness that was effective in commanding the officers underneath him.

Chief Bright was more con man than lawman, but quite a good one. He could control people, and he kept close track of those who owed him. By grammar school, Adrian Bright himself had adopted his father's always smiling on the outside yet nut-cracking behind-the-scenes manner. Which is why he had been both his high school and college president and valedictorian.

And why in DC his star had risen so far and so fast.

Bright had higher political ambitions, but he was a realist and knew that at five foot six with middling looks, it just wasn't going to happen for him in the Bigs. That's why he had leaped into the shadows where in DC, a person like Bright—a small bland-faced, dapperly dressed man who left no personal impression on the memory—was actually ideal. He had no real expertise except that he could convincingly conjure up the impression that he could tackle whatever was needed. Kissing an ass, rooting out a traitor, or giving a speech stuffed with red tape statistics and regulatory jargon that could make a problem go away.

He soon became known around town as not just *a* turd polisher but *the* turd polisher.

His entree into the Company had been a fluke. It was at the insistence of his own patron, the senior senator from Missouri who was on the Intelligence Committee, who had needed someone on the inside.

Once in, Bright had been astounded at what was going on. He thought he had been a grifter? It turned out, he hadn't even become acquainted with the term. It was a madhouse, a literal madhouse where the inmates in management could do anything, get away with anything, because no one was watching. They weren't *allowed* to watch. The whole Top Secret National Security cover story. Never in the history of the world had crooks come up with a more secure smoke screen behind which they could rob and pillage. Especially in the very beginning of the war on terror when literal ton-weight pallets of hundred-dollar bills were raining down out of the sky.

There was just one rule in the mayhem. Don't get caught. Don't embarrass your boss because if you got caught, there was a place they would put you, he had been told in no uncertain terms by his boss.

On the marble wall in the front hall of Langley with all the other mistakes.

Since he had started a dozen years before, Bright had amassed ten million dollars. Ten million freaking dollars. That was his own money. Not Claudette's. Her blueblood Virginia family was loaded, of course. They probably had a hundred million, which with her two siblings meant probably a thirty-three-mil payout when Mémé kicked it.

But who cared? Bright thought as he hoovered up a little more stardust.

He had his own nut. He kept it offshore in several Swiss bank accounts managed by a lawyer he met once a year at his thirtieth-floor Fifth Avenue office in New York.

A tax-free ten was really like twenty, he thought, smiling. Maybe twenty-five depending which state you lived in.

He laughed as he remembered Momma getting them all to cut coupons out of the Sunday paper.

It astounded him that he had gotten his hands on such an incredible amount of loot.

Then he laughed as he thought of the fire emoji.

And only more to come!

Fire was the word, he thought as he lifted the phone again.

He brought up the song "Fire Woman" by the Cult, a fave, as he leaped from the bed.

And by the time it started, he was in front of the full-length mirror in complete unabashed headbanger mode, air guitaring its opening riff.

60

When his phone rang an hour later, Bright was halfway through his playlist and stoned out of his gourd. Done dancing with himself (Billy Idol track 21), he had busted out his night vision spotting scope and was watching a middle-aged couple dancing in a curtainless room three floors down across the courtyard.

The woman, also naked under her almost fully open robe, had a most incredible body, he thought as he watched her do a drunken spin.

Bright, an avid Peeping Tom, knew that some people knew that they were being watched. He felt the butterflies swirl in his stomach.

But not these folks.

When the phone rang a second time, he was going to ignore it until he saw it was from Devine.

Finally, he thought as he closed his curtains. The prodigal son returns.

"Hey, buddy," Bright said.

"Hey, yourself," Devine said. "I got your message. What's up?"

"Gannon," Bright said as he began to pace. "He's still alive, right?"

"Yep," Devine said.

"Our agreement was—"

"Was what?" Devine said.

"That he wouldn't leave Mexico. That you'd put him in the Concurso and take care of him. I didn't even want him to go there really. I just needed you to put a bullet in his head and bury him in a deep hole. Alaska was perfect for that. Now you've taken him back to the compound, right?"

"I wonder who told you that. Bouthier? Or was it Nevin? I don't trust him. I really think I need to recycle some of my security team. Everybody has such a big mouth."

"It doesn't matter, James. What matters is Gannon being dead and he's not. Why? What the hell are you doing?"

"What is it, Adrian? I've never seen you so…worked up. What did Gannon do to you? Kill one of Claudies's dogs?"

Bright closed his eyes. Devine had never called him Adrian like that before. It had always been with respect.

And why wouldn't it be? It was Bright who had saved him, gotten him out of Iran, nursed him back to health.

Sheep-dipping Bright was one of the first real field assignments he'd been in charge of when he started at the Company.

He'd even helped him psychologically repair from all the trauma and torture of Iran with a series of psychedelics in his food that the Company used on special cases. For months, he kept visiting him at the Company funny farm in Switzerland. He had really helped him work on his hang-ups, his childishness, his manic-depressive nature. He'd even gotten him to start reading.

"I just need it done, Jimmy," Bright cried.

"Just?" Devine said. "There's nothing 'just' about killing a man,

Adrian, which is why you came to me. The way I go about it is my business, so back off."

"Came to you?" Bright said, outraged. "I paid you three million dollars. You work for me!"

"Do I really, Adrian? Then fire me. I can take it. Give me my pink slip. I'll give back the money and I'll let Gannon go. I'm waiting. Hello? Adrian, are you still there?"

Bright's mouth opened. That hurt. That really stung.

"I knew it."

"Knew what?"

"You don't respect me anymore. I really thought we were friends."

"Bravo on the uptake."

"Screw you," Bright said. "After all I've done for you."

"Adrian, please. I'm teasing. Why do you think I called you? I'm going to take care of Gannon tomorrow. Give me twenty-four hours and I will send you pictures of his bullet-riddled body. Or better yet, I will send you a body part of your choice in a dry ice shipment free of charge. How does that sound, um, boss? I'll even call you boss, see?"

"Screw you, James," Bright said, smiling. "I know you're wasted so I'm going to forgive the insults. Just get rid of this guy. Twenty-four hours."

"Twenty-four hours, Adrian, and I will present you one dead Gannon or your money back," Devine said. "Cross my heart and hope to die."

PART THREE

CALL TO ACTION

61

The National Reconnaissance Office was on a sprawling campus in Chantilly, Virginia, and at its center was an unmarked beige hangar-like building where all the action happened.

At the hangar's top floor was a black-walled room they called the tank.

The tank was like a massive Best Buy TV section with a catwalk-like loft of elevated offices above it that were almost like skyboxes at a stadium. In the tank's center were screens. Screens on the wall, screens of laptops along a block-long line of communal desks.

On most of the screens were feeds of the United States's vast array of orbiting military satellites, moving maps showing urban and remote terrains.

In the aquarium blue-light glow of these maps and screens, Ed Navarro poked his head out of his office up on the catwalk and surveyed his kingdom to check to see if busy fingers were typing at keyboards and gleaming off glasses.

Ed liked his section chief job here on the third watch. He had always liked the Orwell line about the rough men on the wall letting everyone else sleep soundly and between the hours of four and eleven, he liked to think he and his ten guys were those rough men.

Besides, the watch he ran was the best one possible. Days had too many bosses and nights were filled with night owls who everyone knew were all nuts. They'd given Ed his pick because he had been at NRO the longest and knew where all the bodies were buried. And he had picked wisely.

No doubt about it, Ed thought as he looked down at them. His small ten-guy crew was the best in the whole shebang. Ed's reputation preceded him so whenever anyone good showed up, they eventually ended up on third watch without Navarro even having to do anything.

What really touched him was that his gang could dress casual these days like the other shifts but they didn't. They all wore the old-school camo fatigues like he did.

Inspection of his troops over, Ed went back into his office to work some more on his own little side project.

Looking for a needle in a haystack.

The needle was called Mike Gannon and the haystack was called the Western Hemisphere south of Mexico.

He had the date locked in, and he was going through the overhead shots of the airports one by one, manually checking every square foot of every tarmac.

It was a rough slog. There were over a hundred airports in Central America alone and in South America, you were talking nearly a thousand.

Not to mention he wasn't supposed to be doing it so he had to change screens whenever anyone came over.

The plane that he was looking for was the one that had taken

Gannon. He could have sketched it with a blindfold on at this point. It was a white Gulfstream V with light blue and dark blue pinstriping and the tail number N556NR.

He'd already checked the number, registered to something called Precision Aviation out of Delaware. The owner of the company, one Arthur H. Percy, didn't even have a LinkedIn, so if the organization wasn't a CIA cutout dummy paper company, Ed would eat his headphones.

"What have we here?" he whispered as he saw something that looked like a Gulfstream. The tail number wasn't even close.

His eyes were starting to melt behind his blue-light reading glasses, and he was thinking about busting out the homemade meatball sandwich he had brought for dinner when he got the call.

"Ed," he said, lifting his iPhone up from beside the mouse.

"I found it," said his little buddy Raymond Cruz.

Raymond was a fifteen-year-old half-autistic kid who lived in New Mexico and ran a website called Jetspot that all the plane spotters subscribed to. Years ago, plane spotters had a radio scanner and binocs but today, they had laptops and Mod5 data receivers. They even had apps now that told you the flight number and even the owner registration of any and all planes overhead. So going to the plane-spotting community where people—mostly kids like Raymond and crusty old ex-pilots—sat around airports watching the comings and goings was a no-brainer.

"N556NR. I found it," he said.

"Where?"

"IQT."

"IQ where?"

"The Coronel FAP Francisco Secada Vignetta International Airport in Iquitos, Peru. It's up in the Amazon."

"Who found it there?"

"Our people are everywhere," Raymond said. "It's actually

quite a busy airport. Lot of green tourism into the Amazon. One of our guys was in there waiting for a flight out."

Ed pumped his fist.

"Raymond, you did good."

"You owe me a beer."

It's what he always said.

"You are learning, grasshopper. But I don't owe you a beer, kid," Ed said. "I owe you a keg."

62

Above the timberline in the cliffs north of John Barber's ranch, there were collections of massive spotted gray boulders with tinges of green on them from the moss.

On a camp chair amid his very own version of Stonehenge, Barber sat with a pair of reading glasses perched on the end of his nose as he messed around with some rabbit hair and duck feathers, tying dry fly-fishing ties.

Declan and Stef were back from their climb and now playing with his pup, Dempsey. Why Barber had tagged along, he wasn't sure.

Probably because he was feeling protective of Mike's son.

Poor kid. The flight back from Alaska had been excruciating for Declan without Mike. Ever since they'd gotten home, Barber had been working him. Had to keep him busy to keep his mind off the horror.

But all the sheep were shorn now and the ewes wouldn't start lambing until the end of April so, here they were. He wasn't even the most avid fly fisherman in the world. That was Mike's thing. Yet, here he was, knitting away his anxiety like an old crone.

He had just seated the next dry fly hook into the little vise between his knees when the sat phone in his knapsack rang.

He loved these damn phones, he thought as he put down the vise and slid it out. Since there were no cell towers to get triangulated on, it was supposedly impossible to track you.

He didn't know about that, but he liked to think that at least it was harder.

He stood immediately when he realized who was calling him. "Ed?"

"John, got news. We found the plane."

"Mike's plane? The G5 with the blue markings? Where?"

"He's in Peru."

"Peru!"

"Maybe at least. The plane that took him was there four days after he went missing."

He looked up at Declan, his mind racing. Mike could still be alive.

"Wow. Where exactly was the plane?"

"On the tarmac of the Coronel FAP Francisco Secada Vignetta International Airport in Iquitos up in the Amazon."

"The Amazon. You have to be kidding me."

"Sorry I don't have any more, man, but I just thought you should know. It's something at least."

"Are you kidding me? It's a lead. They have to have security video at this airport, right?"

"I'd say so. I'll stay on it and see if I can come up with anything else."

"Ed, brother, you really are the man, you know that?"

"Anytime, Kemosabe. Be well," Ed said.

"Declan," Barber called over as he hung up.

"What?"

"Come here, son. I need to tell you something."

63

Gannon tried unsuccessfully to contact his buddy Paolo by pipe phone twice during the day but it was only late at night when he was just about to go to sleep that he decided to try one last time.

"Miguel," Paolo called up merrily from the stainless-steel pipe after a half minute of tapping.

"Where were you, man? I tried twice," Gannon said.

"I went out for a jog and then I went to the cinema," he said. "Ha ha. Only kidding. I was here but I must have been listening to my headphones."

"I'm going tomorrow," Gannon said. "The lunatic told me he was going to hunt my ass down."

"As I said would happen. Miguel, a question. You are a Catholic, right? Most Irish are Catholic?"

"Yes."

"In good standing?"

"Somewhat. I've missed a lot of Mass lately."

"Have you ever received last rites?"

"No."

"Well," Paolo said. "Technically I was defrocked by my corrupt bishop but wrongly. It does not matter. I will give you last rites if you wish. I cannot anoint you with oil obviously, but we can do the rest if you would like. Reconciliation and all the prayers."

"Yes, please."

"Let us begin as we live, in the name of the Father and of the Son and of the Holy Ghost," Paolo said.

"Thank you, Father," Gannon said when they were done.

"No, I am Paolo, Mike. Just Paolo to you, please."

"Thank you, Paolo."

"You are welcome. Now, I want you to go to sleep but I need you to remember something. Listen to me very carefully."

"I'm listening."

"Every second that you are incarcerated, Miguel, every millisecond, remember it is a continuation of the outrageously astronomical crime they are perpetrating not just against you but against God. God who sees all and knows all sits resolutely by the spring of the scale of justice that millimeter by millimeter they are wrongly pulling and drawing down as they diabolically push you toward the abyss.

"But God knows what these reprobates, who are unworthy to house the Divinely connected human spirit, do not. That the strings that draw down lower and lower do not hold your bucket to hell but instead are the strings of a bow notched with an arrow of righteousness that they are aiming at their own throats.

"They do not know that at a moment of God's choosing as the bowstring of outrage against Him reaches a point where no further tautness is possible, the degeneracy perpetrated against you and against myself and against all who are wronged will be avenged in the blink of an eye."

"Wow," Gannon said quietly.

"Mark my words, Miguel. In your coming times of trial, have faith. Have happy faith. For all is possible with God."

"Paolo?"

"Yes?"

"When I win, when I put this lunatic six feet under, I will come back for you. I promise."

"Ah, that's the spirit, Miguel," he said. "You hold on to that as tightly as possible. That spirit that makes God smile. Now go to bed, my friend."

64

When they came in to wake him at sunup, Gannon was already waiting for them. After he changed into the camouflage uniform and combat boots Too Tall and Button Eyes had brought, he was told to put out his hands.

Onto his wrists went under-over cuffs with a dead bolt locking mechanism that couldn't be shimmed. The stiff cuffs were secured with a plastic transport box around the center of them and after they locked the box in place with a padlock, the whole thing was hooked to a waist chain that they looped around the small of his back. When he was a cop, Gannon had seen the same kind of setup placed on violent incarcerated defendants for trials back in New York.

Gannon looked down as Button Eyes tugged at the heavy chain to make sure the slack was tight. His arm movement was completely restricted.

"Pulling out all the stops, huh?" Gannon said.

"You manage to pull a Harry Houdini in this get-up, Mikey," Button Eyes said, smiling as he finished inspecting the restraints, "I'll give you the watch back."

At the end of the corridor, they led him through a new door that opened outside into some sort of stone-walled courtyard with an exterior set of stone steps.

The steps let them out near the front of the castle-like building, and he was brought down a gravel path that was bookended by tall strange trees. At the end of this elegantly landscaped corridor was a stone gatehouse that, like the chateau behind him, appeared to have been airlifted from a small French town.

A small French *prison* town, Gannon thought as he took in the elevated guard shack and not one but two rolling gates with a security gap in between.

As Gannon looked back at the building, he thought that the river had to be nearby. Because how else could they have brought in all of this elaborate Disney World bullshit?

Left of the gatehouse was a hangar-like building and as they approached it, there was a loud metal squeal and out from between faded green metal doors emerged a vehicle. Staring at the blocky 4X4 SUV with the spare visible to the rear in its short pickup bed, Gannon thought it was one of the fancy Mercedes ones until he came closer and read Toyota Land Cruiser on its side.

Jimmy Devine came out of the hangar himself a moment later. With him were three soldiers in the same type of camo as Gannon was wearing. Two of them were white with football-player shoulders and wore Oakley sport sunglasses, and the third was a hard-faced and hard-eyed slim Hispanic who looked like he didn't suffer fools too gladly.

"You have some kennel here, Jimmy," Gannon said, tossing a chin at the soldiers.

"Oh, these two should be familiar to you, Mike, from Alaska. Mr. Grabowski and Mr. Nevin and with them is Manuel, our scout and tracker."

"My bad," Gannon said. "I remember now. Grabowski is the one who really likes to ride bitch."

Jimmy eyed Grabowski before he could open his mouth to reply. The scout then handed Jimmy a carbine and Jimmy stood before Gannon and leaned back a little the way some athletes do, poised and graceful even at rest. He held it in a high compress hold, his eye line with the muzzle, fastidious and reverent. Like all SEALs, Jimmy had been a very fine soldier.

Gannon stood staring at him. All night long, he had been searching his memory, scouring all of his deployments with the man trying to figure out why Jimmy had fixated on him. He had thought they were cool. Truly cool. Not overly friendly. Competitive, of course, but all of them were. Two pros. Two climbers at the top of Mount Everest, giving each other the tip of the hat.

He'd just about relegated the man's insanity to the torture he'd received when he suddenly remembered an incident back at the base in San Diego.

Coming out of the bars one night, they'd gotten into a play wrestling match, and it had become a little heated. Jimmy had bashed him in the nose pretty good as he tried to hook him around the neck with an elbow, but Gannon had repaid the favor by slipping it and tripping him and pinning him down between the curb and the tire of a parked car.

He remembered Jimmy getting really worked up at this turnaround. Calling Gannon every name in the book as he unsuccessfully tried to break free. The man had started crying a little at some point.

"Say uncle, Jimmy," he had drunkenly taunted as he sat on his back. "Just say uncle." Gannon had let him go a moment later when the rest of the guys came out, and they had played it off as it were nothing.

But it was only nothing for Gannon, he realized now as he studied him.

For Jimmy, apparently, it had been everything.

Jimmy had reinvented himself. He was Mr. Wonderful now. The world's most interesting, most dangerous man. In this new 2.0 version, this one memory of being fully and completely dominated by another could not be allowed to stand now, could it?

No. That's why it and Gannon needed to be erased, Gannon knew.

Jimmy was still in the war zone. The bastards had really done it. They had stripped him of his ability to ever come home.

Gannon winced as Jimmy suddenly let off a burst of the fully automatic fire into the air. When he was done, he dropped out the magazine and slapped in another that he was handed.

"I present to you," he said as he lifted the weapon before Gannon, "one fully automatic M4 carbine rifle with a fourteen-and-a-half-inch barrel, dead air brake, with flash light and holographic sight attached."

"Wow, you remembered my setup," Gannon said with a smile. "That's touching, Jimmy. Now, if you would undo the cuffs."

"Not just yet," Jimmy said with a wink. "This will be given to you when you reach your destination. Now, remember when you are inserted, you can do whatever you wish. Dig in, run, set up an ambush. I will give you twenty-four hours. That should be sufficient time for you to prepare."

"Twenty-four? Shit. You really are a sport. That'll be plenty of time."

"Gentlemen, did I tell you or what?" Jimmy said to his soldiers. "Look at the calm on this man. Did I not tell you we have a gentleman in our midst?"

They all turned as the morose Hispanic waiter from dinner appeared from the shed doors, bearing a tray.

"Ah, yes, a toast," Jimmy said.

Into Gannon's cuffed top hand was placed a champagne flute with a long straw in it.

"See, Mike? I even had a straw put in yours so you can toast with us."

"How thoughtful," Gannon said.

"You really are like me, Mike," Jimmy said, raising his flute. "So many fools think hunting is about killing. You and I both know that it's about one thing. The action. The crackling electricity of the risk. The kill is just the cherry on top. We both know the kill is actually sad in a way as it brings the glorious hunt to an end. The high comes at the moment of the ball being hiked. Not the touchdown being scored. Isn't that true, Mike?"

"Sure," Gannon said. "I couldn't agree more."

"Irony and sarcasm even now, Mike," Jimmy said, coming over and palming Gannon's shoulder. "More pandering even now? Moments of reconciliation are quite brief in our species' history. Let's just enjoy each other's company for a moment, shall we? Have a moment of mutual respect and admiration."

Jimmy lifted his flute.

"A toast," he said. "To the old brothers-in-arms we used to be."

Gannon went as if to sip as well.

But then with a sudden jerk of his hands and torso at the waist, he tossed the whole thing over his shoulder instead. Straw and all.

"The only thing that's true, Jimmy," Gannon said as he crushed the flute with his boot, "is that you're crazier than a shithouse rat. None of all that stuff about me setting you up is true. None of it. That's just all bullshit to justify murdering my ass in cold blood. Which even at this moment is shocking. How can you do this? Only a freaking mind-blown animal could hunt down a former brother-in-arms, an old friend who watched his back and would have laid down his life for him."

"How can I do this?" Jimmy said, smiling as he wiped champagne from his lips. "Why, with a playful ease is how."

"The spooks that broke you out set you up, Jimmy. They set all of us up. And whatever experimentation the Iranians did on you, that wasn't the Iranians, Jimmy. That was them. These bastards, our old bosses, run the Iranians. They run damn everything. All they did was put you in a damn Skinner box to screw with you. Then they just pretended to break you out in order to play you some more. They just put it all on me because I've become an issue for them."

"Please go on. This is fascinating."

"Some clever inbred pencil neck from Langley with a micropenis is smiling right now, Jimmy. From ear to fricking ear. Because you are being one hell of a tool to help them wipe up their mess. You think you're some sophisticate now or something? Some kind of great man in history? South America's Alexander the Great? You're just another disposable meat robot. A damn wind-up toy and a roll of Charmin all in one. They're not laughing at me, Jimmy. They're laughing at you."

Jimmy laughed then.

"I love it, Mike. You're getting pissed. Finally, the fire is being lit. This tragic dance of ours is going to be epic. I can already tell."

Gannon squinted coldly into Jimmy's eyes.

"I saw you murder that kid in Mexico. Hell, two hundred people saw it. For what? Who would shoot some poor stupid kid in the head for nothing? A lunatic, Jimmy. Only a lunatic would do that. You want tragedy? That you weren't killed in that helicopter we were on. That's the real tragedy. Because look at yourself. Find a mirror and look in it. You're a lunatic."

"That's it. Talk dirty to me, Mike," Jimmy said, squinting back. "And as you are about to leave, please take a look at everything around you. A last look."

"Screw you. Seen enough. Let's go already. I'd rather get my brains blown out than listen to another of your insane TED Talks."

"You're right. Talk is cheap, Mike. Now, for the only thing that matters."

"Which is?" Gannon said.

"Your next step."

65

Grabowski drove and Nevin rode in the front-side passenger seat and Gannon sat behind Grabowski with the tracker beside him. As they entered the jungle, it started raining almost immediately and out through the sloshing wipers, the red mud road quickly became the consistency of melting chocolate ice cream.

Gannon tried to keep track of his orientation back to the compound, but with all the slip sliding and bumping up and down, by the third corkscrewing turn, he soon gave up.

He sized up his handlers. They all had Browning Hi-Power 9mm sidearms, and Nevin had the barrel of a cut-down carbine, perhaps some type of Heckler & Koch, standing up between his legs.

When they finally slid out from the jungle canopy to an intersection of a larger wider mud road, it was about three quarters of an hour later. Gannon was shocked to hear a rumbling from his left, and he turned as a truck rattled past.

It was a white work flatbed with long planks of new sawn lumber on the back of it, tied down with an orange tarp.

Lumber, Gannon thought, watching it disappear from sight. Lumber, the jungle, and drugs. It really was the Amazon. Had to be.

I knew I should have paid more attention in fifth-grade geography class, Gannon thought, as they swung into the wider dirt road the way the truck had gone.

The drab-colored jungle passed by out the window. This new road, despite not being paved, seemed much firmer than the jungle path and was well graded and cut back deep on both sides to about the width of a two-lane parkway.

A faint Spanish-language station came in when Grabowski put on the radio. Gannon didn't need to speak Spanish to know it was some religious thing, some guy preaching. After a minute of it, Gannon laughed as the tracker next to him said in Spanish to shut it the hell off.

Just as Grabowski did so, they began to slow at something ahead in the curve in the road. A stopped bus, a modern tourist one, was almost sideways in the left ditch with the truck that had passed them stopped sideways beside it on the right. Three workmen from the truck were out in the street, talking to the bus driver.

Immediately, Grabowski gave a series of baps on the horn, gesturing at the workmen to move their truck. But the lead workman, an old Spanish guy in a stained gray fedora talking to the bus driver, waved him off.

When he honked full-on a few times, the old timer only turned, smiling, and mocked honking a horn back at him. Then he gave Grabowski the finger and went back to talking to the bus driver.

Gannon had started laughing at this, but as soon as the cursing Grabowski's hand touched the door handle, Gannon stopped.

Because he realized it had finally come.

The chance he had been waiting the last several weeks for.

Gannon already had his left boot planted against the door beside him when Grabowski arrived by the workmen outside.

Then he kicked out and launched himself up and sideways at the Hispanic scout beside him with everything he had.

The guy's nose shattered as Gannon's savagely swung elbow smashed into it.

Screaming bloody murder, the guy immediately started punching and pushing back, but Gannon, with his feet up on the back of the driver's seat now, only screamed himself as he leaned back and felt the guy's teeth cut the back of his head as he smashed his skull into the guy's face like a bowling ball.

He was up on top of the soldier, ripping more elbows into his ribs, practically sitting in his lap, when the face of Nevin appeared in the gap between the front seats. Gannon drew his legs up until his thighs were almost touching his chest. Then he kicked out as hard as he could and broke Nevin's nose as he stove in his sunglasses.

Gannon kept coming. Half leaping and half somersaulting himself forward off the soldier in the back seat, he managed to slide himself down through the front seat gap into the empty driver's seat. The engine, still in Park, screamed as he buried the accelerator. Then he elbowed the transmission down into reverse with his manacled hands.

They flew backward. They had to be doing up to nearly forty when the shooting started. The deafening explosion of the scout almost blowing Gannon's head off with the Browning went off right beside Gannon's ear, and he wrenched the wheel counterclockwise without letting up on the gas, and they were off the road, rocketing backward through the jungle trees.

Two things happened all but simultaneously a split second later. There was a crisp cough of metal as the trunk of a king palm ripped off the still-open door beside Gannon.

And then solid ground suddenly disappeared from beneath the vehicle's tires.

Gannon felt it in his stomach as the sky suddenly swung up in the windshield.

In the weird horrifying sense of backward free fall, Gannon seized hold of the wheel to brace himself. Then the back window exploded in with a sound like thunder, and his head slammed back into the headrest and he went out cold.

66

When the shock wore off, Gannon found himself still in the driver's seat in the running vehicle, looking up at the sky through its bashed-to-shit windshield. He turned to the right to see Nevin there staring back at him groggily. Both dazed with their backs parallel to the ground in their seats, they looked like drunken astronauts waiting for Houston to give them the go-ahead for a moon shot.

The second thing he noticed was a smell that made his eyes go instantly wide.

Gasoline.

Gannon turned to the other side. Between the ripped-open doorway and the tree they'd become wedged against, there was space. He listed left and rolled into it. When the ground hit harder than he expected, Gannon even surprised himself by actually staying upright.

Then his training kicked in. He looked around and determined where the road was and he chose the direction directly away from it and ran as hard as he could into the jungle.

The only way to survive now was to get to a range beyond where they thought he would be capable of getting to, he knew. He turned his emotions off and set his determined eyes downward to look for foot purchase in the green blur, pushing his legs as fast as they would go.

The first time he tripped and went sprawling, it was ten minutes later. Some underbrush scraped at his cheek as he fell face-first, and it felt like the cuffs cut into his wrists as he landed in a jangle of chains on top of the transport box. He lay for a second, gasping for breath. His heart actually hurt as he lay there face-down. It was like there was an overheated engine in his chest, and it was about to chuck a rod.

"Get your shit together," he cried at his heart through the pain as he got his feet back underneath him again and started jogging and then full-on running again.

"Or burst," he cried.

When he found the jungle clearing about an hour later, it had just stopped raining. He dropped to his knees, gasping again like a fresh-caught fish. When he heard water, he looked over to see he was beside a thin creek. He lurched over to it and dropped on his belly and drank, slurping noisily at it like a dog at a bowl. Done, he lay for a minute with his head in its cool stream. Then he sat up and looked around at the tangled underbrush.

The creek meandered around a small tumble of pale rocks that had a murky, milky green water hole at its center. Sweating from every pore in his body, Gannon gazed at the pale white rough rocks of the creek, at the small hole of bright muggy sky above, listening intently for pursuit.

The birdcalls in the mist behind him were like none he'd ever heard before. His belly chain and padlocked transport box jingled and held up his hands as he instinctually tried to slap at the buzz of a mosquito in his ear.

"Son of a bitch," he yelled as he leaped to his feet, wanting to kill something.

Sick of his blind jungle run, he decided to change directions and follow the creek upstream. It meandered upward for three or four miles before it went straight into the dripping cliff of a high box canyon.

Gannon stood below it, staring up. In the pale gray cliff face, there were stripes of some other kind of dark glossy rock with sparkling bits of quartz or something in it. Beside these veins were shadowed cave-like fissures.

In the heat and buzz of insects, Gannon stared at the strange dark holes, shaking his head.

The actual Amazon jungle, he thought. With his luck, damn vampire bats would start coming out of the caves at any second, wouldn't they? Or pumas maybe. Followed immediately by projectile volcanic lava.

Cliff or no cliff, going back wasn't an option, so he scrambled up the talus of the least steep of the cliff slopes and gripped at a vine-like tree and started climbing. At the steepest parts, he had to lean sideways all the way into the rocky dirt hill and dig himself up foot by foot by using his elbows.

"You never saw workouts like this in those CrossFit videos," he mumbled as he side-crawled his bleeding elbows up the blasted rock.

He actually had to do a rock climber's lay-back at the top through a chimney-like column of rock before he was finally able to flop himself over the lip of the ridge.

Atop the ridge, he closed his eyes and lay down for a spell, allowing his lower back time to stop spasming. When he opened them again, he noticed that there was actually a hell of a view on the other side. The sun had come out more, and the emerald green of the jungle below was beyond startling with blue hills glowing in the distance.

What was even more beautiful was off to the right. Not too

far off, maybe five miles or so, were the terraced fields of some kind of farm.

"A farm means a vehicle. Let's go," he said to himself as he stood.

The soft loose dirt sloping down was a joke compared to the other side. The cleared grass field he came upon an hour later had a wire cattle fence around it. The posts of it were just primitive-looking warped sticks.

When he touched the wire, he smiled as he quickly drew back.

There was electric current running through it.

He followed the fencing to a ragged footpath through a jungle tree line heading down. In the next field, he came upon the cattle. They were like no kind of cows he'd ever seen. Gray and feral-looking things, thin enough to see their ribs. When he caught the scent of woodsmoke through the mist ahead, he began jogging again.

The farmhouse he came upon another quarter mile down was as sad looking as the cows. It was a bark-colored old cabin with a red rusted tin roof lifted off the wet ground on small crooked wood stilts. In another primitive animal fence arranged around it were some chickens and a mule and some clothes drying out on a long wooden pole.

As he came closer, deep under the tin eave sitting on a bench, he suddenly noticed a young woman staring back at him. She was Hispanic and pudgy and had an equally pudgy baby, naked but for a diaper, sitting in her lap.

"Hola," he said smiling, trying not to seem threatening in his shackles and blood-covered clothes. "¿Agua? Por favor?"

She stood with the baby, staring at him. She was wearing a halter top and shorts that were too small for her big-boned frame. Or was she pregnant? Gannon thought. She was maybe sixteen. The baby stared at him as well. It was a boy. A spitting image of the mother. He was very cute.

"¿Agua?" he said again.

She stared at him warily some more, at his shackled hands. Then she chinned at something to Gannon's left. There was a pump in the ground beside the mule pen. The young woman stood and went inside as he headed toward it.

He pumped until the water came up, cloudy at first, then clear. It was surprisingly cold and had a mineral taste to it.

He drank and looked around. Catty-corner to the right of this jungle farm homestead back toward the tree line, there was another structure. This one was on lower stilts and had a thatched roof. It looked like a witch doctor's house. Something out of the primordial mists of time. But he saw there was some junk out in front of this open-fronted shed-like building, old tires, a mud-splattered spackle bucket, and he stepped over the cattle fence and approached.

The inside of it was dark except for some shafts of light that came down from gaps in the overhead thatch. It was some sort of milking barn with pens and the strong smell of cow shit. To the back of it, a ladder led up into a hayloft and to the left, there was a workbench with a toolbox on it.

After he let his eyes adjust to the dimness, Gannon saw wood shavings on the floor beneath the bench. He came in deeper looking for tools. If there was a vise, he could snap the padlock and his cuffs with it.

He'd just opened the toolbox to see that there was some red double-aught shotgun shells inside of it when there was a sound, a jingle of metal behind them.

He turned. It was the young woman.

She was standing in the doorway, pointing a shotgun at his head.

67

They stood staring at each other silently.

After a minute she stepped through the shadows into the light. The soft chubby features of her brown face were hard now, her expression grim.

She said something in Spanish.

As if in response, Gannon sat at the workbench behind him without turning around.

She said something in Spanish again.

Gannon shook his head no. He stooped his shoulders in a protective gesture as if he were cold.

When she spoke again, she was closer. Gannon bowed his head, his shoulders shaking slightly as he pretended to weep. He half turned to her pleadingly, showing his scratched hands.

"Help me," he said sorrowfully without looking at her. "Look, I'm bleeding."

The quickness and fierceness with which he spun and seized

the barrel that came into contact with his elbow a split second later shocked even himself. The lady screamed as he grabbed the gun in a death grip and jumped up and turned hard at his hip and wrenched it out of her hands before she could pull the trigger.

As she went sprawling, he spread out his manacled hands just wide enough for him to grip the gun. In one of the shafts of light, he saw it was a Remington Wingmaster.

Pulling the action back slightly, he saw a red double-aught-buck shell peeking from the pump gun's chamber.

By its blued barrel, he could tell it was old, but it must have been well cared for because the action was quite smooth.

He shucked it back.

"You don't mess around, do you, sweetie," he said with a whistle. "Me neither. Move and I'll kill you. I'm not kidding. I'm having myself a real rough morning."

As the young lady put her hands up, the baby started crying from the other house. It was a high, surprisingly loud and forlorn wail. Gannon chained, aching, bloody and battered and bent over the shotgun like the hunchback of Notre Dame, wanted to join in. The lady balanced herself up on one foot.

"Don't move, remember?" he said. "No move."

"Mi niño. Mi niño," she said.

"Oh, your baby needs his bottle now, huh?" Gannon said. "Maybe. Or maybe you go back and get another gun and blow my head off? Right? Kill the gringo?"

She stared at him and started to cry herself now.

He knew this young lady was only protecting her family, and he hated to terrify her.

But then again, tough shit.

If the cost of him living was inconveniencing others to help keep him alive, why, that was a price he was more than willing to pay at this point, wasn't it? Many hands lighten the load.

He dumped out the toolbox. Four shells rolled out. When

he tried to load one in the shotgun, there was no room, which meant there were five shells already in the shotgun.

He managed to pocket the four extra shells in the cargo pocket of his camo pants by rolling them off the bench with his elbow. Then he motioned for the girl to sit as he sat down on the bench, thinking. He needed the cuffs off; that was for sure. But would shooting them off even work? And how would he pull that off? Get the nice young lady to help? Pull the trigger with a toe? Sounded like someone could get pretty hurt doing something like that.

No, he thought. He had a gun now. That was a game changer even with the cuffs. By bending awkwardly, he'd be able to work with it. He loved shotguns. At long range, they were useless, but even at semishort range, the spread could really get some lead out there on your side. Like all SEALs, he'd actually been well trained to shoot from the hip.

He could put a real damper on someone else's day now for a change, he thought as he nodded at the trusty Wingmaster. One you could put your entire arm through.

They both turned at a sound through the open barn door.

It was a truck engine.

"Oh, would you please just go to hell already?" Gannon said as he arrived at the shed opening.

Up the drive came the lumber truck from the dirt highway. The damn lumber truck with the orange tarp.

He couldn't see who was in it yet.

But he had a pretty damn good idea.

How? he thought.

He looked down at his shackles. The freaking transport box, he realized. There must have been some sort of tracker inside of it.

But that didn't matter right now, did it? he thought as he heard the truck shriek to a stop by the cabin.

"The hayloft. Now! Get up. Let's go," he said to the young woman, gesturing her deeper into the shed with the gun.

They were just at its ladder when the big-boned young lady had another idea. She suddenly turned and bolted for the shed opening instead.

"Shit," Gannon said, watching her go. "What now?"

He looked straight up at the thatched-roof ceiling. When he saw that there was a gap in it above the hayloft, he hurried up the ladder and then kicked it loose from where it was nailed to the loft and then pulled the ladder up after him.

After he placed the ladder against the grass wall just beneath the opening, he hurried back to the loft edge and swung the shotgun at the opening of the barn.

He let off a blasting round and shucked the gun.

"Come in and get me, you stupid pricks!" he yelled. "You'll never take me alive!"

Then he scurried over the loft and up the ladder out onto the top of the thatched roof.

He lay still on his back down in the straw, waiting. He heard them call to each other in the farmyard. Then he heard their footsteps. They were coming around the front of the barn now. When he heard their footsteps stop, he knew that they had taken up firing positions.

It sounded like the shattering end of the world as all three of them opened up at the same time with their automatic weapons a second later. Gannon's stomach felt like water as he heard and even felt the bullets spraying through the thatch walls of the rickety barn beneath him. *So, this is what a range target feels like!* he thought, wincing.

But even through the terrifying racket of gunfire, he crouched up with the shotgun and crawled to the top point of the thatch, praying it would hold his weight. When he made the top, he saw the two Americans twenty feet to the left below, standing and shooting side by side. Staring into the mouth of the barn, they didn't even so much as glance at him as he stood straight up with his awkward sideways crouch and fired.

It was a very good shot. They both stopped firing immediately as they fell back to the dirt in a bloody sprawl.

But the Hispanic scout was still firing obliviously from even closer.

Gannon racked the gun as he hurried forward.

The firing stopped just as he peeked out over the rim of the thatch. The scout was standing right there directly beneath him, changing out a magazine.

Gannon stood on the rim of the roof and had just completed flipping the pump gun barrel down when the scout looked up and their eyes met.

"No! Don't!" Gannon said as the young man swung up with the rifle.

"No!" Gannon shouted as he pulled the trigger.

"Why!" Gannon said as he hurried back down.

As he came out into the barnyard, he saw that the young scout was still alive. Despite his grievous wounds to the head and neck, his boot scuffed at the dirt as his left hand idly tried to undo the snap on his sidearm thigh holster.

Gannon stepped up quickly, ready to shoot him again, when he saw him stop breathing.

He looked down at him through the already gathered flies.

"You think I wanted to kill you?" Gannon said, kicking at his boot. "We should be drinking cervezas together, homey! I'm retired. Done with all this stupid shit. All I want to do is go home."

When he looked toward the house, he saw the young mother in the far cow field beyond it, running for the tree line with her baby.

In the silence, one of the calves out in the field bawled loudly. Gannon shook his head at the ground, the jungle, the foreign sky.

"All I want to do is go home," he said again.

Then he bent and knelt in the heat and stench of blood and cordite and cow shit and began rifling through the dead man's pockets for the cuff keys.

68

In his career as a drug smuggler, Lou had done four jungle run-ways. Two that he was actually proud of.

But wow was this not one of them, he thought, standing in the center of the ragged and raw twenty-football-field-long jungle clearing with his arms folded.

His international crime spree wasn't over yet, now was it? he thought as he gaped at all the jutting stumps, the knocked-over trees, the blackened marks along the sides where they'd piled and burned the brush.

He unfolded his arms where he stood at the open tailgate of the Land Cruiser and began massaging one of the stress lines above his right eye.

Now he was committing freaking environmental crimes, he thought. Slash-and-burn agriculture.

But on the positive side, at least everything was ready to go for when his plane arrived, he thought as he glanced at the fuel drums beside the SUV. They were already filled to the brim with fifty-five gallons of high test each and ready to be fitted with an electric transfer pump that plugged into the truck's generator.

If the plane arrived, said a nasty voice in his head as he lifted the sat phone off the top of the fuel drum.

"Please ring now," he said to it as he checked the battery charge for the thousandth time.

It was pretty much all set up now. Both the coke and the plane were on their way.

But, of course, there still was a bit of a snag on his end.

Lou wanted Angel, his best pilot, to do this crucial first run. But Angel, not for the first time, was a no-show so they had to give Reggie, his Australian pilot, the gig.

He liked Reggie as a person. He was a nice guy. And being a vet of the Australian air force for ten years, he had great credentials.

But he sucked under pressure. He sometimes freaked out. He'd have panic attacks and you had to guide him onto the runways with kid gloves. Sometimes it was like talking a suicide off a ledge. He'd actually crashed two planes.

The guy was a world-class sweat hog, too. Never saw a guy sweat so much in his life. When he landed, it would be dripping off him like a faucet. Guy could soak through a wool blanket. Made you nervous just being around him.

They'd heard from Reggie when he passed the Peruvian border an hour before, and he really should have been here by now. Lou wanted to try him again, but the Aussie was already nervous. With his tank low, things could spiral into an emotional disaster very quickly. Last thing he wanted was for the dude to melt down again and flip out.

Lou took a deep soothing breath himself. Reggie wasn't the only one losing his grip, was he? he thought. Like on every big deal he'd ever done, ever since he'd woken up, his stomach was a knot.

"Any word?" Alessandra said, awaking from the beauty nap she'd been taking in the Land Cruiser's front passenger seat.

"Not yet," Lou said, glancing back at her lovely pink-toenail-polished feet sticking up on the dashboard.

Now that all the dirty man work was done, she had deigned to grace him with her presence, he thought.

Actually, that wasn't fair, Lou thought. She didn't even have to be here. The agreement was for her to be there for their meeting with James. After that, she could have headed back to Lima and gone home already. But instead, she'd insisted on coming to the transfer to watch his back and to help videotape everything with her phone so no one could play games later about the count.

It was his nerves, Lou thought. They turned him into a complete asshole.

Lou almost dropped the sat phone as it suddenly blipped.

"Okay, I think I'm close," Reggie said.

"Good. That's good, Reg. What do you see?" Lou said, looking up at the sky.

"I see the seahorse-looking river. You're parallel to it, right?"

"No, perpendicular," Lou said, looking at his own map. "Right at the back of the seahorse's neck. We are dead east. From there, you come straight in at it."

"Okay, okay. I think I got it."

"Are you ready for a flare?" Lou said, turning and taking the flare gun from the back of the Land Cruiser.

"Okay, okay. Yes, give me a flare."

Alessandra sat up in the truck as Lou shot the red flare straight up. As it reached its apex, in the distance he thought he could hear a faint droning.

"I think I can actually hear you," Lou said. "Do you see the runway?"

"No, no. There's nothing," Reggie said.

Lou dropped his head. He wanted to murder this guy. With his bare hands. Get your shit together, Reggie, he wanted to scream.

"That's okay, buddy," he said soothingly instead. "Not a problem. Just look at the map again. You got this, brother. This is going to go as smooth as silk."

"I'm doing the best I can, man. The best I can, man," Reggie said.

Mama mia, you could practically hear the guy sweating, Lou thought.

"I know you are, man," Lou said, wiping his own now-sweating hands.

As he turned, his nerves hit a new high when he saw the two trucks emerge at the end of the jungle runway.

The coke had arrived.

"You got this, brother. Honestly," Lou said to Reggie as the trucks bearing the ticket to the first day of the rest of his happy retirement rolled closer and closer.

69

There was a high, almost earsplitting whine, and the twin blades of the tan-and-green camo-patterned Chinook transport helicopter began to blur above the helipad tarmac to the north of Devine's compound.

To the rear of its hold through the terrible sound and vibration, Bouthier watched as his boss, Devine, attached the Russian RPD light machine gun that he was carrying to the door-gunner rail.

Bouthier had thought about offering him a hand until he had glanced at the dark expression on his face.

Then he thought again. He knew by hard lesson that when the boss's ducks fell out of row, someone had to pay for it, and anyone convenient would do.

And Devine's ducks weren't just out of their row.

Devine's ducks apparently were all dead.

There was radio silence from the men transporting Gannon to the jungle hunting ground. As radio silence wasn't part of the plan, Devine had become quite wound up. The heat of his white-hot rage had been steadily building.

Devine's anger was well past blistering now, Bouthier thought, glancing at his steady grim expression. And was now into surface-of-the-sun territory.

"Sir," came the pilot over the comm as Devine finally secured the weapon.

"What now!" Devine screamed.

"I just need to repeat that I do not recommend we take her up so soon since we still have not received that back rotor service adjustment I asked for, sir. The vibration is really bad. Can't you feel it?"

"Feel it?" Devine cried. "The only thing that's going to be felt around here is my boot up your ass if you don't take this bird up now."

Case in point, Bouthier thought, shaking his head.

Bouthier's father was the same way, he thought as he took a retreating step back into the shaking shadows of the helicopter's hold. He, too, was a born rageaholic.

Which was why their mother had left and why Bouthier had lied himself out of the house and into the army at the age of sixteen.

"You want something done?" he heard the boss yell as he finally seated the drum magazine and pulled the charging handle. "Guess who's got to do it?"

Bouthier went to the other open bay door as the heavy aircraft slowly lifted off. As they achieved some altitude, the curling mist off the nearby Amazon tributary looked like a giant gray snake on the move atop the intense green of the triple canopy jungle. The overhead rotors cut its haze into silver curlicue ribbons as their elephantine aircraft plunged through it heading south.

When he turned back, he saw Devine was up in the cockpit with the pilot, showing him a tablet. He knew the truck had a GPS unit, so he must have been showing him that.

When they arrived at the gas station at the outskirts of Iquitos, it was coming on half an hour later. Coming to a halt at a hover thirty feet over it, Bouthier saw tin shacks filled with fruit for sale, and across a muddy yard from the station was a dock along the water with several barges.

Bouthier, who had been to Iquitos several times to pick up whores for Devine, knew that the dock was a place where American and European tourists took river tours into the jungle.

Without comment or order, Devine unhitched the rolled-up ladder and dropped it out of the side of the aircraft and climbed down into the dirt street before the station. Bouthier followed along with Llewellyn behind him and as he arrived on the muddy street, he saw that Devine was already entering the station's garage door.

The local Peruvians came out of their listing tin structures and stood, gaping. About fifty people and growing, men and women. Barefoot children. Dogs.

Not good, Bouthier thought as he followed Devine into the station.

Inside the garage bay, a young man wearing blasting headphones was squatting in the dirt before a cannibalized scooter engine, holding a power drill.

He looked up as Devine tapped him hard on the shoulder. Devine pointed at the crushed Toyota Land Cruiser sitting in the garage's other bay.

"That is my truck," Devine said in his excellent Spanish. "Tell me exactly how you have come to possess it."

"What's your problem?" the man said, taking off the headphones. "It was on the side of the road. What the hell is that sound?"

Devine removed his Browning Hi-Power 9mm from its holster. The young Peruvian did that goofy eyeballs-crossing thing as Devine placed its barrel on his forehead and cocked back its hammer with his thumb.

"That sound is my helicopter, and I would like to hear more details, please," he said.

The young man quickly explained how he had heard about the wreck from a passing bus driver. How three men in military dress had been driving it, but it had crashed along the road, and the military men had left the wreck behind in a lumber truck that they had stolen at gunpoint.

"Thank you," Devine said, tossing him a roll of money from his pocket as he turned.

Outside, Devine politely gestured for Bouthier and Llewellyn to get back on the ladder first.

Uh-oh, Bouthier thought, having a bad feeling about the boss's sudden manners as he started up the ladder.

When Bouthier finally got up the ladder to the door of the still-hovering helicopter, he looked down and saw that the boss wasn't on the ladder. He was by the rusting gasoline pump of the battered station, holding its spilling nozzle, and as Bouthier watched, he lifted it out and laid it on the ground.

Some of the smarter onlookers began to run, immediately grabbing up children, as the rapidly growing puddle of flammable liquid began to run into the gutter.

As he made the hanging ladder, Devine gave a thumbs-up gesture with the arm he had crooked over one of the rungs, and as the aircraft ascended, he lit a flare and tossed it.

The red-and-orange fireball that formed when the flame ignited the fumes engulfed the entirety of the station. Bouthier, from the open bay of the aircraft, watched Devine watching the destruction.

When the man looked up, he thought he might see him smiling or some other wickedness or craziness.

But what he saw shocked him even more.

The man was weeping. Devine was sobbing like a baby as the helicopter swung him around through the rising vortex of black smoke.

This was becoming unstable, Bouthier thought with a nod. Devine had been flirting with insanity down here in his jungle coke-laced hideaway, and now this had done it. Had pushed him right over the edge. The man had freaking lost it. The center here was losing hold.

Bouthier had seen some downfalls before in his mercenary travels, and if this wasn't a downfall in the making, what was it? He was a contractor and the contract here was definitely up. He needed to get out at the right moment. That was his priority.

He looked over at Llewellyn.

"Are you thinking what I'm thinking?" Llewellyn yelled over the rotor as Devine began to climb the ladder toward them.

"All over it, brother," Bouthier said. "We need to think about jumping off this gravy train before it derails."

70

The lumber truck Gannon left the body-strewn farmyard in was surprisingly modern. It had a touchscreen radio and an empty dashboard tablet holder above the glove box and best of all an AC that he immediately cranked.

What it didn't have was a lot of gas left in its tank, Gannon couldn't help but notice as he rumbled it through the pasture.

"But we beggars can't be choosers, can we?" he cried out crazily as he parted the jungle cows like Moses through the Red Sea.

He still had no idea where he was, but on the plus side his hands were freed now and he had a fresh change of underwear and a new camo shirt from Nevin's kit bag. The neatly packed bag had also contained lunch with a sleeve of crackers and a banana and a brick of cheese, all of which he instantly devoured.

Most important of all, he was armed to the teeth now. On the passenger seat beside him he had not one, not two, but three locked and loaded fully automatic M4 rifles. There were cleaning kits with them as well and before he even started out in the truck, he made sure they were all zeroed in exactly the way he liked. Along with them was a duffel bag with a sweet sixteen extra magazines, all of them holding twenty-eight rounds of lovely 5.56.

As he drove, Gannon's right hand softly stroked the butt of one of the rifles as he thought in minute detail about all the crimes that his old buddy, psycho Jimmy Devine, had perpetrated against him.

How the son of a bitch (with the help of satanically evil CIA buddies) had drugged him and starved him and beaten him and dragged him down here in the muck of this filthy shithole jungle in order to play a game of patty-cake with him.

He thought about how broken-hearted his son probably was and about how they would have killed him in a New York minute had he not had the luck of leaving with the guide.

"Careful what you wish for, Jimmy," Gannon yelled as he felt the rage inside him begin to build.

The horn honked as he punched at the steering wheel.

"You want to play pin the tail on the jackass with me, brother?" he screamed. "Okay, let's play, Jimmy!"

Beyond the field was a tire-tracked path that he hooked a left on for no particular reason and began rolling bumpily down a hill. After ten minutes or so, the "road" connected to what looked like the bed of a dried creek.

Gannon winced as the underside of the truck scraped and screeched as he bottomed out on a boulder.

"Woopsie daisy!" Gannon cried as the truck listed left, and he heard several boards klonk together and slide off of the back.

At the bottom of this creek run was what looked like a newly graded dirt road. And beside it, he saw there was an open cleared field.

A freshly cleared one, he thought as he rolled down the window and caught the cloying green smell of cut foliage mixed with woodsmoke.

He had just stopped to look around for another farmhouse when he heard something. There was the drone of an engine and a moment later, a small plane suddenly appeared over the top of the tree line at the end of the field to Gannon's left.

It was a white-and-grayish-green twin-engine prop, and it was flying at about the height of an elevated subway train and still descending as it blew past him.

Holy shit! It was landing, Gannon thought. The field to his left was some kind of airstrip.

"Thank you, God!" Gannon said, immediately sliding one of the rifles over onto his lap as he stomped on the gas and took off after the plane.

71

For all of Lou's worrying about the crap runway and the nervous Reggie, the landing had been perfect.

The gliding touchdown couldn't have gone more smoothly
at Kennedy Airport and now after they loaded up and turned
Reggie around, it would be all she wrote.

He had worried for nothing, it had turned out.

Escorting the half ton of cocaine in a jacked-up Nissan Path-
finder and a Ford Expedition were two young unarmed Peruvian workers and Alberto, James's lizard-like lawyer.

As they began to unload, Lou gave himself the job of jungle plane pump jockey, while Alberto joined Alessandra in the
front of the Toyota.

Lou smiled as he watched them chatting and laughing.

Could this be any easier or more civilized? he thought.

When the sat phone in Lou's pocket trilled a minute later,
he smiled as he lifted it out and saw it was Reggie. He looked

across the runway where his Australian top gun had gone off a few minutes before to water the jungle.

"What now, Reggie? I'm not bringing the TP. Use a leaf, bro," he said.

"Lou, there's…there's…a guy here," Reggie said. "He, um, he has a gun to my head. He wants to talk to you."

"Very funny, Reggie," Lou said.

"Hi, Lou. My name's Mike. Thanks for your help back in the garage in Mexico," said a voice. "That garage was hotter than a pizza oven. That was real nice of you."

It was an American voice.

Holy shit, Lou thought. *This cannot be happening. The gringo from the Concurso? This is impossible.*

"Um…hi?" Lou tried. "What's up?"

"What's up is I'm running for my life, Lou. Since you did me such a solid back in Mexico, I decided to maybe give you a chance to not get your brains blown out of your shiny bald head. But you have to listen to me very carefully."

"Okay. I like the sound of that," Lou said.

"I thought you might. Reggie tells me you're from New York. Me, too. I've met New York players before. Smart people. That's why I'm giving you a chance. Let's put our heads together. Work something out."

"Definitely," Lou said, forcing himself to smile. "Let's make a deal."

"That's it. Smile, Lou. Make the others think all is well. Here's the deal. Reg tells me he's heading out of here. I need a ride out. Those jackasses loading the plane work for Jimmy, right? James Devine?"

"Yes, with James."

"See, that's the problem. Jimmy's guys are the ones I need to avoid."

This is all I need, Lou thought.

"There's no problem with them," Lou said quickly. "They're kids. Not even armed."

"How about the ugly guy and the woman in the truck?" Gannon asked.

Lou looked at the front of the truck, then at the back of the slimy Alberto's head.

"The woman is not armed. She's with me," Lou said. "She and me and Reggie are just the transportation brokers."

"That's what Reggie says, too," Mike said. "The ugly guy is with Devine?"

"Yes," Lou said. "He's Devine's lawyer. Alberto is his name."

"He have a gun on him?"

"I don't know. He might have a pistol on him. I didn't see one, but it's definitely possible. He's the one we're doing the deal with."

"Good. Now, I'm only going to say this once, Lou. I just took out three highly trained special forces guys about five minutes ago, so if you think you're going to make points with Devine or something by screwing around with me, you're not. You're simply going to make me shoot you in your head. Do you understand?"

Lou swallowed. "I understand," he said.

"Okay. Tell the men to stop loading and to get out of the plane. Do it now."

"Hey, you," Lou called to one of the loaders by the truck. "Stop what you're doing and tell your friend to get out of the plane."

"What?"

"You deaf? Do what I tell you."

The kid went inside the hot plane and then both young men came out.

"Now tell the woman to come back to you to help you for a second. Do it now," Gannon said.

Lou lowered the phone. "Hey, Alessandra, this thing is stuck. Could you help me for a sec?"

Alessandra exited the truck and walked over to Lou. "What is it? Who's on the phone?" she asked.

"Good," Gannon said in Lou's ear. "Now don't hang up. I'm going to put you down for a sec."

The rifle crack and the crash of glass that sounded out a split second later made Lou jump. When he looked over, Alberto's silhouette was replaced by blood all over the inside of the truck's windshield.

Lou grabbed Alessandra, who began screaming, and when he turned, the American, wearing camo and strapping an M4, was already out of the tree line, pushing Reggie before him.

"Unload the plane," Gannon called out.

"What is this?" Alessandra said.

"You think I know?" Lou said. "Just calm down. I think we can get through this, Alessandra. This has nothing to do with us. We step back and stay out of the way. There'll be other deals."

They all turned as they heard a sound in the east. It was a low thump. A helicopter. It was approaching.

"Unload the plane now!" Gannon called again, running now as he began to drag Reggie beside him.

72

They'd scanned the area where the garage people had told them they'd found the lumber truck, but there was no sign of it. No truck, no nothing. And they had looked. Came down and checked tire tracks then took the chopper up high, maybe ten thousand feet, and had a good look-see all around.

When Bouthier noticed that the boss was on his sat phone, they were down along a back jungle logging facility near one of the Amazon's tributaries.

Staring at the endless matted and tangled jungle, Bouthier rolled his stiff neck and adjusted his earmuffs to tamp down the eggbeater shriek knifing through his skull.

Why didn't I just go to college? he thought.

At least gas had to be getting low, near the red line, Bouthier thought, scanning the mushroom-gravy-colored river. Jimmy's rage aside, this needle-in-a-jungle-haystack game was coming to a close.

At least for now, he thought. Which was good because he had skipped lunch, and he was starving.

"Scan the riverbanks," Devine called through the headset.

Bouthier scanned the riverbanks.

How had Gannon done all this? he thought. How he had caused so much mayhem so quickly was incredibly hard to fathom. The team that had escorted him weren't exactly the JV team.

That's why he had to give it to Gannon. There was no doubt about it at this point.

Bouthier stared down at all the floating logs in the gray water.

They were dealing with one highly dangerous and resourceful crackerjack commando son of a bitch.

But would they refuel and come back? Probably, he thought. With how worked up Devine was, they would be out all night with night vision no doubt.

Bouthier pondered on the boss. He kept thinking about how unnecessary it was to set the gas station on fire. He didn't mind cruel. Cruel he could deal with. Cruel was a weapon just like Machiavelli said. A damn good one. After his time as a private merc, he knew that more than most.

But cruelty for the heck of it was like a professional arsonist standing around after the job was done, getting his jollies off. It was useless. Just indicated dangerously unloosened screws.

Which sucked because it was actually fun when they'd first arrived. They'd gone hunting several times with the chopper. He'd actually bagged a giant armadillo one night. Ugliest thing he ever saw. Something out of a nightmare. They'd gutted it, cut it into strips, and grilled it right in camp. Tasted like an old shoelace covered in BBQ sauce but with the primest of prime Peruvian flake and some of the fancy French wine they'd brought along, no one cared. They'd really had some laughs.

"Something wrong?" Bouthier said as he saw the boss slap the phone off.

"Alberto tried to contact me, but broke off and I can't regain contact."

No, Bouthier thought.

"We need to go to the new strip," Devine called to the pilot, pointing. "Head south over that ridge."

They saw the airstrip right off as they came over the top of it. If you could call it that. It looked like a torn wound in the jungle. Like it just got shanked with something rusty. It was three or maybe four miles off.

The boss, looking out with his glasses, suddenly screamed over the headset.

"No!" he yelled. "No!"

Bouthier swung up his own glasses, zoomed in.

Midstrip there were three vehicles and to the right of them, a plane, some kind of Cessna twin prop, was turning at the other end of it about to take off.

That's when the boss said exactly what Bouthier was thinking.

"It's Gannon!" he screamed. "He's on the plane. Faster! Down the ridge! Drop the hammer! Get to the end of the strip. Block them in!"

"I told you, sir," came the pilot over the comm. "I'm reluctant to take it to top speed. It needs servicing. The rotors are out of sync."

"I don't give a shit. I'll out-of-sync you, you son of a bitch. Down now!" he screamed.

They tilted and roared down the ridge, the rushing wind battering at Bouthier's face through the open door. Bouthier watched the plane. It was picking up speed now, starting its takeoff.

He swallowed as his mind instantly did the terrible math and geometry of where it and they were about to converge.

Shit, was this going to be close, he thought.

The plane left the earth as the helicopter dropped lower with a stomach-dropping sensation, the dense vegetation suddenly swaying beneath. Bouthier had to hand it to the pilot. He made it to the end of the runway and stopped the big lumbering monster almost on a dime. It flared up as it entered into the slash right in front of the plane like a linebacker trying to block a field goal.

"No!" Bouthier screamed.

They were too close. As he turned, he saw that the plane was right there in the door gap. Its twin props roaring right at them.

But the plane tipped down at the last second. Bouthier dry mouthed and swallowed, could have reached out and touched the end of its wingtip as, by some miracle—the hand of Almighty God maybe—it banked sideways and down.

As it zoomed under the chopper, he heard its undercarriage trim the foliage with a sound like a Weedwhacker and he waited for a crash. But there was none. He moved to the other side and saw the beat-up plane zipping along the jungle canopy, heading higher now. It had made it. It had successfully gone under them.

"No!" Devine was screaming.

Then the real bad shit started happening.

The back end of the chopper started tilting up as everywhere alarms, sharp and blaringly loud, started bleeping out from the cockpit like crazy.

"I told you! It's out of sync. The back rotor. I can't make it come down. It just keeps ascending!"

Up they went in the horrid beeping like victims on a merry-go-round gone wild. They got up high, incredibly high. Way too high to around fifteen thousand feet when the back rotor tossed a bearing or something.

Bouthier, truly terrified, now looked up at the ceiling of the craft as he heard the machinery up there slowly whining down. He smelled oily smoke. Then they began to plummet.

As they began leaning ass down, he slid into the rear wall of the helicopter. Glued to the back of it, he stared helpless, watching the pilot. He was fighting the stick between his legs like a panicked snake charmer battling a suddenly rebellious cobra. Bouthier glanced out the doorway. They were practically free-falling now. A megaton chunk of metal and plastic and glass coming down as fast as a Wile E. Coyote anvil.

When they hit the top of the triple canopy, Bouthier felt it through his back and then it was their turn to do the Weed-whacking. Bouthier grabbed the cargo netting and wrapped himself up in it, waiting to die.

73

The aircraft had been torn asunder in the impact and in the rear part where Bouthier lay half-conscious in a haze of pain, there was a not unpleasant smoky smell of burning.

His right arm was broken. Very badly broken and twisted up behind his back at an angle that he didn't like to even think about. His right knee had hit something as well but he didn't think it was that bad. As soon as his concussion wore off a little more, he would think about moving, maybe.

As he began to nod out again, his eyes shot open as out from the jungle in the distance suddenly a kind of long and loud out-rushing wheeze that morphed into a low spine-tingling rumble was emitted.

As it dissipated, he stared out the still-open port side of the chopper at all the green.

It was a monkey or something, he thought, swallowing. He patted with his free hand for the rifle he had brought with him.

Nope, no rifle. He couldn't find shit.

He was still listening, straining to hear it again, when he detected another sound. Something tramping through underbrush. It stopped then started again. He listened to it. It was getting closer.

Screw me, no! Bouthier thought, panicked. It really was a damn monkey or something! No, no, no. No monkeys!

When the face appeared in the bottom of the broken Chinook's side door a minute and a half later, it did so suddenly like a jack-in-the-box.

But it wasn't a monkey.

It was far, far worse.

"Hey, jackass," Gannon said as he climbed up into the broken craft.

Gannon came over and stood looking down where Bouthier lay sprawled in the netting like a broken doll.

"Haven't you ever heard the expression, you can run but you can't hide?" he said.

"My arm," was all Bouthier could think to say.

Gannon squatted. He whistled as he took a good look at Bouthier's arm, which had become wedged behind his back.

"The appendage formerly known as your arm, you mean. Yikes. I never saw an arm go so far behind someone's back like that. Looks like you have an extra elbow or two back there now, buddy. Real sideshow-freak stuff. I really hope you're up to date on your health insurance premiums."

"Where's Jimmy?" Bouthier said.

"Jimmy? Yeah, smell that burning barbecue-ish smell? That's Jimmy's flesh converting into carbon down the hill a little there. Jimmy's dead. Humpty Dumpty of the Amazon took a great fall along with all the king's horses and all the king's men apparently. What a mess!"

"You came back. I thought you got away in the plane."

"I did, but when we saw the crash, I turned it around."

"Why?"

"Because I'm a commando, that's why," Gannon said, giving him a noogie. "Commandos always come back. That's what makes us commandos. We don't ever leave. Not until the job is done."

Bouthier stared at him, baffled.

"But isn't it done? I thought you said Jimmy is dead."

"He is. The king is dead but his castle still stands. We're going to correct that."

"You're going back to the compound?"

"Yep, and guess who's coming back with me?" Gannon said as he grabbed Bouthier by his ankle.

"No, wait! My arm! No!" Bouthier said as Gannon began to drag him toward the opening.

"Please!" he said. "Just wait. My arm is caught in the netting. Undo the strap, please. It's cutting my arm like a knife. Please!"

"Cuts like a knife," Gannon said, pausing to snap his fingers. "I love that song. Bryan Adams. Good call, bro."

"Please," Bouthier said.

Gannon tugged all the harder.

Bouthier screamed.

"A little on the high side with the chorus, buddy," Gannon said as he retightened his grip on his ankle. "But I like the enthusiasm. Now, ready for the big finale?"

Bouthier moaned.

"And a one and a two and 'Nana na, nana na, nana, nana!'" Gannon sang over the screaming as he finally pulled Bouthier free.

74

"Okay. Devine's dead. So, what now, Mike?" Lou said.

Gannon slammed the tailgate of the Ford Expedition over Button Eyes where he lay gagged and hogtied, and they walked off a ways onto the runway toward the plane.

"There's another prisoner," Gannon said. "Back at the compound. I need to go back and get him out."

"Wow. That's, um, unexpected. You want me to come with you?"

"No, I move quicker alone," Gannon said. "You hang here with your buddies. Make sure they stick around. I'll be back soon enough. But if I'm not, wait three hours, then take off."

"Here, take this," Lou said, handing Gannon Reggie's sat phone. "Just hit Redial on the last call."

"Okay. We'll stay in touch."

"One other thing," Lou said.

"What?"

"I'm a cop."

"What?" Gannon said, blinking.

"Undercover DEA. The others don't know."

"No," Gannon said, smiling. "I knew there was something I liked about you. Out of where? New York?"

"Yeah."

"Get out of here. You know Jerry Murphy?"

"Know him? He was doing belly flops on the dance floor at my wedding. He was my boss for years."

"I worked with Frank, his brother, in the seven-two."

"Screw off! You're a cop, too?"

Gannon nodded.

"Retired. Small world, huh?"

"Were you NYPD before or after you became Rambo?"

"After," he said with a wink. "Actually, also during. They gave me permission to get deployed a few times when shit came up."

"I can imagine. You seem pretty good at solving problems."

"Yeah, lucky me," Gannon said, shaking his head. "You must be in pretty deep to get into the Amazon, huh? What's the story with your backup? Have you checked in lately or..."

"No backup with this one. I'm... I'm..."

Gannon squinted at him.

"It's a long story," Lou finished.

"I see," Gannon said. "You got money problems or something? The boss doesn't know? Doing a little side deal? Something like that?"

"Pretty much. I thought I could smooth something out, but I got in over my head. Way, way over my head, Mike. I mean, take a look."

He gestured at the ragged runway, the smoke of the burning helicopter rising in the distance.

"Could this have turned out worse?"

Gannon laughed.

"Look on the bright side. It's over now. And at the end of the day, you didn't go full dark side."

"What do you mean?"

"What you did for me in the garage. You didn't have to do that. Jimmy and his guys easily could have killed you for that. When it mattered, you stood up. You remembered who you really are."

"Yeah, what's that?"

"A cop, dummy. One of the good guys."

Lou smiled.

"You're right. I actually did remember, didn't I?"

"I'm always right," Gannon said with a wink as he headed for the truck. "Sit tight. I'll see you in a bit."

75

When Gannon arrived back at the compound, it was dark and the gate was wide-open. As he pulled through, he could see that the front door of the chateau was open and all the lights were on and there was the sound of techno dance music.

"When the cat's away," Gannon said as he pulled up before the castle steps and came out carrying the rifle.

He went up into the hall. Rifle butt to his shoulder, muzzle up and forward as he checked the corners, he passed an office. Then he came to the dining room he had been in.

In the kitchen beyond it, an old man sat with his back to him on a spackle bucket, peeling potatoes. He stopped peeling and turned when Gannon poked him in the back of his head with the muzzle of the rifle.

"Get up," Gannon said.

He got up. A little old roly-poly man with a slick of combed-over hair in chef's whites. He looked Italian maybe.

"Where's the butler?" Gannon said after he hogtied his hands. "Pedro?"

"Yes. Pedro."

He tied the chef to an industrial mixer and found the stairs he had described and crept up. Pedro was in his luxurious quarters on the second floor, taking a shower. He looked more morose than usual as Gannon swung open the steamed-up glass.

Pedro surprised him by being a fighter. The shaving cream can he flung just missed Gannon as he ducked. When he went for the shampoo, Gannon lunged in and delivered a crisp and quick rifle butt to the man's nuts to calm him down a little.

Pedro hit the deck, moaning, then he crawled into the corner and assumed the fetal position.

Mission accomplished, Gannon thought as he squealed off the water.

"Hey, loser. Guess what? There's a new sheriff in town," Gannon said. "You want to keep breathing, you're going to get up now and throw on some clothes and do exactly what I tell you. You got it?"

He started babbling in Spanish then. No tengo this and that.

But the chef had already told Gannon that Pedro spoke English.

"What was that? What did you just say in Spanish? Yo necessito plomo en mi cabeza. You need a bullet in your head?"

Gannon loudly flicked the charging handle of the rifle back and forth.

"Okay, compadre. Vaya con Dios coming up," he said.

"I'll do whatever you need," Pedro said in clear perfect English as he got to his feet. "Please don't kill me."

"Now you're talking business. Turn around."

After he let the butler put some shorts on, he ziptied him facedown in the bedroom and took a leak.

At the sink, washing his hands, he grinned at himself.

"So far, so lucky, you crazy son of a bitch. Now finish this," he said.

"Who's playing that music?" he said to the butler as he went back into the bedroom.

"The women. James's women."

"What are we talking here? Hookers?"

"Yes."

"How many?"

"Four."

"Who else is here?"

"No one."

"What about a pimp or something? Their pimp?"

"No pimp. We bring them up from Iquitos."

"Who else is here?"

"No one. There are workers, but they are off today. Since James left with his men, it is just me and the chef and the women."

"Where is Paolo?"

"He's in his cell."

"How many other prisoners are here?"

"None."

"No one else is here? Are you sure? Think hard. Because if you're lying to me, I'm going to kill your ass."

"I swear it!"

He helped the butler up and brought him back downstairs to the pool. They stood at the open French door, watching the four ladies of the evening, who were sitting at a poolside table. Festive in their sequined minidresses and heels, they looked like they were ready to hit the discoteca.

The laughing ladies were completely oblivious until Gannon, still holding the rifle, thumbed off the phone playing the tunes on the bar.

"Good news, ladies. Your prince has come," he said as they sat there in shock.

He held up his zipties as walked toward them.

"And look, I've brought you all some bracelets."

Back inside two stories down in the subbasement, Paolo was in bed reading as Gannon clacked open the door lock.

"Paolo," Gannon said. "Hate to barge in like this."

"Miguel," he said, leaping up and embracing him. "What about the guards and James and—"

"They're dead."

Paolo danced around the room pumping his fists.

"That is incredible! A miracle, did I not say?"

"You called it, brother."

"Thank you, God. But how did you win the hunt?"

"The luck of the Irish," Gannon said. "Put your shoes on. We need to get the hell out of here and quick. But before we go, I need to do something. After being cooped up for so long, I feel a real urgent need for something."

"For revenge?" Paolo said as he tied his sneakers.

"No," Gannon said as he helped up his friend. "Combustion."

76

Outside, Gannon immediately headed through the back garden and down the stairs toward the barracks. Behind them was a large warehouse with a padlock that Gannon made the butler unlock at gunpoint.

Inside of it, stacked floor to ceiling, were pallets and packed on the pallets was cocaine wrapped in kilo packets like discount Costco bars of soap. There were hundreds of pallets. Maybe a thousand of them.

"Looks like we found something," Gannon said.

"How much is there?" Paolo said.

"Oh, about a hundred," Gannon said.

"A hundred?"

"Metric tons," Gannon said.

"¡Ay carumba!" Paolo said.

With canisters of helicopter fuel that Gannon found in a utility shed beside the helipad and a grill lighter that Paolo found in the kitchen, it only took a little under an hour to douse and set the dormitories and lab and the massive cocaine warehouse ablaze.

They saved the chateau for last. He and Paolo started at the top with two fresh five-gallon fuel cans and began emptying them as they made their way down.

Gannon paused as he came to Jimmy's quarters. There was a baronial bed up on a platform and a camera mounted on the ceiling and mirrors everywhere. In the master bath, there was a massive sunken tub and more mirrors and another camera.

In the boutique-like closet drawers that he opened and closed were Rolex watches and silk ties that he ignored. Though when he opened a drawer filled with stacks of euro hundreds and hundred-dollar US bills, he found a small knapsack and decided to fill it.

He found what he had been looking for in a cigar box under some T-shirts in the bottom drawer and put it in his pocket. He lifted his gas can again and splashed fuel on the closet cabinets, on the bedroom window draperies, on the porno movie set bed.

When they were back outside again by the front steps, he handed Paolo the lighter to do the honors.

"No, you, Mike. You were the one who did it."

"You were here longer, Paolo. I insist."

As Paolo set it off, they stood with an almost ceremonial attitude and watched the line of flame run down the hallway and up the stairs they'd just come down. One by one, they watched flame flicker in all the windows until the Disney castle was fully enflamed. When he turned to Paolo, the defrocked priest's eyes were filled with wonder like a child before a Christmas tree lighting.

The others—the women and the butler and chef and Button Eyes—were all sitting behind them in the gravel drive ziptied beside the Expedition. Gannon dragged Button Eyes closer to the flames and then squatted down beside him.

"You think I got a soft spot for you, think again, jackass," Gannon said. "The only reason you're not sitting in the front hall there tossed into the hellfire where you belong is because I need you alive to tell the tale.

"You tell your boss the lion is coming for him."

The fire was reflected in the man's eyes as he blinked up at him.

"Lion?"

Gannon nodded.

"You see, almost every animal survives by hiding, right? By stealth, by creeping around. Almost every one. But not the lion. The lion comes into an area. He takes a different approach. He roars. When you're king of the jungle, you tell everyone around that you're there."

Bouthier swallowed.

"You tell to whom it may concern, they made one mistake. They tried to break me. Now it's my turn to break them instead."

They looked up to where the flames crackling the windows were blackening the white of the brick.

"You tell them I got Jimmy, and you tell them how I came back and smiled and took selfies as I piled up every last gram and stick of their shit and then burned it all to the ground. You tell them, they're my work now, and my work is only half-done.

"And wait, one more thing."

Gannon stood and face-planted Bouthier into the gravel with a boot between his shoulder blades. The zip ties popped easily under the insanely sharp blade that Gannon had taken from him. Then Bouthier cried out as Gannon ripped Declan's Rolex off the wrist of his mangled arm.

"There we go. Much better," Gannon said as rezipped the crying muscular man extra snug.

77

After word of the fiasco from Bouthier, Bright thought he'd have time to prep himself for the carpet call from his boss.

He didn't.

He was actually still wrapping things up at the gym that he went to before work when he saw the screen on his iPhone flash.

"Oh, boy," he said.

When he arrived at the building in Foggy Bottom fifteen minutes later, his hair was still wet from his shower. The office was on Twenty-Second across from the Truman Building, an unmarked square four-story building neatly trimmed in beige stone. He'd been to it before, so after he showed his badge to security, he knew which side of the parking lot to use.

He headed from the garage into the main floor lobby, and he pushed through the door to the firm's duplex office suite and said hi to Ingrid, the receptionist.

"You can go right up, Mr. Bright," she said.

The office was fancy even by DC standards. He practically couldn't hear his footsteps on the plush baby blue carpet runner that carried him up the polished mahogany steps.

The door was open and he stepped through it and stood motionless.

Behind the bulky antique desk hung a yellow-orange modern print and along the walls were framed photographs. The photographs were of his boss, Alex Sarris, at various points in his storied career. Alex teaching at Harvard. Alex as deputy secretary of defense somewhere in Iraq. Alex at the ceremony where he was installed as the director of National Intelligence. The most up-to-date one showed Alex in the Oval Office working as the national security advisor of the previous president.

Now Alex was the State Department director of Policy Planning with Bright himself being his off-site ombudsman assistant and liaison at Langley.

Bright's was a plum job not just because it had a GS-15 level of pay with hardly any official duties, but because it placed his mouth near the ears of legendary men behind the throne like Alex.

Behind a door left of the desk there were muffled voices. He wondered if the delay was a psychological punishment or a freeze-the-kicker sort of thing. He knew what he was in for. He'd been bracing himself. It wasn't going to be pleasant.

The door opened after a moment and a well-dressed man with slightly frizzy copper hair came out. He moved quickly for a short man. He gave Bright a shake of his surprisingly strong little hand.

"Adrian, I appreciate you coming by," he said in his thick New York accent.

"Anytime, Alex."

"Could you take a seat for a minute? I'll be right back. I'm waiting for an email."

"No problem at all," Bright said.

He sat on the couch as Alex reentered the side office. The clatter of a truck outside drew Bright's eyes to the window. Dawn was lighting the sky behind the Washington Monument's immense obelisk. As he stared at the icon, he remembered that around the block nearby there was a bar in a hotel where he'd practically lived while he was a congressional aide. Feeling his mouth go suddenly dry, he wondered if it was still there.

"Thanks, Adrian," Alex said as he came back in and sat.

"Anytime," Bright said.

Alex stared at him as if searching for the right opening. Bright could smell the scent of his aftershave, some spice in it—jasmine? Was jasmine a spice?

The ginger-headed man searched around his desk and lifted something. It looked like a small baseball, a child's toy. It was a stress ball, Bright realized as Alex started squeezing it.

Then the boss stretched back and breathed slowly as if trying to calm himself. "Okay, don't bullshit me here. Bullshit time is over."

Bright nodded.

"Articulate the mission again."

"The Gannon mission?"

"Yes, the Gannon mission. The one you talked me into approving the funding for. I know I said I didn't want to know about it, but now I do. Tell me everything. Starting with whom you gave the contract to."

"I gave it to a former agent of mine from when I was in the clandestine service. He worked for the Company but then he quit and became, well, he became a drug dealer. A very powerful one. His name is—"

"James Devine," Alex said.

"Yes."

"Go on."

"Gannon was grabbed by Devine's men in Alaska while he was on vacation and was brought to Mexico. There he was supposed to have been eliminated. But without my consent or even my input, Devine suddenly decided to—"

"Bring him to his compound in Peru," Alex said.

"Yes."

"I thought I told you that I would approve the contract if there was zero, zilch, nada chance of it coming back to me. No company assets, remember?"

"But I didn't use any. That's why I went with Devine. He's a drug dealer!"

"Yes, you idiot," Alex said, swiveling in his chair. "But he's *our* drug dealer."

"What?"

"Were you also not aware that Devine and Gannon were in the same unit in Iraq?"

"What!"

"Is there an echo in here? My goodness, you are completely—and I mean completely—full of shit. Breeze into me with this song and dance about this plan you came up with. Had the whole thing ready to go off like clockwork. Just need my signature on the paperwork.

"Then you hire an assassin—one of our most precious assets—to kill a man he once fought shoulder to shoulder with? I mean, is your last name like a joke or something? The same way they call big men Tiny? You're about the biggest dumbass I ever met!"

"How was I supposed to know all this?"

"Enough. Now, Adrian, there is only one reason why we are still conversing so cordially. Do you know what that reason is?"

"No."

"Because the fiasco *you* have caused has not been traced back to *me*. But it may yet. Not only was an unholy amount of product destroyed, but this former compound was about to be rolled out as one of the Company's state-of-the-art insurgency training centers."

"I didn't know," Bright said.

"Here is what we are going to do now. Or should I say, here is what you are going to do. Listening?"

Bright nodded.

"No one knows who destroyed this compound and no one is going to know. It will remain a mystery to the 'last syllable of recorded time,' to quote the bard."

"Which means?"

"The mission still stands. Gannon in a body bag still solves all of our problems. But there will be no more help from the Company. Things are way too hot."

"But—"

"But nothing. Don't cry poverty, Mr. Slick. You know everyone in town, especially on the other side of the Potomac."

The Pentagon, Bright thought. That actually was a good idea.

When Alex whistled a split second later, Bright turned as the side office door opened. Two men were standing there, large beefy men. One was Black and the other looked Samoan or something. They both had shaved heads. Though they were wearing suits, they seemed like bouncers.

Bright sat up, staring at them. His brain tried to square a rational reason for their presence. It failed.

"Do you see these two men, Adrian?"

Bright shook his head, his mouth dry.

"You know what I call them?"

"No."

"The secret to my success. They solve all my problems. If Gannon isn't in a body bag in seventy-two hours, you become one of my problems. Understand?"

"Completely," Bright said.

PART FOUR

THE FRIENDLY SKIES

78

Gannon woke up on a plane for the second time in a month.

Well, he thought, peering out at the hazy morning light on the water below. At least this time, it's heading in the right direction.

They were heading to Panama now. To another remote jungle strip Lou used working undercover as a drug dealer. From there, it was going to be a piece of cake as Lou knew people who could get Mike papers for a flight home.

Gannon crossed his fingers, thinking about his son.

Home, he thought. Please be true.

It was just the two of them now. After some discussion, Alessandra and Reggie had been left to their own devices with a Land Cruiser full of coke back near Iquitos.

"Are we there yet?" he called loudly over to Lou at the instruments.

"Very close now," Lou said as Gannon looked out and saw land.

Lou was a good pilot. As they touched down in the middle of yet another dense jungle, he might as well have been on a 747.

"Nice job, Lou. Very smooth," Gannon said as they taxied over to what looked like a shipping container.

"No problemo. Thanks for flying the friendly skies."

Inside the triple-locked container, there were supplies. Stacks of water bottles, AR-15s and ammo, dried food. Lou rummaged around and tossed Gannon a Hawaiian shirt.

"All the comforts of home, huh?" Gannon said as he got changed. "Surprised no one's broken in."

"No," Lou said. "We pay the farmer who owns the land very well to make sure it doesn't happen."

"This is okay?" Gannon said as Lou handed him a Tracfone still in its packaging.

"Squeaky clean, bro. I bought all of it."

"Shut the front door," Gannon said, laughing, as Lou went to the back and wheeled out a moped. He handed it to him and went back and wheeled out another.

"Why walk when you can ride? There's a town nearby. The highway to Panama City is only a few miles away down that trail. Follow me."

Fifteen minutes of off-road mopeding later, the trail dumped them out into the narrow back street of a run-down little town with two-story painted houses and bars on the windows.

Lou waved as they passed a little restaurant on the corner where a hefty Panamanian woman with a crew cut was putting tables out. A small dog came out of the back of it, barking at them, as they took off down the road.

Deeper into the town, there were sidewalk markets, a food truck selling fish tacos beside an old baroque church. A line of cars was waiting at the first light. One of them, a brown jacked-up Tacoma pickup, was playing a festive reggae Latin rap.

Listening to it and looking around at the sky and trees, Gannon found himself overwhelmed by a feeling of gratefulness, of rushing freedom and hope.

The incredible luck it had taken to get him out of there.

He looked up at the sunrise clouds stacked up above the steeple. They were the color of old gold.

It wasn't luck, dummy, he thought.

"Lou," Gannon said as the light went green.

"What's up, Mike?"

"Thank you."

"De nada," Lou said with a wink as he hit the throttle.

79

Bright's first move the next day was in town and it was a no-brainer.

Admiral Mickelson's secretary told him he was nearby at an event, heading up a round-table brunch with some college kids at the famous DC mortgage company he was on the board of, and Bright got to the manicured grounds of the redbrick building on Wisconsin Street around ten thirty.

After he was given a name tag, the large high-ceilinged room he was guided to had a solemn air about it. A church without its stained-glass windows. One thing corporations rarely skimped on, Bright thought as he took in the sideboards and massive fireplace that could roast an ox, was their obnoxious self-important inner sanctums.

The boardroom table at its center was the size of a small helipad, and at it were over a dozen people. Sitting at one side of the table were old male and female well-heeled fat-cat mortgage executives and on the other side were young nervous college students in cheap suits who wished to be them one day. When Bright saw the C-SPAN camera in the room's corner, he realized the reason for the nerves.

When Mickelson came in ten minutes later, he made quite the entrance in his pristine white naval uniform. Every eye was on the admiral as he walked around the acre of table to the sole empty center seat that was waiting for him.

Bright watched as Mickelson opened the folder that was placed there and licked his finger. One of the white-haired gents beside him leaned in and said something to him, flipping through the folder pages. Mickelson laughed.

The admiral had turned his retirement years into pure gold. Besides this one, Mickelson was on the boards of five other Fortune 500 companies and was corner-office consultant at a multi-billion-dollar venture capitalist outfit that specialized in the defense industry. Bright wondered if Mickelson was the most connected person in DC. His day was filled with power breakfasts with lobbyists, board meeting brunches, lunches with book editors. He even taught a class over at Annapolis.

Bright paid him the best compliment he was capable of paying. He envied the man.

Mickelson looked up and cleared his throat. As he smoothed his snow white naval tunic, he put a more serious, time-to-get-down-to-business expression on his solid trustworthy face.

"Good morning, everyone," he said with his bright white smile and his beautiful speaking voice as soft as the velvet on the chair beneath Bright's ass.

The apple didn't fall far from the tree, Bright thought as he remembered how talented Mickelson's daughter Ginny also was at slinging it.

The next hour was filled with a back-and-forth discussion to make tax accountants long for the grave. Talk droned on about exposure complements, capital requirements, single counter-party risks. When one of the students spoke nonstop for five minutes about the need to implement broader quantitative-impact study issues, Bright thought one of his blood vessels was going to rupture.

"We need to talk, Paul," he said to Mickelson as he came up behind him at the sideboard coffee service during the break.

"What is it, Adrian?" he said out in the hallway.

As they strolled past oil portraits of forgotten old greedy men, Bright told him.

Oh, was he a bullshit artist, Bright thought. He actually seemed to take the news well.

"What do you want me to do about it?"

"The Company is out of this now. That door is closed. We need your contacts in the Pentagon."

"And tell them what?"

Bright shrugged.

"It's up to you, Paul. I know you wanted to avoid getting your fingerprints on this. But our little plan of using your resources to budget this operation under the umbrella of the Company is over now. He's still on the run. Still down south. If you get your people across the Potomac to find him, my guys will do the rest. Everything can still come up roses for us. But we need to find him."

"This is where we're at now?" Mickelson said, sipping his coffee.

"Yes, Paul. This is where we're at."

"I'll get back to you," he said.

80

Ed Navarro, early into work, crossed the parking lot and came around the corner of his building and jogged his two hundred and seventy pounds up the outside steps.

He laughed as he remembered that his daughter had once called his jogging watching a baked potato run on toothpicks. He sighed. His daughter was a brat but a funny one. It sucked that she didn't call him anymore since she went away to school, had this very angry seeming attitude toward him now.

Atop the steps, he pressed his card pass to the reader and the lock clacked and he pushed in.

Even more irritating given that he was picking up her tab.

Ever quick on the uptake, as he entered the fishbowl, Navarro immediately noticed that the big boss man's corner office light was on.

His boss, Rob Carmichael—or Rob Car-meleon as Navarro called him—was a tall nice-looking Black guy from South Carolina. Back when it was all men at the NRO, he, like all the rest of them, had worn camo fatigues and had acted like a man's man, a good ol' boy. But as the men were phased out and the ladies and snowflake college kids and the Silicon Valley start-up people were brought in, he had morphed into a kind of college professor replacing the camo with tweed coats and rep ties.

If the Amish had come to work there, Navarro liked to tell people, Car-meleon would be wearing suspenders with a chin beard, warning about the English as he handed out flyers to the next quilting bee.

He looked back at the light on as he found his desk. It was weird that the boss was there. Navarro came in earlier than his crew to pick up the squeal on anything new that had come up and his boss was always long gone.

Down the line of desks, dayshift section chief Barry Hulse tossed a chin hello at him from where he sat on his phone.

"What's up with Car-meleon?" Navarro said.

"Got a visitor."

"Who?"

Barry shrugged.

"Dunno. Just came in," he said.

They both watched as the door opened and out came a white-haired hearty and handsome military-looking man. He was photogenic, the creases of his dress casual khakis sharp enough to split a hair. He seemed vaguely familiar. Some younger guy was with him, big dude, short hair, shoulders like a tight end.

"Heavy hitter, huh?" Navarro said.

Barry chinned the phone and did the "see no evil, hear no evil, speak no evil" thing with his hands.

"Ed, could you come in here?" Carmichael called up as the two mysterious visitors left.

"Afternoon, Rob," Navarro said as his boss closed the door behind him.

"Hey, Ed. Have a seat. I got a red ball just came in."

"That so?" Navarro said as he sat.

"Yes," Rob said as he unlocked his desk and took out a blue electronic pass and placed it on the table.

Navarro looked at it as Carmichael locked the desk again.

Whoa, he thought. Red ball indeed.

The pass was the golden invite to the chocolate factory. In the corner of the fishbowl was a SCIF with full unrestricted, and as was rumored, unrecorded access to all the birds, even the ones the guys on the floor didn't know about.

From the corner of his desk, Carmichael moved over a paper-clipped printout stack.

He placed the SCIF pass on top of it.

"Ed, there was a flight out of South America twenty-four hours ago. The details are there. They want the plane found and I mean yesterday."

"They?"

Carmichael played with his rep tie.

"Did you say something?"

"Gotcha. I take it you don't want this in the log."

"You take it right, Ed. Hit me up when you find it."

As Ed pulled the paper toward him and saw the Iquitos, Peru, line at the top, he was glad for the office dimness. Because as his boss stood, Navarro's eyes went full-aperture wide.

81

There was the boom of construction in the hazy distance and then the discordant echo of a siren.

But all was well, Gannon thought as he sipped his second ice-cold Heineken draft.

The hotel in the fancy Punta Pacifica area of downtown Panama City was a shocker. The fifty-story modern glass behemoth looked like something from midtown Manhattan or maybe Dubai where it stared off into the Pacific. The showstopper was the thirty-ninth-floor infinity pool Gannon was sitting beside with good ol' Lou, his best new buddy.

"There are nice places to have lunch, Lou," he said to his buddy in the other chaise, "then there is Punta Pacifica."

"Yeah, funny what kind of accommodations a magic back-pack full of twenties and fifties can get you these days," Lou said.

After their moped road trip into the city, Lou had called up his passport buddy, and then they had had some fun doing some shopping. Wearing designer jeans and sneakers and soccer shirts, they'd taken their photos in a downtown Walgreens and were waiting on Lou's boy to do the rest. If all went well, Gannon was going to be on an American Airlines flight tonight to Dallas.

"So, Mike, you don't have to tell me if you don't want but—"

"You actually want to know what got me brought down to a secret CIA political prison."

Gannon told him. About how his postretirement Bahamian fishing dreams were dashed by a run-in with a bag of money that turned out to belong to a group of corrupt FBI agents. About how he had also banged heads with some other corrupt folks in the Justice Department. How he was hiding out on his buddy's weekend warrior ranch in Utah with his son.

"The hunting trip seemed like a safe bet. Hell, I figured Alaska would be the last place I'd run into them."

"But they were watching you. Why not grab you in Utah?"

"Not positive. Maybe because my buddy's actually crazier and more paranoid than I am," Gannon said. "His ranch is no joke. But don't worry. I'll find out. I'm done running. Past done."

"Turning it around and taking it straight up the gut, huh?"

Gannon nodded.

"That's the only play I got left. Time to send a message they won't soon forget. I try to be peaceful, try to mind my own business, but head-on collisions seem to be the only thing these sick puppies seem to understand."

"What is this going to mean for me, do you think? They'll come for me, right? I already called my wife to head to a place we set up, but what about the future? I need to be looking over my shoulder now. At the very least, they could jam me up big-time at work."

"I think you're good. You met with Jimmy and the lawyer, right? They're both dead. You can still tell work that you got into an undercover scenario where you had to make moves where you couldn't call in. If they ask, tell them you came down to Lima to follow a lead, but it dried up so you left. What happened at the runway, you have no idea. They can't prove you were there."

"But I'm in charge of the plane."

"Reggie did it on his own or maybe one of your other pilots. You're not sure which. All you need is plausible deniability, right? You think these guys want this can of worms to deal with? They don't."

"But that CIA merc guy saw me at the beach house in Mexico. One of Jimmy's thugs."

"The bean pole guy? Don't worry about him. He's dead, too. He died in the helicopter with Jimmy."

Lou smiled.

"You're right," he said.

"I'm always right," Gannon said, smiling back. "Technically, you're still on vacation. Go back to work like nothing happened."

"That seems just crazy enough to work. In that case, where's the waiter?" Lou said.

82

The waiter had just brought a pitcher when Gannon heard the overhead speaker.

"Bronson. Bronson," said a female voice before saying something in Spanish.

"What is that they're saying about Bronson?" Gannon said.

"Call for Bronson at the desk."

Gannon sat up.

"What is it?"

"Bronson was my call sign."

"McGyver. Bronson," the overhead said now. "McGyver. Bronson."

"Get the hell out of here. Now what?" Gannon said, standing and walking over to the bar.

"Bronson," he said into the phone the guy handed him.

"Mike! Holy shit!"

It was him. His old buddy, Ed Navarro. McGyver himself.

"What on earth?"

"Mike, you're alive!" Navarro said.

"Yes."

"There's no time. Listen, they're on to you. You need to get out of there."

"Why? What, Ed? Slow down."

"Can't. They're coming for you. I'm at NRO and I got an eye on your hotel in Punta Pacifica right now."

"What?"

"I came in this afternoon and got put on a special assignment on the down low to find a small plane out of Iquitos. When I saw that, I could have had a heart attack. Barber contacted me two weeks ago about you, and I had already traced the G5 they put you on so I put two and two together. I'm in the candy store right now with all the birds. I'm staring at your hotel."

"Like live? Right now?"

"Yes."

"How many fingers am I holding up?" Gannon said.

"Screw you. Get out of there!"

"Who put you on to me?"

"Don't know. But this guy looked like a heavy hitter. I already pulled his face off the office video feed. You have a phone?"

"Yes."

"Give me the number."

"Holy shit," Gannon said as the photo hit his Tracfone. "Admiral Mickelson."

"You know this guy?"

"Yep," Gannon said. "I worked for him."

"He's a SEAL?"

"No, this was before I became a SEAL. I was his aide de camp for about a year when I first joined the navy. He was the commander of the Tenth Fleet who had just become CNO at the Pentagon. They needed bodies to get him in there quick so I was sent out of training in Virginia with a bunch of other Dixie Cups to help him move. It was like twenty years ago."

"Oh, that's where I recognized him from. He's that navy guy who was on TV. He did a graduation speech or something that went viral. Then he wrote that best seller. Bootstraps something."

"*Bootstrap Your Life.* That's him. Admiral Paul Mickelson."

"Why is he gunning for you, Mike? What the hell did you do to him?"

"Nothing!" Gannon cried. "I was his chauffeur from the airport and he liked me so he kept me on. I was his Mr. Fetch. I'd get DVDs for his daughters, walked his dog. He was like a father figure, a mentor. He actually taught me how to ride a motorcycle. He helped me apply to the SEALs. Why the hell is he doing this?"

"Beats me. I guess you forgot to use your turn signal one time too many because he's got a hard-on for you like I've never seen. He's got the full weight and focus of the US Armed Forces pointed at your sorry ass, Mike.

"They know exactly where you are. After I hang up, my boss is going to be expecting my report. I could fake like I'm sick or something, spill coffee on the keyboard, but if I don't send it in five minutes, someone else will find you. So, run, you crazy son of a bitch!"

Gannon thought a moment.

"No, Ed," he finally said. "Wait a half an hour and tell them exactly where I am. I'll rent a room here for a week. It'll keep them busy focused here, getting a team of idiots together, while I skedaddle stage left. But wait, one more thing."

"What?"

"You're in the candy store with the birds, you said. Run a trace program on Mickelson for me and find out where he lives now."

"No! What are you nuts?"

"I am and so are you or am I talking to a different Ed McGyver Navarro? He's cheating to get me. Two can play at this game."

Navarro let out a breath.

"I'll send it to your phone. You have half an hour. Now run."

"You're a lifesaver, brother. I knew I had friends in high places."

"Yeah, yeah. I'm hanging up now."

Lou was standing when Gannon rushed back.

"Grab your shades, Lou. Change of plans," Gannon said.

83

It turned out Admiral Mickelson's house was actually a bayside compound out on a jut into the Chesapeake in a town called Shady Side.

The main house was a modern glass job. A huge one. Ten thousand square feet, seven bedrooms.

It even had a glass guardhouse.

With one guard in it. A linebacker-size guy in his late twenties, Gannon knew.

Oh, yeah. He knew all about it.

He had been watching it across the water from a marina parking lot on Kent Island with his Walmart binoculars for thirteen hours straight ever since he'd gotten off the plane.

The passport had come through an hour after he and Lou had sneaked out of the hotel back in Panama. It was Canadian and even better than he had expected. After they'd said goodbye at the airport, Gannon had no trouble at all getting through customs and onto his nine-hour Delta flight.

Instead of calling home, when he left DCA, he rented a van and bought some supplies and came straight out to the admiral's for a look-see.

The best vantage point he sussed out was across the bay from his house here in a town called Romancoke. He had laughed when he saw the sign, the irony of which was not lost on him as Jimmy Devine, his old buddy-turned-political-prison-warden, was an imperial fool who dealt coke.

Besides going to Starbucks and getting one of those coffee boxes, he'd been eyes on it.

He was on a time crunch now, and if he wanted to catch Mickelson on his back heels, time was of the essence.

When he decided to go into the freezing late-March water, it was around eleven in the morning. He couldn't find any neoprene suits at the Walmart so, as he came out of the van and into the water with his snorkel already on, he was in waterproof rain gear duct taped at the ankles and wrists.

Leaving his fins on the rocky shore on Mickelson's property, he was in his bare feet as he went straight to the guardhouse. He was lying on the ground under a hedge by the door for an hour, listening, when he heard the guy head into the bathroom. He took out the lockpicks he had put together from his Walmart purchases and had just made entry when a guard emerged from the bathroom dead ahead.

Gannon in his odd dark green Gorton's fisherman gear calmly kicked the door shut behind him as the guy came flying at him. As they collided, the guy went for a chin grab but he missed, and Gannon slammed the heel of his hand into his meaty throat as he gasped. He got a good grip on the man's hair and searched and reached and grabbed a small coffee mug from a side table beside the couch.

The guy screamed as Gannon broke his nose with it. But the

guy, to his credit, instead of crumpling, stomped Gannon's instep and pivoted and hammer-punched Gannon in the side of his neck just under his jaw.

Gannon's head made a dent in the Sheetrock as it bounced off it, and then he grabbed at the big son of a bitch's ugly face and got a thumb in under his lip and the guy howled as Gannon clamped down and pulled hard, doing a pretty good job of trying to rip his face open.

As the guy yelled some more and grabbed at him, Gannon let go of his brutal hold of the guy's lip and got in under his massive arms and wrapped him and kicked the column of his legs out from underneath him as he reared back at the window.

He was able to swing the big bastard around just enough to make sure he hit the glass first, and out the window they went along with the blinds. Gannon just missed hitting the side of the air conditioning unit, but the kid wasn't so lucky. Its metal edge caught him flush in the face, and he fell back, moaning and crying out like an animal being treated to a cruel and unusual slaughter.

The guy, blinded by the blood in his eyes, was trying to take his gun out—some kind of concealment Glock—when Gannon did it for him.

There was the sharp hard sound of pool balls clacking together as he plastered the Glock's barrel off the guy's lantern jaw.

The next blow after that to the guy's Cro-Magnon temple did the trick.

"Goodnight, Irene," Gannon said as the guy's bucket-size head lolled over.

"Windows, please be double-paned," Gannon said at the main glass house as he ran at it with the Glock down low by his side.

84

A lot of people had basement home theaters these days, but Admiral Mickelson, who was still very much a player with his fingers in many military industrial pies, liked to think of his jungle room as his basement theater of war.

The dedicated fiber trunk line he had the telephone company run in up through his million-dollar shoreline neighborhood had cost a literal fortune.

"Worth every penny," he said as he sat in his inner sanctum, watching the live feed from Panama City.

On it, downtown Panama City was rolling past. Men and women in office clothes, a Nautica billboard, busy shops and bus stops. As the vehicle and pedestrian traffic blurred past, the body camera swung toward the car's interior revealing three large men in Panama City PD uniforms with black Kevlar vests.

It was his and Bright's rapid response team of mercenaries.

They were about to hit Gannon at the hotel. He'd been staying there all week, keeping his head down.

"About to get the shock of his life," Mickelson said under his breath.

"Dammit, look at this traffic," one of the mercs said as they stopped.

Mickelson, just as impatient or probably even more, sitting in one of the oversize leather power recliners, drummed his fingers on a knee then he snapped them.

"Exactly," he said to himself. "This calls for actual popcorn."

As Mickelson arrived at the top of the staircase to the ground floor level, his spider sense tingled. Something was weird. The air was cold. Had his wife left the door open when she went out to go to the gym?

As he rounded the corner toward the kitchen, Gannon, standing there beside the wine fridge, delivered an eyeblink instant and perfectly brutal chopping left to Mickelson's torso that sounded like it had cracked a rib as it knocked the wind out of him.

His knees blasted painfully off the Brazilian cherry as he collapsed, gasping.

"Have a seat, Admiral," Gannon said as he looked down at him. "Take a breather, sir. Good idea."

85

After taping up the still pretty spry old codger with some vinyl electrical tape he'd found in a drawer, Gannon guided him into his wood-paneled home office.

"Mike?" Mickelson said as Gannon sat him on his leather couch.

"Are you really that surprised?" Gannon said, rolling the office chair over the Persian rug to sit in front of him. "You were the one who taught me all the *Art of War* stuff, sir, remember? When far away, appear near. When near, far away. It's even in your best seller that I read on the plane."

The admiral stared pensively at the wooden blinds.

"You have a son, Mike. What would you do for your son?"

"Spare me the tear-jerking family sob story, Admiral. I've been having a long couple of weeks so my compassion meter is on E."

"You know my daughter Ginny. Are you aware of her run for Senate?"

"You mean the one that got kicked off just around the same time I was getting a bag over my head?"

"Mike, bear with me," he said glancing out at his lawn again.

"Stop stalling," Gannon said. "Your watch dog won't be done licking his wounds for quite a while."

"No," Mickelson said, looking concerned. "What did you do to Kevin? Don't tell me you killed him. He's a SEAL like you, you know."

"Is he? Well, they don't make them like they used to anymore, do they? Screw Kevin, sir. You care about him as much as you care about anyone else. Namely, zero, zilch, nada. So, cut the bullshit, Admiral. It's storytelling time. I'll even start it off for you. Once upon a time, Ginny was away at school at UCLA."

"Right," he said, staring down at his lap. "Ginny was away at school at UCLA and she called to tell me that her car broke down."

"I remember," Gannon said.

"That's all I knew at the time, Mike. I heard about all of the rest of it from her very recently, okay? You have to believe me about that."

"I don't have to believe anything, Admiral. Especially anything that comes out of your dirty treacherous backstabbing mouth. But do go on."

"That's when I called you in San Diego to pick her up."

Gannon nodded.

"I thought it was weird going all the way out there to get her in the desert. Where the hell was it? Shandon? Some rest stop out in the middle of nowhere. Took me hours to get there. Kept thinking, why not triple-A? So, what the hell did she do?"

He looked at him, opened his mouth then closed it.

"What the hell did she do?" Gannon repeated. "Must have been a doozy since you decided to try to lay me out in order to cover it up. Right before her big press event for Senate, too. I was the loose end, huh. For what? What the hell did she do in college?"

"There was a road trip up to the big game with Berkeley. Ginny had to go as she was dating the star cornerback at UCLA."

"Charles Chambers," Gannon said. "I've been googling. That's her husband now. The ESPN guy. He played in the NFL for a bit. Now he's a man ball sports Muppet."

The admiral nodded.

"Yep, that's Charlie. Anyway, she and all her friends all went up to Berkeley for the big game. On the way up there the night before, they stopped off at a honky-tonk bar. A lot of drinking went on, a lot of drugs. Charlie had a friend, a very close friend from his high school, a young man named Peter McNulty. Who knows how these things happen, but he and Ginny had a romantic encounter in the parking lot."

Mickelson paused, let out a long breath.

"We're getting to the good part now, Admiral. I can tell."

"They fell asleep in the car afterward, and when Ginny woke up and realized what she had done, she panicked. She's always been very, um, circumspect. Very controlled. She had selected Charles Chambers to be her boyfriend, knew that he was going places, the same places she wanted to go. She also knew he was shopping for an engagement ring. But when he found what she had done with his buddy, it would be over between them so..."

"So?"

"Peter McNulty was reported missing two days later."

"No one had seen them together?" Gannon said.

Mickelson shook his head.

"Everybody was wasted and he had driven up by himself. They found his car in the lot of the place, but they couldn't find him. He'd simply disappeared."

"What did she do? Strangle him with her panties?"

The admiral pursed his lips and looked down at the floor.

"They were in her car and she got him to chug some more

vodka on a dare and when he got it all down, she suffocated him while he was passed out then drove out and dumped him in the desert."

"Your daughter is a psychopath?"

The admiral said nothing.

"Then her car died?"

"She ran out of gas as she was coming back. She called me in Virginia Beach, where I was stuck at a conference. I knew you were in San Diego on your next assignment, which is why I called you."

"But this happened twenty years ago," Gannon said. "Why take me out now?"

"They found McNulty's remains two years ago. Three miles from where you brought her the gas. The family hired a detective, who's been poking around. You would be the only link. I know you're a straight shooter, Mike. If you heard about it, you would've told. You would have put her right there at the scene."

"You're wrong," Gannon said.

"You wouldn't have told?"

"No, I definitely would have told. You're wrong that I'm the only link. You knew about it, too."

"My family traces its public service back to the Civil War, Mike. My grandfather was in WWI, my father a colonel under Eisenhower. I did my duty, but I never had a son to pass on the chain. Just three daughters. Ginny is it. Her talent. Her Senate run. She'll win, too. She's next in the chain."

"Correction," Gannon said as he showed the admiral the recording app up on his iPhone. "Ginny *was* the next in the chain."

86

"What are you going to do now?" the admiral said.

"How was Devine involved with you?" Gannon said.

"Who's Devine?"

"My host in South America."

"I don't know what you're talking about. That's not on my end. I partnered with a CIA case officer who's been helping with Ginny's campaign."

"Hired out, huh? What's this case officer's name?"

"Bright," he said immediately. "Adrian Bright."

"Never heard of him."

"Well, he's heard of you. When he found out there was already a concern about you in the Agency, he devised a way to kill two birds with one stone."

"Yeah, sucks for him. Turns out this bird's got a hard fricking head. Now this bird is pissed and his sharp beak and talons are itching for a nice soft neck to tuck into."

"Just make it quick. I helped you, remember?"

Gannon peered at him.

"You're a sorry sack of shit, Admiral. You were a good man, but you let money and power corrupt you. There's no way around it. Now, you have to pay the price."

He fell to his knees, moaning.

"Get up, you blubbering jackass. I'm not going to kill you."

He looked up hopefully.

"I'm just going to teach you a lesson. I'm going to take all your money instead."

"What?"

"Your money. You know, your assets," Gannon said, cutting off the tape around his wrists. "Sit in the chair and bring them up on the computer there. All of your brokerage accounts. Don't you love banking from home? Go straight to bank transfers. I saw you made what? Six mil last year at that venture thing? Good work, if you can find it."

"But…"

"Or we can go for what's behind door number two."

Gannon took out the karambit knife he had taken off Button Eyes and lifted a sheet of printer paper. When he made a slight motion with it, the bottom half of the paper separated almost silently before wafting to the floor.

The admiral blinked down at the paper.

Then he turned in the office chair toward the computer, and there was a rapid sound of clicking in the quiet of the room.

"Everything is at Schwab. Good," Gannon said, looking at the screen over his shoulder. "Let's see. Holy moly, is that a typo? Quite the day trader, aren't we? That's a hell a lot of money. Now cash out all your positions."

"What?"

"Into your joint tenant account there. Move all of it now."

After he was done, he said, "Now what?"

"Send it here," Gannon said, handing him a slip of paper.

"Wait, that's a—"

"Bitcoin exchange, yep. Convert it to Bitcoin."

The admiral did as he was told.

"Okay. Put it all on a thumb drive." When that was finished, Gannon said, "Nice." Then he pulled it out and put it into his pocket. "Now get up."

"Where are we going?"

"Move it," Gannon said as he took him back out into the kitchen. "Whoa, a Ninja blender. I love these," Gannon said as he took it out from a shelf on the granite island.

The tiny plastic thumb drive gave off a tiny clatter from the inside glass of the blender as Gannon dropped it in.

"No!" the admiral said as Gannon plugged the blender in. "That's f-f-fifty—"

"Uh-huh. Fifty million dollars. But not for long."

"You're joking. You wouldn't."

"I wouldn't," Gannon said, smiling. "But you will. You're going to press Ice Crush in a second. With the last of your broken fingers if you want to do it the hard way."

The admiral shook his head.

"Easy come, easy go, Admiral. I figure ending Ginny's political aspirations and getting her put in the slammer while stripping you of all your hard-scammed loot should be punishment enough."

"But why not take it?"

"Because I'm not a piece of shit like you. That's what all you dirty traitors think. That enough money can corrupt anyone. That anyone would have done what you did for that amount of loot. Guess again."

The admiral had a blank look on his face.

"Don't worry, Admiral. It'll be good for your character. Your number one best seller is all about pulling yourself up by your bootstraps, right? Well, old age is no excuse. It's never too late to get the old fingers around the old bootstraps. Good thing, too. With a zero balance now, bootstraps are about all you'll have left."

"But…" he said again.

Gannon's face darkened.

"Oh, and Admiral, when we're finished…"

He lifted his white head.

"Bright's phone number?" the admiral said.

"Uh-huh and his address, too. And one last thing. You still ride, Admiral, don't you?"

87

Bright made it to the end of the pool and tucked his knees and did his flip turn and pushed the soles of his feet off the wall.

The lap pool was in an indoor pool house beside the garden. Claudette was the swimmer. Had swum in college and was actually an Olympic alternate. The winter pool was the only reason she had agreed to the house.

As he swam, he remembered how she had cried when he brought her in to see it, saving it for last, the Realtor smiling at him. "I think we're taking it," Bright had said.

He got to the end of the pool and checked his phone on the towel.

No Mickelson yet. *What was the holdup?*

Bright laid the phone back down and bobbed in the pool, looking out the French door. In the garden, the sunset sky beyond the rose trellis was the color of honey. He took it as a positive sign.

Relax, killer, he told himself in his head. You still got it, remember?

Almost cooler than the dip in the pool was the bracing cold of running in his robe across the path into the side door off the kitchen. As he pushed it open and heard the classical music, he smiled. Claudette's flight must have been early.

He heard a bang in the back of the pantry.

"Honey!" he called out.

"There you are," Alex Sarris said, coming into the kitchen. He was wearing his wife's polka dot apron.

"Have a nice swim, Adrian?" he said.

He placed the Duncan Hines box he was holding onto the countertop next to a bag of Nestle milk chocolate morsels.

"Alex?" Bright said, tightening his robe.

"Sorry for letting myself in, Adrian. I know Claudette is coming home so I thought she would like some brownies."

Bright took a deep breath. There was a crackle sound and when he turned, he saw the other two men from Alex's office sitting in his living room. One was reading Claudette's *Real Simple* magazine while the other one, the Samoan, was staring into the fire they had made, still as a totem pole.

His Persian rug was covered in plastic now and there was a hook in the ceiling with the tripoded camera ready to go.

Alex smiled as he opened the subzero. He slid open a drawer and perused the beer selection.

"This is... Spaten!" he called out merrily as he clinked out a bottle of the German lager onto the marble. "Can I get you one, Adrian?"

"No, thanks," Bright said as his heart began a speed metal drum solo inside of his chest.

Handel's masterpiece, "Sarabande," started from the Bluetooth speakers as Alex poured beer into a glass. Stanley trotted in.

"How about some for faithful Stanley here in his bowl then?" Alex said. "But no, Stanley doesn't drink beer, does he? That would be too...double-wide. I know how hard you've worked to get the taste of the Ozarks off that silver tongue of yours. Almost succeeded, too."

"Almost," Bright agreed.

"But, Alex, I thought you said tomorrow. I'm about to wrap all of this up. I really am."

"No, you're not, Adrian. You failed."

"I—"

"He wasn't there."

"At the hotel in Panama City?"

"No, some homeless guy was in there. They found him in the tub. Gannon snookered you again. Why don't you have a seat there and think about that? How you did this all to yourself."

Alex had just poured the last of the batter when Bright's phone, charging on the kitchen desk, emitted its electro-chirp through the Baroque dirge.

Alex went over and checked it.

"Ah, splendid. Claudette just landed, Adrian. Perfect timing. Won't be long now," he said.

88

There were many bikes in the admiral's toy box of a garage, but as he was in a hurry after he leathered up, Gannon selected the matte black Suzuki SV650.

As he got on and pointed it north toward Bright's address, he picked up the tempo. At the next exit, there was some kind of pileup, a jack-knifed tanker truck and a Toyota SUV crumpled beside a tree. As he zoomed along in the shoulder, a trooper appeared, waving him to slow.

"Not on your life," Gannon mumbled under the helmet as he checked his mirror and swung left around the trooper and the rollover, full throttle, digging up the base of the Virginia hill.

A mile north, he took the next on-ramp and he came down onto the smaller parkway at speed, threading the gap between a heavy truck and a tour bus. He pounded north, howling the bike up through a canyon. It was watershed area around here near the Appalachian foothills, rivers and lakes, one-car bridges. Must have been where a lot of the DC parasites had their bugouts, he thought, passing a nice house with subtle yet solid security fencing.

Bright's town of Nokesville seemed to be all cattle farms. He actually passed a slaughterhouse truck as he came through its tiny main square, the stink of it matching his mood perfectly.

He saw the smoke as he came to a rise five miles north.

"You have to be shitting me," he said as he pulled over to let a growling fire truck pass.

He turned around and got a coffee at the nearest Starbucks and when he got back, the fire trucks were gone, replaced by police cars.

He found a spot on a hill a few miles to the north and stood in the woods with his binoculars.

When they took out the body bag, he wondered what the story was.

Did Bright's upperclassmen pull the plug on him?

Or did he do it himself?

He thought about things. Then he finally came back up through the trees where his bike was waiting.

"Saved me the trouble either way," Gannon said as he spun the throttle and whipped the bike around.

89

The gas station down south in Rockbridge County near the West Virginia border was a something from an older, kinder time.

It was coming on dinnertime when Adrian Bright pulled his vintage green tea Porsche in beside its faded red-painted clapboard and stopped by the first of its two pumps.

After killing his boss and the other two men and setting his place on fire, he'd been driving around, trying to collect his thoughts.

Just as Bright had underestimated Gannon, Alex had underestimated him. The stupid bastard was still playing patty-cake, bent getting the brownies out of the oven, when Bright pulled the subcompact SIG P365 Nitron he always carried in his swimming robe and double-tapped both of his two thugs where they sat. Alex himself didn't get as far as the back door before Bright steadied and fired a 147 grain hollow point straight through his left ear and out his right.

After he dressed and grabbed his bugout bag with all the appropriate traveling items, he'd called Claudette, who was still at the airport, and delivered the bad news. They had spoken of this many times, that his job might one day force him into running. The code word was asking her to pick up chocolate milk, which he despised.

When he said it, he heard her breath catch.

Then he lit a match and backed out of the garage with Stanley in the passenger seat of the Porsche.

Stanley was sitting there, happy as could be, Bright saw as he turned. He shut off the engine and scruffed his buddy's perfect little head.

"Well, at least I still have you," he said.

The interior of the gas station was a throwback as well with a sweet smoky odor of old cigarettes and deer antlers up above the counter.

"Thirty on pump one," he said, tossing the money down before some bored-looking high school kid watching the beginning of *Jeopardy!* on his phone.

When the black Japanese bike and black-clad rider with a black helmet roared in behind his Porsche, Bright's radar immediately went off.

The rider wasn't overly tall, but even with his helmet still on, you could tell he was rugged and thick muscled, dense as a soda machine.

It was Gannon, he thought with a swallow.

Gannon black on black on black. Angel of death and ace of spades. There he stood.

It took a long minute of sheer crazy glued-to-the-floorboards panic before he realized that it was just a coincidence, a crazy coincidence. He watched as Gannon began filling the Suzuki's tank.

Then he suddenly remembered something else.

The gun that he had used to kill Alex and the two thugs had been replaced with something much more formidable, a Beretta

PM12 that was in a custom-made sling under his right armpit. As he watched Gannon fuel up with his back to him, he realized that all it would take was a quick swing up with Pistola Mitragliatice toward the plate glass and a flick of the safety, and the extremely reliable open-bolt blowback weapon would do the rest.

"What is...?" said the contestant from the clerk's phone.

What if I miss? Bright said in his head.

Bright swallowed as he watched Gannon go over and pat Stanley on the head. Then Gannon's pump clicked and he headed back toward the bike.

"Um, anything else?" the clerk said.

Bright turned to him with a look of joyful relief as he heard the bike roar on.

"Nope, that's all. Thanks."

But that wasn't all.

"No!" Bright screamed at the bike's now-tiny red taillights as he got to his car to see the passenger seat empty.

EPILOGUE

HOME SWEET HOME

90

The town where Jimmy Devine grew up looked pretty much exactly the same since the last time Gannon had been there for the memorial.

Pulling into its main street Dunkin' Donuts in the Chevy Silverado he had rented that morning, Gannon smiled over at the dog he had stolen off Adrian Bright.

Tracking Bright down hadn't been a problem in the slightest with his buddy Ed's big eye in the sky. His old pal McGyver still had one more favor in him, it had turned out.

And stealing the man's dog, Gannon thought with a laugh, was truly the best revenge possible. It was better than taking his life. Or his cojones.

Come to think of it, it was the actually same thing, wasn't it? he thought, laughing some more.

"Why, that's a nice dog. What's his name?" said the smiling salty middle-aged lady who handed over his coffee and bagel.

"Moonshine," Gannon said, making it up on the spot.

Moonshine barked.

Gannon laughed. He liked it. You could tell.

"He's cute," she said. "So, where are you headed, fella, all dressed up like that? A wedding or something?"

The opposite, Gannon thought.

"Something like that. Thanks for everything," he said with a wave.

"That's the spirit, Moonshine," Gannon said, petting him as they continued down Main Street. "Dog in a Porsche. Who ever heard of such a thing, huh, boy? Even a city boy like me knows that the only acceptable vehicle a dog can ever be seen in is a big ol' truck. You're going to love Utah by the way. But I just have one more thing to do first."

When he knocked at the door, an elderly lady appeared a few moments later walking behind a red walker.

"Yes? Can I help you?"

"Ma'am, my name is Michael Gannon. I don't know if you remember me, but I was stationed overseas with your son. I was at the memorial for Jimmy."

"Oh, of course," she said, her face lighting up. "I do remember you. You were in the crash with him. I remember all of you, the way you showed up in your whites. My goodness."

A tear sprung in her blue eyes.

"You don't understand how helpful that was. To see you all there. How much you loved him. You have no idea."

"Well, ma'am, I have, um, maybe some good news. I'm still connected with the military, and we had people near the crash site recently. It's all sort of unofficial, if you know what I mean, but they...they found something that we think might have belonged to Jimmy."

"His remains? He can finally come home?"

"No, not his remains, ma'am. Something that might have belonged to him."

"Wait," she said. "Don't show me yet. I need to call Joyce, his wife. She needs to be here, okay? Just let me make a call."

Gannon was sitting on the porch with a cup of tea and was just about to take a sip when a Dakota pulled in behind his pickup. Out of it came a pretty forty-something woman with blond hair and two pretty daughters who were probably in high school.

Jimmy's wife, Joyce, was already crying.

"Mike," she said, clinging to him like a person falling off a cliff. She was shaking. She'd done the same at Jimmy's memorial, he remembered.

Gannon suddenly doubted himself, wondered if he should have done this, dredged all of this back up.

Then he reached into his pocket and held out his hand.

Joyce and the mother reached out for it together there on the porch.

They all stood there, crying, as they held the ends of the chain of Jimmy's gold crucifix.

91

An hour after he left the home where his old friend Jimmy Devine was born and raised, Gannon, taking the back streets, came across a Little League baseball game.

In the distance, the field was startling. There was a softness of evening light on it and its flatness and its pale green color gave a feeling of openness and hope. He pulled up to watch the kids taking the field.

As he stood watching them, he saw in the crowd a woman with the sunlight on her face as well, a brunette woman in her twenties, and in her pale delicate hands was a child of maybe two. A cute little blond boy.

Just then, a high school boy with a bugle began to play "The Star-Spangled Banner."

Gannon thought he'd done enough crying for one day.

But there are times in life when emotions you don't even know you've been suppressing sneak up and catch you cold with a startling force like you just stepped face-first into the path of a speeding freight train.

Because the woman reminded him of his wife, Annette. And she was gone. She was dead. Irrevocably, irretrievably dead. And the knowledge and memory of this, as he watched the young woman, reminded Gannon of all of her efforts, all of her hopes, her struggles. Their struggles together, their work together, and their life raising their son.

And as the bugler played the hopeful song of their country, there suddenly was such an incredible sadness in it.

And in that sadness was an echo of all the struggles of all the people he had ever known. His mom and dad and brothers and sisters and uncles and aunts. And when he looked at the crowd, the echo of the sadness resounded through those people as well. And in the memory of all their families and friends who were alive and who had died.

Gannon felt his breath catch.

A moment before, they had been strangers to him. But as he looked at them now, he saw that they were connected. All of them together in a communion of struggling and hoping and sadness.

As he sat there, it was like all the lives of people living everywhere on the planet became manifest. From the field beyond, it all seemed to come forward on the breeze. From Virginia, from Mexico, where the boy had died atop the old prison roof. From the little farmhouse where he had killed those men in Peru. Suddenly there in the evening air came all the hoping and struggling and innocent dreams of every human being who had ever lived and the weight seemed to press in around him as he sat there, and as this happened, something inside of Gannon seemed to break.

He was still bent forward against the steering wheel, weeping, when Bright's dog began licking at his cheeks.

Gannon looked at him and then laughed as he scratched at his fuzzy head.

"You're right, Moonshine," he said. "I know, I know. No crying in baseball."

★ ★ ★ ★ ★